CW01281469

James Page was born and educated in Australia. He worked in the public and private sectors, including the occasional interaction with, and writing speeches for government ministers, and projects with corporate Australia. Hoping to rediscover his soul, he turned to writing. His other work is *The Chancer's Corp*.

To Gloria and Denise.

James Page

A Slaver's Tide

Austin Macauley Publishers

London * Cambridge * New York * Sharjah

Copyright © James Page 2023

The right of James Page to be identified as author of this work has been asserted by the author in accordance with sections 77 and 78 of the Copyright, Designs and Patents Act 1988.

All rights reserved. No part of this publication may be reproduced, stored in a retrieval system, or transmitted in any form or by any means, electronic, mechanical, photocopying, recording, or otherwise, without the prior permission of the publishers.

Any person who commits any unauthorised act in relation to this publication may be liable to criminal prosecution and civil claims for damages.

This is a work of fiction. Names, characters, businesses, places, events, locales, and incidents are either the products of the author's imagination or used in a fictitious manner. Any resemblance to actual persons, living or dead, or actual events is purely coincidental.

A CIP catalogue record for this title is available from the British Library.

ISBN 9781035806850 (Paperback)
ISBN 9781035806867 (Hardback)
ISBN 9781035806881 (ePub e-book)
ISBN 9781035806874 (Audiobook)

www.austinmacauley.com

First Published 2023
Austin Macauley Publishers Ltd®
1 Canada Square
Canary Wharf
London
E14 5AA

The list of people who helped shape this book is long, so apologies to any I have omitted. Amongst those who deserve credit for shaping my writing are Liz Hardy, copy editor from whom I learnt so much, Brad, Gio, Adi and the team at Coretext who taught me a great deal about the power of writing, Janet Lawrence, taken too soon from us and from whom I was fortunate to learn a great deal from. And to Gloria and Denise, to whom this book is dedicated, thanks for your unwavering support and encouragement. Finally to Dad, gone but not forgotten for pushing on this, it meant a lot.

One

He hangs suspended in the water, motionless, as the bodies plunge into the dark waters from above. Always in pairs, chained together. They are mainly men and a few women, destined for slavery in the West Indies now tossed aside, like garbage, to disappear into the abyss.

They hit the water hard, creating clouds of bubbles that quickly disperse, leaving thrashing bodies behind. Pairs that cannot overcome the weight of their chains and the pull of the water.

The shafts of sunlight that penetrate the blue waters illuminate the scene, creating horrid beauty amongst the chaos. Some of the chained try to reach the shafts of light, perhaps in the hope it will lift them, or as a last act of life, embracing the light before the darkness of the deep grabs them and pulls them under.

He watches, calmly. Floating. In the murk of the water and yet beyond it. The dark sleek shapes, the large sharks approach. They begin to feast, blood filling the water. The scent of it filled his nostrils. He dreams this dream each time he sleeps. It is as familiar to him as the creaking of a ship at night or the shores of the Slave Coast he has visited many times.

*

The carriage turned onto a cobblestoned street, clattering and lurching sideways. Tyler woke with a start and looked around, taking several moments to realise where he was. Images of slaves in the water still filled his vision. The priest watched him quietly from the opposite seat.

'We'll be there soon. Are you still sure you want to do this?' Father Albert said.

'Yes, Father. I need to. I want to look Carrington in the eye when I speak. I want him to hear it from me, not second hand.'

The priest studied Tyler closely. To another, the worn look of frustration on Tyler's face, the bitterness and anger in his voice would have been a cause for alarm. Cause to ensure that George Tyler, the slave-boat captain tried for murdering hundreds, should never meet Yorke Carrington, the very man who had prosecuted that trial. But Tyler was insistent and the priest knew that Tyler needed to tell his story and most of all to Carrington.

Tyler looked away, out the window to the streets of London. They drifted by, as meaningless to Tyler as everything else. The only thing that mattered now was squaring the ledger with Carrington. A reckoning lay ahead and Tyler was determined to see it through.

*

Yorke Carrington pulled the curtain back and peered out into the street again. Then he dropped the curtain as another carriage passed, paced across the room to the door and put his hand on the handle. He flicked the lock back and forward, locking and unlocking the door, his hand shaking.

When the priest had written to him and said Tyler wanted to visit, Carrington had started shaking. He has barely stopped since. What could Tyler want other than revenge? He flicked the lock again, trembling.

'Yorke, you must calm down,' Sophie said. 'Father Albert would not bring this man here unless he was sure it was safe.'

'I want that man hanged for murder. Now he wants to see me. Why?' A carriage made its familiar sound as it neared and Carrington raced to the curtain, pulled it back and watched. It continued up the street. Carrington sighed and walked back to the door, flicking the lock again and again.

'Trust in Father Albert. He knows this man, Tyler.'

'And if he's wrong? Tyler murdered those slaves. And now he wants to see me. Oh God, Sophie, what does he want?'

Carrington walked over to a chair and slumped down, head in hands. 'I can't do this. I can't.'

'Yorke.'

Carrington continued muttering to himself. 'Yorke! It will be alright.'

The knock on the door made them both jump. Carrington looked at his wife, then to the door. He stayed slumped in the chair. Again knocking, only this time louder, more insistent.

Sophie Carrington looked at her husband. Then she walked over and opened the door.

'Father Albert, Mr Tyler, please come in,' Sophie said. She ushered the men to a sofa. 'Would you like tea?'

'Sophie that would be delightful,' Albert said. 'Mr Tyler?'

'No thank you, I would rather have this over and done with.'

'Yorke, are you going to greet our guests,' Sophie said to Carrington who still sat on the chair. 'You will have to forgive my husband, Mr Tyler, he is convinced that you are here to wreak some kind of revenge on him. Perhaps you could reassure him that is not your intent.'

'Your husband thinks he knows me, knows who I am because of what I did. I want him, of all people, to hear my story, to understand it. Then he will know who I am,' Tyler said.

Carrington still sat in his chair. He looked at the man sitting in front of him, still so defiant. 'Then tell us, tell us why you threw 130 men and women into the Atlantic to die.'

George Tyler looked at Carrington and then looked at the floor. 'I did what I did because at the time…'

Tyler looked from the floor to the window and swallowed hard. 'At the time, I thought it right, but now, well now things are different.'

'I beg to differ,' Carrington said. 'The lives of men always mattered.'

'Not in the slave trade. Not the lives of sailors or slaves. Not then,' Tyler said. 'Especially not on the Slave coast.'

'Must you call it that?' Carrington said.

'Mr Carrington, if you are to understand my story, to understand why I am here today there are realities of the slave trade that must be spoken of. They are brutal and searing. I can't bear justice to my story if I can't tell those truths. Can you manage your distaste for the trade long enough for me to finish?'

The colour drained from Carrington's face. He nodded.

'The Slave coast is a curious mix of inactivity and rapid action, of churches built inside slave forts. Life is cheap there but slaves are expensive. There are lost souls both amongst the slaves and the traders. It's odd how I never saw that before. I guess I just never wanted to.

'And it's worth remembering that back then, before Wilberforce spoke against the trade, before the pamphlets and the sermons denouncing the trade people were happy to own slaves. To see grand buildings erected in Bristol or

Liverpool and paid for by slave traders. And people are still happy to sit in the coffee houses and drop sugar into their coffee or tea. Sugar that comes from slavery.'

Carrington looked at the tea that Sophie had made. There was no sugar bowl. He sighed remembering how hard it was to take tea without sugar. It was an affectation and sign within the world of the abolitionists that you were serious. That you were prepared to sacrifice to end the slave trade. It also made the tea and coffee miserable to drink. Sugar, England's all-consuming craving was delivered on the back of the slave trade that Carrington worked every day to end. Yet even here, at home, he still craved tea mixed with sugar.

'Yorke, are you listening?' Sophie said. 'George is talking.'

'Yes, dear. I was wondering, Mr Tyler, if perhaps you could describe the voyage, of the Charlotte?' Carrington shivered when he said the ship's name. Few slave ships had ever been as notorious.

'Yorke, I think you should call George by his given name. He is helping us, in return we should extend him some courtesy,' Sophie said. 'Don't you agree, Albert?'

'Yes. And perhaps it's worth outlining a little for us how the trade works, George.'

Tyler sat quietly for a moment. 'We call it a triangular voyage. From Bristol, we sail to the Slave coast of west Africa, pick up a boatload of cargo and then run east towards where the African coast turns south. At that point, we pick up the Atlantic current that heads westwards, to the Americas. The middle passage across the Atlantic you hope passes quickly, without incident, then we would put in at Jamaica. The cargo is offloaded, either sold directly to market or more usually we would use an agent with ties to Mr Pennington.'

'Pennington being the slave trader who owned the Charlotte?' Sophie said.

'That's right. The agent would have a consignment of sugar ready for us to collect and load, then it was back to Bristol completing the triangle so to speak.'

'You make it sound so mundane,' Sophie said.

'It was. It always was, until that last voyage anyway.'

'So you sailed to Africa and raided some villages for slaves. Then what?' Sophie said.

'The biggest misconception of the trade is that we go inland looking for slaves,' Tyler said.

'How do the slaves then get to the coast?' Sophie said.

'African traders bring them down to the coast,' Tyler said.

'Surely not,' Sophie said.

'The trade is run by Africans and some Arabs. The Africans round up their own and bring them to a series of trading forts on the coast where they are sold to Europeans. These forts house the cargo until it is sold to the slave ships. The forts each have governors, who ensure the traders that bring the slaves from inland are treated fairly,' Tyler said.

'Treated fairly?' Sophie said in shock.

'Sophie, if this is too much perhaps you should leave,' Carrington said.

'I would rather she stayed,' Albert said.

'Do you think that wise?'

'Yorke, if Sophie is shocked by this then so will others be. And that is what we want, to shock people when they see how this trade is run. I have set aside any personal feelings for this horrific trade, so as to help George tell his story. With that story, we can change public opinion and get this vile trade outlawed once and for all.'

'Do you think you can swallow your contempt and call me George?' Tyler said. 'And maybe let me call you by your name.'

'I do not like you, or what you stand for, Mr Tyler. If you hope to ease that contempt through familiarity you will be gravely disappointed.'

'I know you have nothing but contempt for me but that's why you keep failing in getting the slave trade outlawed. Your hatred for the trade blinds you to the single reason you and your abolitionist friends keep failing. Too many people care less about slavery than they do their own convenience. Do you think when a man has a cup of coffee in one of London's coffee houses he stops and thinks of where that sugar comes from?

'Because it comes from people like me risking their lives to sail cargoes around the world. And it comes from slavery. You don't like me, I understand that, but if you can't even extend some basic courtesy to me, when I am offering to help you, well perhaps I should go elsewhere.'

Carrington stared at Tyler for a long time. 'So do you think this makes you a good man, that this redeems you?'

'Nothing will redeem me and I'm as far from a good man as you'll find. All I want is for you to understand me and what I did, and then you will understand what this trade really is.'

There was a long silence in the room.

'I apologise, I am angry with you because of the trial. I thought the trial would be…would be enough to end slavery. And to fail, it is a bitter taste in the mouth.'

'A bit like tea without sugar right, Yorke?' Albert said and then laughed.

'Really, Albert, that is in poor taste,' Sophie said.

'Try a strong coffee without sugar, that's poor taste,' Tyler said.

'Perhaps we can get on with things?' Carrington said.

'Alright, but answer this for me. Do you like your tea better with or without sugar?' Tyler said.

'I hardly think that matters,' Carrington said.

'I could ask your wife, she'll know,' Tyler said.

Sophie smiled a little at the corners of her mouth. Yorke Carrington hated tea without sugar. He barely drank it. She willed her husband to answer.

'Alright, with sugar. But I have vowed not to take tea with sugar until the trade is outlawed here in Britain.'

'Good for you,' Tyler said.

'Now can we get on with things?' Carrington said.

'Certainly, right after you call me George.'

'Does it matter so much?'

'Slaves are given new names when they are sold in Jamaica. It's the last step in erasing their past, in cementing their servitude. I don't deserve to be called by my name, not after what I did. But to be able to forget that for a short time, to be treated as an equal, that still matters to me. As ironic and awful as that may be to you, my name and story are all that I have left. If you want the story, you need to use my name.'

For the first time, Carrington saw the man rather than the monster. A man who had dumped more than 100 slaves into the Atlantic, but a man nonetheless. For the briefest moment, he felt pity for George Tyler. For the man whose name now represented all the evils of the slave trade.

'Carry on then, George.'

'I always hated being in port. Give me the deck of a ship at sea. The way the whole world contracts to become that ship. That's my world, that's what I loved. That's why I captained a slaver, to command that ship and that world we sailors alone inhabit.'

'But that's not why we're here, is it? You want to hear about the Charlotte.' Tyler sat back and looked at the ceiling, his thoughts thousands of miles away.

'We left Bristol like on any other voyage, tacking out into the Downs and from there out to sea. And it was uneventful, like any other voyage. Of course, you're always wary of the Channel and its surroundings 'cause the weather can turn so quickly and push the full force of the Atlantic into that small space. When that happens ships go down, so we always worked hard to clear that area as quickly as possible. Once past the Isles of Scilly, you breathe a little easier.'

'And then what? Did you have orders from Pennington?' Yorke Carrington said.

'They came from Mr Pennington by way of a letter. I still have that letter.'

Tyler pulled a crumpled paper out and carefully unfolded it. 'I don't know why I kept this,' Tyler said before he read the letter.

Bristol April 1804
Sir,

My ship, the Charlotte, being fully outfitted by Mr Weldon and now ready for sea, you are to proceed in her and make the best way to Cape Coast, on the coast of Africa. Included within is a copy of the invoice from the said Mr Weldon outlining cargo on board the Charlotte, which you are to barter for best negroes, and should any cargo remain thereafter, for palm oil. Do not exceed the 300 negro limit by law that Charlotte is entitled to carry. Included is the fit-out plan for loose packing of the cargo for the middle passage.

Where possible, make all negroes purchased male, though a small number of not more than 10 per cent are entitled to be female and 2 per cent be children below 12 years but not below 7 years. They are all for sale to Jamaica through the house of Messrs. Barton, Higgins and Co whereupon landing you will find lodged with their representative instructions for prosecuting the remaining part of the voyage. With regards to those negroes purchased, make them strong of body and sufficient of mind, but no greater age than 24, for above this in Jamaica sales for such above 24 years attract duty of £10 each head. During the middle passage, take care in exercising the cargo on deck for a time each day, keep conditions as clean as possible and make good that the cargo is not ill-treated to diminish value upon arrival in Jamaica. Discipline is yours and yours alone to keep, with rules and laws to be laid down by you and ensured by you.

Your crew are Second Captain Lawson Miles, your Lieutenant Thomas Franklin, and your Mate Gilbert Calum. Of Surgeon Mr McDougal. Upon reaching Jamaica and the House of Barton and Co, you will find your coast commissions; £3 gross sales on £103, with Second Captain's privilege, Surgeon's privilege and all gratuities and head monies being fully deducted you may then draw your commission of £4 in £104 on the remaining account. Your Lieutenant is to receive two slaves on average of the cargo, your Mate one slave on average. Your Surgeon will receive 1 shilling for every head of cargo sold. These above for each officer are forfeit in whole and for perpetuity upon any private, illegal trade in any cargo by any officer or proof of embezzlement or other loss or waste of the cargo through idleness or neglect. Of insurance, only the middle passage is underwritten for the number of 300 cargo.

I wish you God's speed and hope for a prosperous and plentiful voyage.

Yours sincerely Charles Pennington Esq, Full share.

'And the truth was we had a prosperous voyage with God's speed behind us all the way down to the equator,' Tyler said. He showed no emotion, of joy or happiness nor did that change as he began telling the story of the Charlotte.

Two

Tyler looked at the sails billowing and filling with wind and felt a surge of joy as the Charlotte picked up speed. The water was calm despite the wind and the ship surged ahead. Several of the crew took to rigging a bosun's chair, dangling a piece of wood secured at the end of a taught and thick rope and took turns sitting in the chair as it was lowered into the wake behind the Charlotte.

Tyler looked at Lawson Miles, who smiled his crooked-teethed smile. Thomas Franklin held a small piece of fish on a thin line of rope and used it to try to distract the ship's cat, Dinks. The cat had other prey in mind, and stiffened and then began stalking a mouse across the decks.

Franklin watched with a smile on his face, one predator appreciating the work of another. Soon Dinks had the mouse trapped and began playing with the doomed animal. Franklin watched in admiration.

'I am Gilbert, Gilbert Calum,' Calum said, approaching Franklin. 'We haven't been properly introduced.'

'And I'm watching the show,' Franklin said, grunting and pointing towards where Dinks was now swatting the mouse from paw to paw. 'So get out of my way. And you don't address me unless I tell ya to, ya understand?'

'I thought as we were both officers that—'

'You're the ship's mate, don't think. Just do what I tell ya and we'll get by.' Franklin stood and walked into Calum, bumping him out of his way and heading below. Calum nearly fell, then recovered his balance and stood pale and white. Memories of his own father came flooding back, of a man more interested in disciplining his children than in nurturing them.

Days slipped by under the prow of the Charlotte as she raced southwards. The tropics neared and the heat rose each day. Shipboard life was one of routine with few interruptions. The weather was pleasant and calm, with the Charlotte encountering only one storm.

The storm came up fast in the night, with little warning. Calum was duty officer and immediately ordered his watch to furl the topsails. Quickly the sailors scrambled aloft, feeling their way through the rain and spray. Climbing barefoot each man moved as rapidly as possible. As the ship began to sway and roll the rigging slanted outwards over the waves below. Sailors would scramble as the ship rolled them away from the ocean, using the angle to climb quickly before clinging on as the ship rolled them towards the ocean below. Where the rigging met the mast, the sailors had to pull themselves up and over the small platforms and reach out and climb onto the next level of rigging.

Then they reached the yard arms and scurried out, their toes gripping the ropes slung below the yard arms, those thick cross beams that bore the weight of the sails. Crabbing their way sideward, leaning out over the yard arms, they reached forward and gathered the sails, bundling them in and lashing the canvass to the arms.

As they did this, the ship rolled from port to starboard and back while plunging forwards into the oncoming waves and then rearing back as it rode the waves upwards. The ship was moving and pitching and rolling across four fields of motion with no discernible pattern to the movement.

On deck, Calum was supervising the sailors loosening the ropes that were used to tighten the unfurled sails. This allowed the sailors above to furl the sails under the yard arms. Judging when and how far to loosen the ropes was tricky; loosen the slack too quickly and the sails could whip and billow in the wind, wrapping themselves around ropes and yards or flicking at the sailors balanced above. Wait too long and the taught sails could tear under tension and the force of the rising wind.

The other officers were gathering on deck. Miles made his way over to Calum in the strange rolling naval gait common to sailors in rough seas, with legs splayed apart and each step taken quickly.

'Need help?'

'No, under control.'

Calum turned and headed to the wheel, located in the stern of the ship. As he did, the Charlotte lurched to port and pitched heavily forwards. Calum stumbled, almost regained his balance and then fell heavily.

He looked up and saw Franklin, standing next to Tyler, smiling wolfishly and saying something to Tyler. Franklin's eyes never left Calum's, a predator sizing up his prey.

A little more than a month after leaving Bristol, the Charlotte reached the Tropic of Cancer.

Tyler was very pleased with the progress. The crew were getting on, which was no small mercy at sea, the Charlotte had sailed well through the storm and was making good time. That helped stop sailors from letting their superstitions get the better of them. Tyler was aware of the fickleness of the sea and of a ship's crew. It took little for fear or trouble to spread. To appease their fears, Tyler turned a blind eye to a number of less-than-Christian ceremonies regularly conducted on the voyage. Many were small, private affairs but crossing into the tropics dictated something grander.

'Mr Franklin, perhaps we should celebrate the Baptism of the Tropics if you please?'

'With pleasure, cap'n. I will organise the godfathers and we shall begin at noon.'

Franklin quietly passed the word around to those crew who had sailed the tropics. Each man was assigned a novice, a sailor who had never ventured this far south. As godfathers, they would initiate their novice.

A large bucket that served as a bath was placed on the deck and filled with seawater. The novices each took a turn hauling buckets of water up and over the railing and into the bath. Every man aboard with the exception of Tyler and Miles took part.

'Here on this ship, in this tub be all the oceans of the world,' Franklin said. 'I, Lord of the Tropics, hereby place my line across the ocean.' With this, Franklin leaned forward and placed an iron bar barely two fingers wide across the makeshift bath.

'To enter my realm, the tropics of the world, let he that be worthy dance upon Cancer. Now let them that may dance upon the tropic line step forwards.'

The first novice named Jones, barely more than a boy, stepped forward. 'Who represents this novice?' Franklin said.

'I am his godfather,' said an older sailor. Then he pointed at Jones. 'This is Flat. Flatulence.'

'Make your vows,' Franklin said. The godfathers then began beating on pots and pans liberated from the kitchen. Jones stepped forward and climbed gingerly upon the iron bar over the makeshift bath.

'I vow that no sailor will ever find or hear of me with his wife. I vow that no sailor shall ever have to carry my load. I ask the Lord God for fair winds. And I ask the Lord of the Tropics for safe passage through his waters. These are my vows.'

Franklin stepped forward and dipped a ladle into the bath and then poured it over Flatulence's head. The novice smiled and bowed carefully to Franklin then stepped down. Jones would later give his daily grog ration to his godfather along with a share of his meal. All the novices would do the same, a small bribe in return for easy passage through the baptism.

Three more novices quickly followed Jones until only one was left, Gilbert Calum. 'Who represents this novice?' Franklin said.

'I am his godfather,' said Rusher. 'This is Stumbles. Stumbles and Falls.' Several of the sailors from Franklin's watch laughed. Calum blushed red.

'Make your vows, Stumbles and Falls,' Franklin said to much amusement.

'I vow that no sailor will ever find or hear of me with his wife. I vow that no sailor shall ever have to carry my load. I ask the Lord God for fair winds. And I ask the Lord of the Tropics for safe passage through his waters.'

Franklin dipped his ladle in the water while behind Calum two sailors stepped forwards and yanked the iron bar from under Calum. He fell awkwardly into the bath.

'I pronounce you initiated, Stumbles and Falls,' Franklin said. Franklin then pushed Calum under the water and filled a bucket and dumped it on Calum as he came up gasping for air. Then other sailors pushed forwards and took turns to force Calum back under. Only the Lord of the Tropics could stop this part of the ceremony.

'Come on, Stumbles, find your feet,' Franklin said laughing.

Many of the sailors now edged backwards, having had their fun they baulked at any further humiliation for Calum. Looks of uncertainty spread and some of the sailors quickly backed away eager to distance themselves from what they were watching. Usually, a novice who was dunked was afforded a chance to beg and bribe his fellows. Still, Franklin and a handful of sailors kept dunking Calum.

Calum swallowed a big gulp of seawater and retched violently. He was pushed under and saw Franklin staring at him and hated him in that moment. From beneath the water, as he choked and gagged he vowed revenge on the older man. Finally, he rose above the water, gulping in the air. As he did, he saw the world anew, with a cold hatred for his tormentor.

'Enough!'

Every head looked around at Tyler, who stood at the stern.

Calum managed to grab the edge of the makeshift bath and haul himself out of it. For several moments, no one moved. Then Calum walked away.

'Mr Carroll, your accordion needs playing now,' Tyler said. Usually, it took cajoling and the promise of an extra rum to get Carroll to play. Now he moved as quickly as he could, trying not to slip as he followed the sodden path that Calum had taken below deck. Moments later, Carroll reappeared and struck up a tune.

*

The Charlotte docked in the Cape Verde Islands a few days later. The islands lay due west from the cape after which they were named and began the trading zones of the African coast from which the continent disgorged much of her wealth, including people, for sale.

South lay 700 miles of French-controlled coast, from the Senegal River to the Sierra Leone River. Then the Charlotte would skirt the Grain Coast, famed for its spices and peppers, past the Ivory and Gold Coasts to the Slave Coast. The Slave Coast ran eastwards until the African continent hooked south past Gabon and the Congo, both rich trade ports for slaves.

But first, the Charlotte needed to resupply. Tyler laid a course for the Isle of May, the smallest and most desolate of the Cape Verde Islands. Once anchored, Miles and Franklin went ashore to trade for salt with the locals, to cure the meats that would also be bought, at La Praya, a day's sail away and more meat to be bought upon arrival at the Slave Coast.

Soon the salt was loaded and the Charlotte left the desolate speck of land behind. The following day, the Charlotte slipped into the port of La Praya. As the ship entered the harbour, a blank cannon round was fired, with a reply coming from the Portuguese fort that sat above the harbour.

At the dual cannon burst, a number of ships dropped long boats and rowed over towards where the Charlotte anchored. Soon Dutch, Portuguese, Scandinavian, Spanish and even French sailors were bumping their long boats alongside the Charlotte, asking of any news, talking sailing conditions and names of sailors and where they were from. Within half an hour, the sport had ceased as there was little else to discuss.

'Did you find anything interesting?' Tyler said to his officers.

'The Elizabeth is in port due to head back to England tomorrow,' Miles said. 'Mr Royce is her captain. Do you know him?'

'That I do, Mr Miles,' Tyler said. 'Lower a long boat and a few sailors to row me over, I will see how Edward is fairing.'

'Why, George, you old sea dog, how wonderful to see you here,' Edward Royce said as Tyler climbed aboard the Elizabeth.

'I may well say the same about you, old timer,' Tyler said.

'Old timer is it now?'

'You have been at sea longer than me.'

'Yes, for all of six months longer, and that makes me an old timer does it?'

'Afraid so, Edward.'

'Well then, you best assist this old timer to his cabin and I have no doubt you will be able to lighten the ballast by drinking more than your share of rum.'

'If you insist, Edward.'

The two captains settled into the small cabin and a sailor bought in a ham, some fruits and cassava and a bottle of rum.

'So, where are you coming back from?' Tyler said.

'India this time, we have spices and tea aboard. The whole ship smells like a perfumed whore house.'

'Did you stop on the coast?'

'Just to resupply and offload some cotton. This time around, the fashion was blue, and of course, our cotton was plain, but we managed to find some blue dye and buy it and I had the sailors dye the cotton.

'As sailors, they know what they're doing but when it comes to dying cloth, well, Pennington will have my guts for garters when he sees our newly dyed blue deck! And some of the sailors will go to their graves, be it tomorrow or in fifty years' time with blue hands and feet. One of the dimmer lads was so silly to scratch his nose several times and now it is blue. The men have taken to calling him "blue-beak". Anyway, we covered the costs.'

'Sounds like you could have made a small fortune charging people to watch the show.'

'For God's sake, George, don't say that near Pennington, or he'll ask me why I didn't do just that. Still, he will clear another handsome profit.'

'Any information on the slave markets?'

'In Senegambia, the price is £29 to £30 a head. I suspect that the price may rise if all the talk of abolishing slavery gathers momentum,' Royce said.

'I've heard far too much of that nonsense of late,' Tyler said.

'Call it what you will, George, but the idea is growing. Before I left, there was talk of a bill in the Commons to abolish the trade.'

'There has been such talk since that fool Wilberforce started pushing for an end to the trade and that was twenty years ago. Nothing will come of it.'

Tyler stared out the window as if seeking to see whether the wind was changing. He was a slave boat captain and had no desire to stare down the precipice of a world without slavery. He could almost sense himself falling, much like the first time he climbed high into the rigging of a ship as a boy. He almost let go then, now he could feel the same sensation pulling at him.

Royce reached out and put an arm on Tyler's shoulder. 'George, what news from Pennington?'

Tyler steadied himself. 'I hear that he is considering running for Parliament, or joining with some other traders to get one of their own elected. Given how few are entitled to vote in Bristol, it should not be that hard.'

'I hear that it is about one in twenty men alone have the right to vote, and I bet Pennington knows most of them and probably employs the rest.'

'It's likely the traders will get a man in Parliament. Pennington believes it's not too late to rally an amendment against Wilberforce and his lies.'

'George, I suspect that it may be too late. Granted, I have not been home for many months but before I left, I visited friends in London. They said the city was alive with the idea of slavery ending. Churches were preaching against it. Seems that Londoners had taken the idea to heart and you know London leads the nation's thinking.'

'Most likely it's another silly new fashion that will quickly pass. That's London's true heart. And will people be so easily convinced when they have to take tea and coffee without sugar? And what of tobacco? People are not so easy to convince when they actually have to do something or go without.'

'There is a poem that circulates from time to time,' Royce said. 'It's called Charity by a fellow named Cowper and it uses lines like "cargoes of despair" and talks of a trade awash in the blood of innocents. They hand out pamphlets describing all this in detail.'

'No doubt lies. How in God's name do people think England will ever be anything great without slavery? It's the engine that drives taxation for goodness sake. Any government that stands against that cannot win.'

'The abolitionists would make this a moral issue. They are humanising slaves by describing the suffering they endure. They are trying to make Londoners and others see blacks as people, not cargoes. They want us to see them as equals of a sort.'

'Us, Edward? Do you support this nonsense?'

'I never gave it a thought until recently. The trade was just always there. No one really thought about it because no one had to. But now, well perhaps it's time to think about it. Nothing will ever change if we do what we've always done.'

Royce stood and walked to his small bureau desk and rummaged through a drawer. 'Here is one of the pamphlets.'

He handed a worn and tattered pamphlet to Tyler who looked at a picture of a black man in chains, down on one knee, his hands raised as though begging. Below was a single line, *Am I not a man and a brother?*

'So you say you agree with this. What are you saying, Edward?'

Royce looked at his friend opposite, deflated and turning inwards. 'I owe it to you to tell you this, George. This current against slavery is too strong. Sooner or later the abolitionists will win. Better to read the winds and ride them, rather than try to sail against them. Be ready for it you old sea dog.'

Royce watched Tyler, waiting for a reaction.

'I…so you are…' Tyler sighed, raised his glass and looked at his friend. 'To the good old days, which seem to be passing too soon for my liking.'

*

Three days later, the Charlotte, resupplied with food and water, raised her anchor and sailed away from La Praya for the African coast. The sailing was fluky at first but soon the Charlotte picked up the beginnings of the Guinea Current that flowed southeast and then eastwards along the coast.

Within a few days, a large river mouth and island came into view. Tyler pulled out his pilot guide, a series of notes, drawings and maps detailing landmarks along the coast. These included forts and factories to house slaves and other trade goods, rivers and bays and depth soundings.

'Mr Miles, I make that out to be Sherbro Island. Do you concur?'

Miles consulted his own pilot guide, like Tyler's a small leather-bound book filled with information.

'Sherbro Island it is,' Miles said.

'We are making excellent time. I think we shall forgo landing at Fort James and push ahead for Elmina,' Tyler said.

'I agree, captain, we are having a very good turn of the weather and currents,' Miles said.

*

For the next three weeks, the Charlotte raced along, propelled by the Guinea Current. The weather was hot but not unpleasant and the crew had little to do. Those who were ambitious compiled information, consulting with Mr Miles and his pilot guide. A keen sailor could easily use such time to begin to make his own guide. The rest of the crew used the time to relax. Soon the cargo hold would be emptied, the ship reconfigured with a barricade put in place between the slaves and the crew quarters, a similar defensive structure erected on the deck and a live cargo in the hold. All sailors had heard stories of slaves trying to rebel. It put a man on edge. For now, though many sailors lay in the sun and enjoyed the freedom of not having to think about such things.

'Mr Tyler, Elmina is on the horizon,' Franklin said.

Many of the sailors raced to the front of the ship, some up into the rigging to spy the fortress of Elmina. It was situated on a promontory above a bustling town. Behind the fort, lay the entrance to the River Anokobra, one of the largest inland trade routes, known to locals as the slave highway.

The coast looked dirty, with a pall of dust and smoke hanging like a low-lying cloud and the water turgid and blue with streaks of brown. Tyler combed the small collection of ships looking for any he knew.

'Master Jones, I will give you an extra dose of grog if you can tell me the name of the most famous sailor to visit that fort,' Miles said to the boy.

'Um, Mr Drake?'

'Not um Mr Drake. Christopher Columbus sailed in these waters. Seems fitting that the man who opened up the Americas should have visited here, don't you think?'

'I suppose so,' Jones said.

Tyler laughed. 'Lawson, leave the poor boy alone. Next, you will be telling him about the Governor's staircase.'

'Governor's staircase, captain?'

'See now he is addressing me directly, wanting salacious titbits about the Governor of Elmina. Well, go ahead and tell him. It will fuel his dreams for nights on end.'

'Master Jones, the Governor of Elmina has a trapdoor built into his bedroom floor. Below it is a staircase that descends directly to the women's prison, to facilitate, shall we say, intimate and immediate access should the Governor have the desire for a woman,' Miles said.

Jones's eyes widened as he realised what was being said. 'Oh, that might be my heaven right there. Are they white or black, these women?'

'Black, young man,' Miles said.

'Exotic black women to entertain him. Wow.'

Tyler and Miles both laughed. 'You realise that the women are not willing participants,' Miles said.

Jones was now over at the railing. 'How exactly does one get to be Governor of Elmina?' Miles and Tyler looked at each other and laughed.

'Well, for a start you have to be Dutch, not English. And you also have to be very smart,' Tyler said.

'So two strikes against young Jones,' Miles whispered. Tyler laughed some more.

'Wait, why aren't we stopping?' Jones said, his dream disappearing in the wake of the Charlotte.

'We are bound for Cape Coast. It's three leagues further along, and it's English,' Miles said.

'Does it need a Governor?' Jones said.

*

Tyler stepped ashore to the familiar sensual assault of Africa. People of all descriptions wandered around dressed in colours bright and vivid. Wild animals were caged, and food markets peppered with aromas of spice. Here fish in abundance, there fruits of every colour and shape. Meat lying in the sun, some of it reeking, some cured. Fish too laid on platters with their attendant retinue of flies. The whole was like closing one's eyes after looking at the sun and seeing colours and patterns dance still.

'Mr Miles, you check in the inn over there, I will check in here for Nagle. Assuming the old shark is still alive,' Tyler said.

'Let's hope so,' Miles said.

Five minutes later, both men met in the same spot. 'No luck, captain, how 'bout you?'

'Same.'

'Perhaps we try around the town square?' Miles said. He could sense Tyler stiffen a little, baulking at heading too far from the Charlotte.

Tyler and Miles entered an alleyway that led between ramshackle warehouses, mostly constructed of wood, with some stonework stitched in here and there for support. Several of the warehouses reeked of rotting food, others of human excrement. These latter all had sturdier foundations and walls, and housed slaves waiting for sale.

Soon the dark alleyway lightened and they emerged into the town square. Several large trees stood at intervals, each with telltale iron chains linking to shackles driven deep into their trunks. Under one tree a slave auction was concluding.

Tyler and Miles did not stay to watch. They crossed the square and entered the largest drinking establishment.

Nagle sat in a corner, leaning back in his chair, almost defying it not to break under his considerable weight. He was talking loudly, slyly watching the men at a nearby table straining to listen to his advice on selling slaves. 'It's all in the wrist, the way you flick the whip and how hard you hit the bastards, and where.'

Sensing the interest from the nearby table, Nagle turned to his companion and spoke quietly. 'Of course, you want to break them enough, but not fully. So they look compliant but not broken.' As he spoke, Nagle lowered the volume of his voice, watching the nearby men edge and strain sideways in their seats, hoping to hear. He loved this sport, baiting listeners and teasing them.

'Tyler, my dear fellow,' Nagle bellowed. One of the men at the next table jumped and nearly fell from his chair.

'Nagle,' Tyler said. Tyler had once seen a dead shark of immense size at the port in Cape Town. His knees had nearly buckled under him seeing the teeth on that shark and its immense girth. What he never forgot above all was the shark's small, dead eyes. Every time he saw Nagle, he was reminded of that shark.

'This is Lawson Miles, second captain of the Charlotte. Lawson, Mr Nagle, Pennington's preferred factor on the coast.'

'Factor extraordinaire, dear fellow. Now you must be thirsty, drinks perhaps and then we can start working on a deal.' Nagle smiled at the mention of the word deal. Tyler shivered.

Nagle snapped his fingers and a small black boy raced over. Drinks were ordered and the three men sat at a table, Nagle's previous compatriot quickly forgotten. Nagle opened the dealings.

'The fort is currently well stocked with slaves, and two caravans are only a day or two away from arriving. How many are you after?'

'Three hundred. Short of that, perhaps palm oil,' Tyler said.

'Three hundred. I think the Governor may have about half of that himself for sale.'

'The Governor is selling. I thought he wasn't allowed to do that under the terms of his administration?' Miles said.

Nagle laughed for several moments. 'Well, what he is expected to do and what he does are very different things. Every Governor for the past half-century has run a profitable sideline in trading slaves. Now, I expect you want them under 24 years. And how about women, do you want women?'

'No more than ten per cent women, maybe a handful of boys too,' Tyler said. Nagle leered and winked at Tyler.

'The boys are for sale in Jamaica I take it?'

'For God's sake, yes. No one on one of my ships is into that sort of thing.'

'Do you want warehouse space or will you trade from the ship?'

'We have manillas, so from the ship should do until we get the slaves,' Tyler said. 'We'll use a place here for the branding if that suits.'

'Alright then, meet me here tomorrow, midday. I will see what is on offer.' With that, Nagle stood and walked out. Tyler and Miles followed.

'So he seems to know his way about?' Miles said.

'Nagle has been down here since I was little more than a boy. He knows the town, the traders, the slaves, which to avoid and why. Without him, Pennington would be just another trader, and you and I probably pressed and serving at His Majesty's pleasure in the royal navy.'

'So he has lived here all the time you have been sailing here?'

'Yes. God alone knows how he does it. I sure couldn't live out here.'

Nagle met the two officers outside the tavern at noon the following day.

'Right, so the Governor can do us for 125 slaves, including your females. That leaves 175 men and boys. There is a caravan of Arab traders due in later today. They are casting about for buyers. Currently, there are two other ships in port, both already with decent complements. One is expected to leave in the next two days for Boston, so little to worry about there. The other is happy to purchase at auction, which will take a number of days. So we should have you sailing soon enough to beat the crowds.

'Nassim, who is negotiating for the Arab caravan is a friend, so I have sent him a message, telling him what we are looking for. He suggests we attend the auction and grab the boys there. If you can swing some sweeteners above the manillas, we can probably tidy everything off with Nassim in private.'

'What is this Nassim looking for?' Miles said.

'This Nassim is a personal friend, so perhaps you should drop the tone that suggests he is, how shall I say it, dodgy. If you want the slaves you want and with little fuss or competition, then Nassim is our man. And Nassim is looking for muskets, and perhaps some tobacco.'

'We have both, along with some fine pipes and some Indian cotton too, though only a few bafts.'

'The muskets and tobacco will suffice,' Nagle said.

'Good. Do we meet this Nassim, or?'

'Leave it with me,' Nagle said. 'It appears you have timed your run well. We should have you underway in a week or two. Do you need any wood for the fit-out?'

'No, the carpenters have it under control. We should have the ship refitted for the middle passage a few days after we offload the cargo,' Tyler said.

'Excellent, then for now we are looking like the weather gauge is on our side, to put it in naval parlance,' Nagle said. 'There is only the matter of my commission.'

Tyler had been waiting for this. Nagle had declined to draw a pay from Pennington, despite the repeated efforts of the Bristol trader to get Nagle on his payroll. Pennington had gone as far as putting together a consortium of several traders with a lucrative offer to fund Nagle in return for exclusive use. Nagle had declined. He had come to Africa searching for freedom and was not prepared to give it up. A factor owned by a trader or group of traders meant money, but not the freedom to do the deals Nagle wanted. And Nagle enjoyed the dealings, the gossip, the pleasures of the coast too much to give it up and be at the call of a master.

'So I will take two per cent total of manillas, and those cotton bafts too if that is agreeable,' Nagle said.

Tyler looked at Miles, who shrugged his shoulders. Pennington had no clear instructions on the matter of Nagle's commission. Tyler thought about it, then agreed. Better to get things done quickly and easily than linger on the Slave Coast for months trying to buy slaves, all the while having to house them, feed them and increase the risk of a rebellion with the coast in sight.

The following day, Tyler led a contingent of his sailors into the town square. Several, led by Rusher, set up shop in a nearby factory rented for the day. Soon they were joined by a few locals, large men hired for their muscle. Miles, Franklin, a handful of sailors and the surgeon McDougal accompanied Tyler as they made their way to the square. Tyler spied Nagle talking to some Arab traders near a corral of sorts. Within it, stood a motley collection of Africans, bound for slavery.

Nagle watched Tyler but made no effort to end his conversation. After several minutes, he strolled across to Tyler.

'So the Arabs are auctioning the men first, of which there are about thirty. The other boat captains will most likely bid for those, and then they will bring out the boys. I suggest we stay and watch.'

'As you wish then,' Tyler said.

'I have had a shaded area reserved for us, by that tree over there.' Nagle led Tyler, McDougal and Miles to the shaded area where four seats were ready for them. The sailors, under the command of Franklin, went and sat in the shade of another large tree, waiting until they were needed to escort the slave boys back to the factory and then the Charlotte.

'So, Mr Miles, is this your first auction?' Nagle said.

'Yes it is,' Miles said. Behind him, there was a cracking sound. Miles jumped. Turning, he saw the slaves being led out, each chained to another. An Arab trader walked near the slaves, cracking the whip that he held to offer encouragement.

The slaves were marched into a corral next to a large tree. Pairs of slaves were then marched out of the corral, their chains attached to the larger chain shackled to the tree.

'So the beauty of the Arab traders is that they really know their merchandise. Some of the other traders, the Africans, bring all sorts of men from a variety of tribes. And the Lord knows you don't want some of them,' Nagle said.

'Aren't they all the same?' Miles said.

McDougal snorted and laughed, as did Nagle. Even Tyler smiled at that.

'Oh, I say, that is a delightful joke,' Nagle said. He looked at Miles and saw the look of confusion. 'Oh, you're serious. You really don't see the difference out there?'

'Look at the group in the corral. Mostly they are Mallais, with a few mixed in from other tribes. The Arab traders have a knack for picking the best slaves, those strong enough to survive in the cane fields, but not so proud as to consider rebellion. You don't want any of the Ayois, for example. They are a proud warrior race. Now get a few of them together and you get rebellion fomenting. You can tell an Ayois from the scars that spread from the corners of their eyes.'

'One should definitely avoid the Foin, for they are truly the dregs of the trade,' McDougal said. Both he and Nagle shared a quiet laugh. 'They have scars on their temples. The men who have dealt with them say it saps their will. Now, Nagle, what are the others to avoid?'

'Those would be the Tebou and Guiamba. They are covered with all sorts of scars and are known to spread a depressive state amongst the slaves.'

'Some of those in the corral have scars on their faces, should we avoid those too?' Miles said.

'No. Those with scarring on their cheeks alone are the Aradas. The ones with their foreheads scarred are the Nago. Both are good at sugar cane harvesting.'

'So there you have it, Mr Miles, your first education of the intricacies and vagaries of these Africans,' McDougal said.

The auction began and soon the slaves were sold. Twenty went to one slave ship captain, the remainder to the other.

'Right, McDougal, shall we inspect the boys?' Nagle said.

He and McDougal stood and walked over to the Arab traders. Two burly Africans stood nearby. A brief conversation took place and the two Africans walked over to a nearby warehouse. They disappeared inside and soon a group of boys were paraded out into the corral. They sat in the dirt and an Arab barked an order at the group. The boys began to sing, in a melancholy tone. One boy refused to sing and the Arab beat him with a long cane until the boy joined in. All the slaves eyed the earth on which they sat, singing with little enthusiasm.

The Arab barked out another order and this time the boys rose and stood. One of the boys was slow to rise and received a whipping from the cane.

Nagle and McDougal walked over to the slaves. Nagle said something to the Arab.

Another order was issued. The slaves tilted their heads back, then left and right. Nagle kept a keen eye on the slaves, then separated out several from the group, tapping them on the shoulder with a cane that the Arab provided him.

Another order. The separated slaves stepped forward, then turned and walked off. The burly Africans secured the boys to a chain. These boys were likely well over twelve or near enough to it. Next, Nagle circled the coffle of slaves. McDougal trailed him. Nagle stopped and said something quietly to McDougal. The surgeon gestured to one of the boys and the Arab issued another order. The boy stepped forward gingerly. McDougal looked at the boy's knee, comparing it to the other. 'It's swollen,' McDougal said.

The Arab nodded and the boy was removed. Two more boys were singled out, both of weak physiques, one with a small chest, the other with weakened arms. Both were marched off. Nagle said something in Arabic and the slaver barked another order. The two weak boys were separated from the others.

'Can I see the teeth?' McDougal said.

Nagle said something in Arabic and the remaining boys were asked to open their mouths. McDougal covered his nose and mouth with a handkerchief and then inspected the teeth of each boy. One more boy was separated out and sent back to the other discarded boys, under the watch of the two Africans.

Nagle nodded and the Arab ordered the remaining boys to run in place, then to bend at the hip. Each boy was asked to lift his arms, then swing them.

McDougal nodded to Tyler. These boys would do. McDougal then nodded to Nagle who spoke to the Arab merchant. Soon after the deal was concluded, the boys exchanged for a manilla a person, with two boxes of muskets also delivered. The slave boys were kept separated from the discarded boys the whole time. Some unscrupulous traders were known to try to substitute a few of the discarded slaves for the chosen slaves.

The chosen boys were taken to a nearby warehouse by a party of sailors led by Miles and McDougal. Franklin and the group of sailors ensured none of the boys tried to escape. Then Franklin went and found Rusher, who merely nodded and pointed at the fire and bellows being operated by two sweating Africans. Sticking out of the fire were several iron bars with wooden handles.

'Bring in 'em, we have the brands nice and hot!' Franklin yelled.

'Thank you, Mr Franklin,' Miles said. 'Let's get them branded and back on board if you please.'

Franklin smiled. He nodded to several solidly built Africans standing nearby. 'Let's get 'em branded.'

The boys were marched over near the fire. The ends of the brands were glowing in the fire, each carrying the mark of the Pennington Africa Company. The Africans grabbed the first boy and held him down. Another African rubbed tallow over the outer thigh of the boy and placed a piece of oily paper over the tallow.

While this was happening, Franklin tested several of the brands, digging the ends around in the fire to ensure each was hot. He grabbed a brand that was glowing near orange-red and as soon as the oiled paper was placed over the tallow, he touched the brand to the paper. The boy screamed. Several of the boys watching nearby tried to back away or run. Africans grabbed each and soon all the boys were branded. As each boy was dragged from the branding McDougal quickly examined the wounds. None looked like they would cause a problem.

While the branding was underway, Tyler and Nagle were concluding the deal for the remaining slaves. Over the next few days, groups of two dozen men would be brought to the same warehouse where Franklin was currently branding slaves. McDougal and Nagle would examine them and if selected, each exchanged for a manilla. Those selected would be held in cells in the warehouse until the refit of the Charlotte was concluded.

All going well, it was likely that Tyler would have three hundred slaves within a week, and be ready to sail soon after.

As the negotiations concluded, Tyler made his farewells. He made to exit the square and then quietly turned and stood in the shade of the alleyway and watched Nagle and the Arab trader. He watched as Nagle passed two manillas over to the Arab trader and then walked over to where the two small boys that had been discarded and separated from the remainder of the rejects stood. Nagle ensured they were well chained and then left with the two boys.

Tyler shivered as he watched, despite the heat. He did not know if the boys were for Nagle's use, or if the factor intended to sell them as part of some awful deal. Either way, their fate was dreadful to contemplate.

*

'So when do the women come aboard?' Jones said, leaning on the side of the Charlotte as she lay at the anchor of the fort.

'Steady on, boy,' Rusher said.

'Steady on! God, I want to do one of 'em blackies so bad,' Jones said.

'Not on the cap'n's boat you don't,' Franklin said from nearby.

Jones's jaw dropped and he stared at Franklin. Finally, after several seconds, he managed to stammer, 'but'.

'Cap'n is very clear about such things. No dalliances aboard with the cargo. Cause no poor bastard in Jamaica wants to buy a negro woman only to have your pathetic sprog pop out of her a few months later. Gawd imagine that, Rusher, a little half-caste bastard Jones running around a sugar plantation.'

'But I gotta do something or I might explode,' Jones said.

Tyler was working on the ledger for the voyage when Franklin knocked and entered the tiny cabin.

'Begging your pardon, cap'n, but Master Jones has a problem,' Franklin said.

'I think I can guess the nature of that problem. Take him a few of the other young ones ashore the night before we load the cargo. That should be in two days' time. Nagle can tell you where you can find a decent whorehouse.'

'Thank you, cap'n,' Franklin said, turning to walk out.

'It's their money and on your head, Mr Franklin. No one misses a watch 'cause he got the crabs from a negro whore. Are we clear?'

'Yes, cap'n.' Franklin ducked under the door and disappeared. Tyler went back to recording the number of slaves in his ledger.

*

Nine days after the auction, the Charlotte raised her anchor and eased away from the coast. Once out to sea she headed east, riding along the current to where it met the Atlantic currents. Here the Charlotte would turn westwards and then northwest, retracing a little of her journey from England. Near the Cape Verde Islands, the trade winds picked up, heading westwards. From that point, the Charlotte would run westwards across the Atlantic for a few weeks.

The shipboard routine was managed by Miles. 'Right, you lads ready?'

'Aye,' came the reply from the non-sailing watch. Most of the group was armed with muskets and swords.

'Mr McDougal, let's go inspect the cargo and begin the exercising,' Miles said.

Miles, McDougal and the non-duty watch gathered behind the barricade separating sailors and slaves. A sailor climbed a crude ladder and carefully peeked over the barricade, inspecting the deck.

'All clear,' he said.

Miles and McDougal unlocked the barricade that stood between the stern of the ship and the cargo hold. Two sailors stood with muskets pointing through embrasures that opened onto the deck. Miles pulled the door open.

'Right, Mr Rusher, your lads in the rigging please,' Miles said. Rusher led his men up into the rigging, one man climbing while another held his own musket and that of the man climbing before each man would switch roles.

'Ready, Mr Miles,' Rusher said when the sailors were in position.

With that, Miles went and inspected the heavy iron grate that secured the cargo hold. The lock was still in place. There were no slaves nearby. Carefully, he unlocked the grate and stepped back. If somehow the slaves had managed to unfasten their chains or break the bindings, this would be the moment they would try to push the grate aside and rush the ship.

'All quiet, Mr Miles,' McDougal said. He peered down into the hold. Slaves were laying side by side in the cramped conditions, packed between bulkheads and next to the wooden planks that formed a path down the spine of the ship. The number of slaves allowed was based on the size of the ship and laid out under laws passed by the British Parliament.

McDougal carefully placed the small ladder that remained on deck unless the hold was unlocked into place and climbed down. Miles and two sailors followed. McDougal sniffed the air. The smell was unpleasant and would be overwhelming by the time they reached Jamaica.

'Why do you do that? It smells bad enough down here?' Miles said.

'That it does, but corruption carries its own smell. It's different to this, this is just waste.'

'You surgeons are an odd breed,' Miles said.

'Right lads, let's start with the left side, groups of twenty,' McDougal said. 'Is Mr Carrol ready with his accordion?'

'Ready as ever,' one of the sailors said.

Each morning, Carrol would play his accordion as groups of slaves were brought on deck.

The sailors went to the rear of the compartment and unlocked a group of slaves from the chain that secured them in place. Then pairs of slaves, shackled together, were marched down the central walkway to the ladder and forced to climb it.

'Good morning, lads, how are we this fine morning?' Rusher yelled from the rigging.

Sailors grabbed each pair of slaves as they made it to the deck and walked them to the side where they were secured to a long chain that ran the length of the deck.

'Right then, lads, dance please!' a sailor yelled. While Carrol played, the slaves danced. Each group of twenty slaves had around fifteen minutes on deck.

One slave refused to dance.

Franklin, who supervised the armed sailors grabbed a cane and walked up and whipped it at the legs of the slave. 'Dance, you black bastard,' Franklin said. 'Rusher, have one of the lads fetch me a whip, please.'

Within moments, a sailor handed Franklin a whip. He cracked it twice near the slave, then smiled and aimed at the slave's face. The whip hit and cracked almost simultaneously and the slave fell holding his face.

'Now, you black bastard, stand and dance,' Franklin said. Then he cracked the whip over the slave who was helped to his feet by his chained partner. After that, all the slaves danced.

Once all the slaves were exercised, a meal of yams, gruel and water was served. Each slave was given a crude wooden spoon to use at meal times. If lost, no replacement was given.

Each afternoon, Tyler had the slaves brought from the hold and chained to the length of chain running the length of each side of the ship.

'Sit 'em down, all of 'em,' Franklin said to the sailors on deck. 'Get 'em fed, lads.' Sailors' offered a second meal similar to the morning meal.

'Duty watch, please scrub out the hold,' Tyler said. Buckets of seawater were pulled in from over the side and the duty watch descended into the hold. Mouths and noses covered by bandanas and kerchiefs, the sailors splashed the water into the bilges and pumped this out, cleaning away a large proportion of the shit and vomit.

'It's ready for inspection, cap'n,' one of the sailors said.

Tyler, Miles and McDougal descended into the hold and carefully looked around. 'Any signs worth pointing out, Mr Smith,' Tyler said to the senior sailor.

'We checked around but nothing wrong, cap'n. No signs of any weapons or scratching near the shackles.'

'Thank you, Mr Smith,' Tyler said. Then he, Miles and McDougal carried out their own inspection.

'Remind me again why we do this?' Miles said to McDougal.

'Too many slavers neglect the hold, leave the excrement to build up, which is how plague ships start. And if rebellion is to foment, it is done in the darkness. Inspecting the hold is the best defence against both,' McDougal said.

'Sit down!' yelled a disembodied voice from above. 'Down, sit down.' More shouting.

Tyler, Miles and McDougal ran as quickly as they could in the cramped conditions, scuttling bent at the waist. At the ladder, Smith and two sailors were climbing quickly. The last sailor stood aside as Tyler, followed by Miles and a puffing McDougal reached the ladder and climbed it. Shouting was still coming from above.

Tyler pulled himself out of the hold to see three sailors, muskets pointed at a group of standing slaves, screaming orders to sit.

'What the bloody hell is happening?' Tyler said to Smith.

'The lads started that group exercising and these negroes stood up too,' Smith said.

Tyler walked over to the slaves who had stood up and balled his fist and hit the nearest as hard as he could in the stomach. The slave collapsed to the deck, dragging his chained partner down. One of the sailors did the same only using the butt of his musket and another slave fell. His chained partner tried to haul the fallen slave up and was also hit with the musket's butt.

Tyler gestured to the remaining slaves to sit, pushing down on the shoulders of another.

Soon the remainder sat.

'Get them below, all of them,' Tyler said.

Within minutes, all the slaves were being pushed back down into the hold.

'Keep them down there tomorrow morning, only let them out in the afternoon. That should teach them.'

*

Gilbert Calum watched Franklin roughly grab Dinks by the scruff of the neck and launch the cat into the air.

'Every time, every bloody time, he lands feet first,' Franklin said in admiration. The cat stalked across the deck to the corner of the stern where Franklin had fashioned a piece of wood as a bench, lay down on Franklin's feet and purred.

Franklin shifted his foot slightly and Dinks stirred. The cat swiped a lazy paw at Franklin, grazing his trousers. Several sailors nearby wondered if this would be the end for Dinks. Franklin smirked, waited for the cat to settle and moved his foot again. Dinks swiped his paw again. Then Franklin reached down and rubbed the cat's back forcefully. Dinks purred in contentment.

Calum watched the rough affection between the two and felt a gnawing inside. He remembered the lack of any affection in his childhood and Franklin's dismissal of him. The pain of his past resurfacing in the spurning by the older Franklin. Calum could taste the saltwater in his mouth, see the joy on Franklin's face as he remembered being pushed under the water in the makeshift bath. He watched Franklin gently shift the cat with his foot and an idea spawned, a way to hurt Franklin, to repay the pain and humiliation Calum still felt.

The Charlotte was making excellent progress across the middle passage. Tyler was pleased. His crew were content, the cargo was subdued and at this rate, Jamaica was little more than two weeks' sail away.

Tyler looked from the wheel across the ship. The sails were billowing nicely and the evening air was pleasant.

'Wonderful evening, cap'n,' Franklin said. He reached down and patted Dinks roughly.

'That it is, Mr Franklin,' Tyler said.

Miles came up from below with young Jones in tow. Jones carried a tray and on Miles's order offered a drink to Tyler and Franklin. 'At this clip, we may be in Jamaica soon,' Miles said.

'All things going well yes,' Tyler said.

'This must be about a perfect voyage, right?' Jones said.

The three officers froze, as did the sailor at the helm. Two more sailors on the deck below the raised stern silently retreated below.

After what felt like an eternity to Jones, Miles spoke. 'We don't say such things, Master Jones. Ever.'

'But why not, things are going—'

'Do shut him up before he Jonah's the lot of us,' Franklin said.

'What do ya mean?' Jones said.

'To say a voyage is, well the word you used…' Miles said.

'Perfect?' Jones said.

'Shut up, boy, or I'll have you in the bosun's chair all bloody night,' Franklin said.

'We don't say how the voyage has gone ever. You may speak of things being maintained, like at this clip, or the weather gauge is fair and if it continues, but don't speak of what has happened or what will happen as though it is a foregone conclusion,' Miles said.

'That is how you Jonah us all,' Franklin said.

'Jonah, like as in Jonah and the whale?' Jones said.

'Now shut up, boy, get down to the deck, get a bucket of seawater and dunk yourself in it,' Tyler said. 'Now.'

Jones looked at Tyler, then to Miles and Franklin. There was no mistaking the looks on their faces. As quickly as he dared, he dropped to the deck, grabbed a bucket and lowered it into the ocean. Then he pulled it up using all his strength and dunked it over his head.

Quietly Franklin said something, with only the word Lord being loud enough to be heard.

Miles crossed himself, as did the sailor at the helm.

'Master Jones is not permitted up here until the voyage ends, is that clear, gentlemen?' Tyler said.

There was a resounding chorus of ayes.

Two nights later, a storm hit the Charlotte hard, tossing her in all the directions a ship at sea did not want to go.

Tyler came up on deck, followed by the rest of the officers. Despite the wind blowing from the starboard side, Tyler was convinced the ship was listing towards the starboard.

'Are we listing starboard?' Tyler said to Miles.

'Again please!' Miles yelled.

Tyler cupped his hands at Miles's ear and yelled, 'Listing starboard?'

'I think so,' Miles said.

'Mr Calum, get down below and check!' Tyler yelled.

Calum carefully but quickly moved below decks. He reached the door to the rear cargo hold where food and water were stored but could not push it inwards.

Putting his shoulder to it still did nothing to move the door. He ducked back to the crew hold.

'You two with me, now.'

The two sailors, grateful to have something to do rather than huddle below decks trying to ride out the storm followed Calum.

'On three, shoulders to the door and push,' Calum said.

Calum counted and on three the sailors and Calum shoved their shoulders against the door as hard as they dared. The door moved slightly inwards and a small wave of water came surging out.

'Tell the captain that there is water in the rear cargo hold,' Calum said to one of the sailors. 'You, get a crew ready to man the bilge pumps,' Calum said to the other sailor.

As more water surged out, Calum was able to force the door open. Barrels of water lay smashed and broken in the watery hold. Calum scooped up a handful of the water and gingerly tasted it. Fresh water. There was no breach in the hull, but many of the precious barrels of drinking water now lay broken in the water sloshing around the hold.

Then Calum saw it. Dinks lay under one of the barrels, his back broken and rear legs crushed. The cat did not move when Calum approached it and for a moment Calum feared his plan for revenge had been taken from him. Dinks moved and looked up at Calum pitifully.

Calum put a foot on the cat's head and pushed down, forcing the broken body under the water. He had watched Franklin, nurturing his hatred for the older man, replacing his fear of his father with hatred for another. And in those days he had planned to kill Dinks, to kill that fear that never left him, by taking something Franklin valued. And what could be more fitting than forcing the cat underwater, just as Franklin had done to him. He would hurt Franklin as the older man had spurned and hurt him.

Now with Dinks under his foot, Calum felt drawn into another self. Warning him of the threshold over which he was crossing and mocking him for the pathetic nature of his revenge. He let the cat up and picked up the lifeless body.

Then, once the pumping started and the water began to drop, he headed up to the deck. He held out Dinks, like a sacrificial offering. Franklin stared at the cat and then at Calum. 'What do ya expect me to do with that? Toss it overboard.'

Calum felt his victory diminish and then disappear. He looked at Tyler and realised the captain was saying something.

'I asked what is happening below?' Tyler said.

'The freshwater barrels broke loose. A lot of them are smashed.'

Tyler went pale. 'How many?'

'Most of them, I think,' Calum said.

'Most of them! Get down there and tell me how many we have left. Exactly,' Tyler said.

Calum stared at Tyler for a long moment. 'What about the pumping?'

'Are the crew pumping the fresh water?' Tyler said. Then he ran to the ladder and disappeared into the hold.

As he approached the hold, he heard a sailor urging the others. 'Pump lads or well be going under, pump for your lives!'

When he saw the smashed barrels, he screamed at the crew, who were furiously pumping the water out. 'Stop pumping, now!' Scoop up as much of this water as you can. Get it into barrels, containers, anything.'

Tyler looked around and counted the remaining barrels. Each barrel held around 60 gallons. Divided between the crew, who drank three quarts each a day, and the slaves, who drank two quarts, he calculated enough water for 12 days. Very quickly, he went through the calculations again. Same result. At best estimation, they were fourteen days from Jamaica.

Two days without water in the tropical heat was just not possible for the crew or slaves. He looked at the tepid water sloshing around his feet and knew that at best the sailors might salvage a barrel, and more likely half a barrel. *Damn this storm and damn Calum. What the hell was the idiot thinking to pump out the fresh water?*

Tyler climbed the ladder and back onto the deck. The storm was now behind them. No chance of collecting more water.

'How is it down there?' Calum said.

'We are short on water, Mr Calum, thanks to you ordering the crew to pump it out. Pray for good sailing from here, boy,' Tyler said.

Calum flushed and looked down. 'I was only thinking—'

'Well, don't. Your judgement was pathetic,' Tyler said. 'I should have sent an experienced officer down there, not you.' He went to say something else and thought better of it.

Calum looked around and saw Franklin smile a dangerous smile. As he did, Calum felt the last of his new self crumble away.

*

At three bells the following morning, Tyler woke up. He lay in the darkness for a moment trying to sense what was wrong. The ship was not rolling and pitching, instead, she felt lifeless. He lay still for a moment and waiting, willing the Charlotte to roll, to pitch forwards over a wave and to lift her bow and rise up the next swell. Nothing. The ship was drifting, not sailing the winds.

Tyler made his way up to the deck. The sails hung limply, without shape.

'How long since the wind died,' Tyler said to Calum. Then he saw Jones standing on deck as part of the crew. A shiver went down his spine. Jones and Calum on the same watch, the Jonah and the fool. And now the wind had given out.

'Forty minutes, captain,' Calum said.

Tyler nodded. He could feel the heat and humidity without the wind. A sense of oppression filled him.

The Charlotte was becalmed.

Instead of rolling, the ship moved almost imperceptibly, tricking the eye and gut. Men were sick, including more than two dozen slaves.

'Can you do anything about that?' Tyler said to McDougal.

'Nothing that isn't a quack's remedy,' McDougal said. 'You know that.'

'Sea sickness dehydrates the men and slaves,' Tyler said. 'And we don't have the water for that.' Tyler looked hopefully at the still sails, willing the wind to blow. Nothing.

'How much can we cut water rations by and still manage?' Tyler said.

'Not a great deal in this heat, maybe by half a quart a slave. Any more and we risk running them down. That is assuming, of course, that we do not dance them.'

'Alright,' Tyler said. 'Mr Franklin, some shade please.'

'Right lads, let's get that old sail up over the deck,' Franklin said.

By noon the following day, things were getting desperate. A solid wall of heat felt like it was pushing down into the Charlotte, draining the men. The crew were idle, left alone with their thoughts. Men turned inward and that, Tyler knew, was a bad place for a crew to be left. He dared not order the men to do much, as work in the heat would only make the lack of fresh water more evident.

By the afternoon of the second day, Tyler acted. 'Mr Miles, would you please organise to have the slaves up on deck? I want a head count of the men and boys.

Mr Franklin, you can count the women. Mr McDougal, please check on the health of the slaves once they are on deck.'

Miles ordered the off-duty watches to gather arms and find places in the rigging and elsewhere to offer covering fire. 'We don't usually have all the male slaves on deck at once, so be ready.'

Then he went and unlocked the grate. 'I can practically feel the heat pulling at my ankles,' Miles said to McDougal.

'There is little to diminish that heat without the wind. Down to it then, dear fellow,' McDougal said.

Slowly, the larboard watch went down below and roused the slaves. 'This is taking far too long,' Miles said.

'The only thing moving quickly down here is the sweat rolling down my back,' one of the sailors said.

'Just get on with it,' Miles said.

More than an hour later, the slaves sat on the deck, chained to the long chain that ran down each side of the ship.

'Two-forty one, two-forty two, two-forty three,' Miles said. 'There should be 270 men and ten boys.' He stopped leaving the idea he did not want to express hanging in the air.

'Who goes down?' Franklin said.

'I will, but I want a party of armed sailors, pistols and knives. You should come, Mr Franklin,' McDougal said.

'I will come too,' Miles said.

'Make sure all the men have bandanas in place. If disease is down there—' McDougal said.

'Or rebellion,' Franklin said. 'Mr Miles, if you don't mind I will lead and if it's a group of slaves out to make rebellion, I would prefer to give the orders.'

'As would I, Mr Franklin. You have the lead,' Miles said.

'And if it's not, every man is to do as I command,' McDougal said. There was no argument.

Gingerly Franklin mounted the ladder, then as quickly as he could he climbed down and faced into the hold, taking only a few steps forwards to allow space for the sailors behind him to stand. Fighting down here would be next to impossible, but he tried to plan an attack.

'In the far corner, there are at least a dozen of them lying there,' Franklin said quietly. As the group of sailors advanced, they passed a few dark bodies laying still.

'Rusher, check those bodies,' Franklin said as they passed the first few lone slaves.

Carefully, Rusher stepped down and aimed a kick at the groin of one of the bodies. Behind him, one of the sailors held careful aim with his pistol at the man's body.

Rusher expected the man to jump up and wrestle him. He paused a half second then kicked as hard as he could. The slave did not move or cry out as Rusher's kick hit him squarely in the genitals.

Franklin stopped and looked at Rusher who rapidly retreated from the man.

'Make a hole,' Franklin said as McDougal came forward. He stepped down and carefully rolled the man sideways into a shaft of light from above. The slave was dead with a grey pallor to his skin.

*

'Get back to the deck and ask for a coil of chain,' Franklin said to one of the sailors. Miles looked at Franklin quizzically. Soon the sailor came back down with the chain.

Franklin took the chain and quietly walked closer to the large group of slaves at the rear of the hold. He motioned back to the sailors to be ready with their pistols and then he lobbed the chain into the group of slaves. Franklin expected the slaves to rise up as one and charge him.

Instead, the sound of the chain clanking and smacking into the slaves resulted only in a soft chorus of sobs and cries.

Several of the sailors pushed back towards the ladder. 'Stay where you are,' Miles said.

McDougal pushed forwards and gently pulled down the bandana that covered his nose and mouth. He sniffed the air. Was that a taint of corruption, he wondered as he took in a bigger sniff of air.

'Right, you,' McDougal said to one of the sailors, 'tell the captain to get down here now.'

Within moments, Tyler stepped off the ladder and stooped down as he walked towards the small party of sailors.

'It would be in our best interests collectively if we disposed of any slave that does not rise up, captain. I cannot express this view forcefully enough,' McDougal said.

'Is it a disease?' Tyler said.

'My preference is not to find out,' McDougal said.

'Grab any slave that does not stand up and throw them overboard. Mr Miles, you do the count please, Mr McDougal you second him,' Tyler said.

Quickly, the sailors grabbed the closest slaves and undid their chains and carried them up to the deck. The first splashes were heard moments later. At this, several of the slaves stood slowly and were escorted above. Some did not rise.

On deck, Miles counted the numbers. 'That is eleven,' he said as another body went overboard.

'I make it eleven as well,' McDougal said.

'Is it a disease?' Miles said.

'We gave the slaves the water we recovered from the broken barrels. I prefer to think that is the cause of our current predicament,' McDougal said. Then he said a quiet prayer, hoping he was right.

*

'Gentlemen, we have a problem,' Tyler said. The officers were gathered at the stern of the Charlotte which still sat becalmed. 'Without rain, we do not have enough water to get the full cargo to Jamaica. We have drifted some small way but even with a stiff wind coming up we cannot make landfall in time. We will be short of water for several days.'

There was silence from the officers.

'Mr McDougal, can you categorically deny this is disease?'

'No, sir, I cannot,' McDougal said.

'But it is not certain that it is either,' Miles said.

'Do you think it best we wait to find out?' Franklin said.

Miles looked at Franklin and then to the deck. He remained silent.

'So then we have a clear course of action open to us,' Tyler said. 'We jettison some of the cargo, enough to ensure we have water for all remaining.'

No man spoke.

'If we do so now, the underwriters can recoup the losses. I am sure of that based on what Pennington outlined in his letter. So I want your consent, each of you, to what we are going to do.'

'Captain, if we reduce the water rations we, could avoid this,' Miles said.

'I agree, I do not think we have come to dumping cargo,' McDougal said.

'We could find a closer port, get water there,' Miles said.

'With what? We have nothing to trade for it,' Tyler said.

'We could trade slaves,' Miles said.

'The cargo is not ours to trade, it is Pennington's so forget that,' Tyler said.

'You could make that decision,' Miles said.

'No I cannot,' Tyler said. 'So that leaves us back with our problem.' There was silence for a few seconds.

'I beg to speak freely, captain,' Franklin said. Tyler nodded in agreement.

'If these negroes are to sell, then they must be presentable right? I don't see too many that are close to that. All of this will be for nothing if we get a low price for them.'

'Is that your main concern, Mr Franklin?' Miles said.

'Absolutely it is. I've worked hard for my share on this voyage and I expect it. Better to get a good return on some and the rest from the underwriters. If we take the lot to Jamaica, God alone knows what pitiful dregs we will end up with.'

'You can't dump some over the side just because they won't get a good price,' Miles said.

'Why not?' Franklin said.

'We could cut the rations for all?' Calum said quietly. Tyler looked at his junior officer, having forgotten that he was present.

'How 'bout we start with your watch then, Calum,' Franklin said. 'If you think you can get 'em to follow your lead.'

Calum looked at Franklin. Then he lowered his gaze and said nothing.

'Shall I go tell your watch that you've volunteered 'em for less water,' Franklin said.

'Gentlemen!' Tyler said. 'The facts are simple. I will not have the men going without, least of all because I do not want them weakened with a hold full of slaves near land. And we are better to land some slaves in good condition than many in poor condition. So here and now, I want each of you to consent to this action. Speak it.'

Tyler looked at Miles, who nodded.

'I want to hear it from you, Mr Miles,' Tyler said.

'Yes,' Miles said quietly.

'I agree, captain,' Franklin said.

'I concur,' McDougal said.

All the men looked to Calum, who seemed to be off in a world of his own. 'Mr Calum?'

Calum looked blankly at Tyler.

'Mr Calum, do you agree?' Tyler said.

'What, umm, yes I suppose so,' Calum said.

'Mr McDougal, select a parcel of the 50 weakest and sickest slaves. Mr Franklin, you have no problem leading this?'

'Pleasure, cap'n,' Franklin said.

'Thank you, gentlemen, for your wise counsel and clear sense on this matter,' Tyler said. Then he turned and went below to his cabin, took the ledger from his bureau drawer and noted that 50 slaves were discarded due to unanticipated circumstances of the middle passage. He noted the date, the consent of the officers and the ship's position. Then he stared off into the distance until the splashes broke him away from his musing.

*

Franklin led his watch below deck. 'Right lads, get 'em all up on deck, and standing.'

'Aye,' Rusher said. Quickly, he unlocked chains from shackles and the sailors moved the slaves onto the deck.

Around two dozen slaves were too weak to stand. Once the healthier slaves were on deck, the sailors quickly unlocked the ankle chains of the slaves still laying down and hauled them out and threw them overboard.

'What was the count, Mr Miles,' McDougal said.

'Twenty-three, we need another twenty-seven,' Miles said.

McDougal walked along the line, examining the slaves. Every few men, he would stop. 'This one,' he said. A sailor would unchain the slave and walk him away from the other slaves and force the man to sit down. Other sailors would pair up the slave's former partner with another who was to be spared. McDougal tapped another slave.

'That's twenty-seven,' Miles said. 'Get the rest fed and watered and back down in the hold.'

If the bulk of the slaves noticed that the twenty-seven men separated out went unfed and without water, none drew attention to it.

'Right, lads, get 'em down below to their rightful place,' Franklin said. He and Rusher led the sailors and soon the cargo was back in the hold.

Many of the twenty-seven sat with heads lolling and hanging, too tired and sick to realise they were still on deck. A few noticed and soon words were flying around between them.

'Mr Rusher, we ask 'em to their feet. Those that don't rise we leave, they can go over last. I would rather not have the black buggers with a fight in 'em watching the weakest go over first. Got it,' Franklin said.

'Aye,' Rusher said. 'Up, up,' Rusher said.

Less than half the twenty-seven rose. 'This way,' Rusher said, gesturing to the standing slaves. The standing slaves milled about, drawn to each other in their uncertainty.

'This way,' Rusher said.

'Come on,' another sailor said, gesturing with his arm for the slaves to walk towards him. He dipped his hand into a barrel and pulled out water that quickly flowed away. Seeing this the slaves moved towards him.

'Now,' Franklin said when the slaves were halfway to the sailor. Quickly, the sailors moved in and grabbed the slaves and pushed them to the railing and overboard. It was over within a moment.

One of the slaves on the deck rose up and ran and jumped overboard. Another rose up and menacingly advanced on Jones. Franklin walked up behind the slave and shot the slave in the head. Two sailors dumped the body overboard. The remainder of the slaves offered no resistance as they were thrown into the water.

The sailors stood around, uncertain of what to do next.

'An extra ration of rum for each of you,' Franklin said. 'Get to quarters and drink it down, lads.'

*

Miles lay awake in his bunk, unable to sleep. For the first time, he questioned the wretched nature of the trade. Until now, the slaves had been cargo, to be managed much as one would manage other livestock on a voyage. There was a sense of pride in looking after the cargo, getting it across the vast blue Atlantic alive and well. How the slaves lived and died after they were offloaded in Jamaica never entered his mind.

And now? Today, he had made that choice for fifty men. How they lived and died. He had helped define the terrible conditions of their last days. He had counted their number as they died. Had seen the looks of terror on their faces as they realised what was to come, even as many lacked the strength to fight it. He had felt as powerless as they did and yet he lived on.

And most painful of all, until now he had been completely immune to their fate, unthinking and unfeeling.

He swallowed hard and it reminded him of the moment earlier in the day when he swallowed down his anger and said yes and consented to the death of fifty humans. *May God forgive me,* he said to himself. Then he stared up at the ceiling a foot above.

*

Tyler was sitting at the bureau desk in his cabin when he heard the cheering and ran and climbed onto the deck as quickly as he could. The sweet tang of rain filled his nostrils and he looked up into the rain falling down. Men were already positioning barrels and buckets to catch as much as they could.

Large fat drops seeped through the canvas where it was swollen downwards as the water collected. The drops were as bright and luminescent as diamonds, a single moment of beauty before their fall. A reminder of a time before yesterday.

A gentle breeze picked up and slowly the Charlotte gained a slight momentum. The rain stopped but the breeze stayed steady.

Tyler called another meeting of the officers. 'How many barrels?' Tyler said.

'We filled four, with maybe enough water still to be collected for two more,' Miles said.

'It's not enough,' Tyler said.

'It could get us to Jamaica on single rations,' Miles said.

'But it's not enough to get the remaining cargo in shape,' Tyler said. 'What of sickness amongst the cargo?'

'In my opinion, the dearth of water is the cause of any malaise, rather than sickness,' McDougal said.

'But can you rule out sickness entirely?' Tyler said.

'Not entirely,' McDougal said.

'So then…' Tyler said. He rubbed his hand over his forehead and then down the side of his face. 'We take another fifty and discard them.'

Tyler looked at Miles, expecting some debate. Miles looked up and closed his eyes. 'Well then, get it done,' Tyler said. 'I need to update the ledger.'

Unlike the day before, all the slaves were brought on deck. Sailors armed with muskets and pistols and swords eyeballed the slaves as they were forced to sit. McDougal walked along the dejected line of slaves and picked out fifty. Most tried to fight back but were either clubbed in the head with a musket or piece of wood. A few simply resigned themselves to their fate.

'There's no point in hiding this so leave the others up here,' Franklin said. He looked at Miles waiting for the order.

Miles could not bring himself to issue the order. It choked in this throat. He tried again, only to be interrupted by Franklin.

'Throw 'em over.'

It went quicker than the day before.

The following day, another eighteen slaves were dumped. No sailor spoke and afterwards most found a solitary place. Some men busied themselves in work, others whittling wood or sleeping. Anything for a diversion. Waiting for the wind to increase and propel them from this misery. Finally, the breeze strengthened, the men grateful to put distance between themselves and what had occurred, to lose themselves in the work of sailing the Charlotte to Jamaica.

*

'Fire the canon please, Mr Franklin,' Tyler said.

Franklin ordered the canon fired, thrilling as he felt the shockwaves reverberating through him.

Within minutes, a tender started to row out from Kingston to the Charlotte. The tender carried a doctor, to inspect the cargo and clear it of disease, and a tax official to draw up the tax bill for the slaves. Once the tender cleared the Charlotte, she would dock in Kingston.

'There she is, lads,' Rusher said. 'Kingston, the pride of Jamaica.'

'If that's the best Jamaica has to offer the sooner we clear out the better,' Jones said. 'But not before a stop ashore in a whorehouse, or two.'

'Probably half a dozen knowing you, lad,' Rusher said.

Jones looked at Kingston. On top of the small hill stood a few nice houses, but much of the rest was little better than London slums. Open dumps stood near houses and sewage ran into the bay.

'I thought Kingston was a tropical paradise?' Jones said.

'All the best houses are on the plantations. The city is little more than an open sewer,' Rusher said. 'Anyways it will be a few days before we see it up close. We have work to do.'

'What sort of work now?' Jones said.

'We've got to get the slaves cleaned, shaved, and the women oiled. And before you ask, no chance in hell you will be involved in that part of things, young Jones. Too much temptation for your horny little soul.'

Tyler met the representative of Barton, Higgins and Co in their port offices. The room was small and cramped, sitting just inside the large warehouse emblazoned with the company name.

'Captain Tyler,' Robert Bennet said. 'How lovely to meet you. We have Mr Pennington's instructions for selling three hundred slaves.'

'Mr Bennet, it is only one hundred and seventy-one slaves. We were becalmed and had to dump some of the cargo.'

'Right you are then,' Bennet said, completely unfazed. 'We have your return cargo, sugar and coffee ready to go. So all is good. Good. Delightful. How long till you sail?'

'A week, once we have the ship refitted and I find a few new crew. When can we begin offloading the slaves?'

Bennet looked around and called a young man over and whispered something in his ear.

The man said something in return and left.

'Afternoon tomorrow, we shall be ready to accommodate the slaves. Good. Excellent. Also, we have a ship leaving for Bristol later today. Do you have dispatches for Mr Pennington?'

Tyler handed over a carefully folded letter. 'Wonderful,' Bennet said.

'What about the shortfall in numbers, is that a problem?' Tyler said.

'Leave that with us, dear fellow, and we shall square the ledger with Mr Pennington,' Bennet said. 'If there is nothing else? Delightful. A pleasure as always. Our man will be out to the Charlotte before noon and we can organise the offloading then. So I think we are done. Yes. Good, wonderful. Until next time, Captain Tyler, and as always a pleasure.'

Then Bennet turned and was gone. Tyler walked out into the sunshine and looked across the bay at the Charlotte. Within weeks, he would be back in Bristol. He smiled at the idea. He had no idea of the storm he was sailing into.

Three

Tyler climbed the small rise to Pennington's offices. For the first time, he felt unsure of himself, having rarely met Pennington, who preferred to do business by correspondence.

'George, you have had a time of it haven't you,' Pennington said as Tyler was ushered into his office. 'Now tell me, you have the ledger and it supports your dumping of cargo?'

Straight to the point, Tyler noticed. 'Yes Mr Pennington, here it is.'

Pennington flicked to the relevant pages. 'Good. I want that kept aboard the Charlotte once we are done. Now don't get comfortable, we have an appointment.'

Pennington ushered Tyler out and the two men walked out into the street. 'We're walking.' With that, Pennington set off at a good clip. Tyler had to quicken his pace to keep up. 'First stop is to visit Taverner. He has already set in motion our claim against the lost cargo. The underwriters have come back contesting certain elements of it but we are confident we can win in court.'

'In court?'

'Yes George, they are not paying yet so we will take the bastards to court if we need to,' Pennington said. 'Do try to keep up.'

Within moments, Pennington led Tyler into an office and soon he was telling his story to Taverner, who like many lawyers stopped and probed the story for holes. Satisfied he nodded at Pennington. 'Nothing Tyler here did was wrong. Legally, a captain has a right to dump any or all of his cargo to ensure his crew's safety. That is our angle, Mr Tyler, and don't forget it. Anyone asks and you did what you did to ensure sufficient water for your crew. Right?' Taverner said.

'Right George,' Pennington added.

'Right,' Tyler said. 'Although there were other considerations too.'

'The times being what they are it was the crew's safety alone, right?' Taverner said.

'Don't worry, I am taking him to hear Clarkson speak, then he will stick with our line,' Pennington said.

'Come, George, we do not wish to be late,' Pennington said. With that, he nodded at Taverner and swept out of the lawyer's office and onto the verge. 'Right, it's about a mile, best we walk it.'

Tyler followed as close as he could. 'Who's Clarkson?'

'Thomas Clarkson, the foremost rabble rouser against slavery. Do keep up.'

'Are we meeting him?'

'Lord no. He is hosting a meeting at the Quaker church. We are going to attend but for both our sakes keep your head down and no names. If you are asked or have to sign something you are George Fisher and I am Charles Kingston.'

What on earth is Pennington leading me into? Tyler thought.

As they approached the church men were handing out pamphlets. Tyler took one and saw the same picture as he had seen in Royce's cabin in Cape Verde, a negro on his knees above the line, *Am I not a man and a brother?*

He followed Pennington inside and the two took a seat in the back row, despite rows closer to the front having space. Pennington leaned in close. 'Turn it over,' he said.

Tyler turned the pamphlet over and froze in shock as he read the headline.

Massacre of the Charlotte
Hundreds of black men thrown overboard

British sailors, from Captain Tyler of the Charlotte to the lowliest hand I call MURDERERS of the worst kind. These took from Africa men, husbands, brothers, sons, and fathers for slavery and then tossed them into the Atlantic for satisfying their own blood lust and depravity.

These British sailors call themselves men and gentlemen and call blacks slaves, yet it is the negro man who acts with dignity as a gentleman and the British sailor who is a slave to his desires for MURDER.

This trade, should it be called such the same as honourable professions, corrupts wholly all those of Britain who are engaged in it.

All will end the same, caring nothing for human dignity and life but giving themselves over to depravity and their basest desires.

A John Smith who sailed on the Charlotte told me of days of lining up negro men to throw over the sides, of whippings and rapes and all manner of debauched congress and conduct that took place aboard that cursed ship.

This conduct is contrary to the nature of man and British men. It must be stopped. End the evil trade in slaves.

The pamphlet shook in Tyler's hand. He went to rip it up but Pennington stopped him and took it. He smiled at a man nearby. 'This should be exciting, finally hearing Mr Clarkson speak.'

'That it will be,' the man said and then turned away.

'Pull yourself together, George, remember where we are and pull it together,' Pennington whispered to Tyler.

Tyler breathed hard, looking at his feet. He fought a desperate impulse to leave but Pennington put a hand on his shoulder, though whether to steady him or stop him he did not know.

Then there was a burst of applause and a curly-haired man of middling age trod onto the stage. 'I thank you, gentlemen, for allowing me to deliver my sentiments. In the first place, I am of the opinion that the condition of slaves in the British colonies should be explained. And in so doing, I am of the strongly held opinion that the conditions of their transport, as made known to you all by the terrible events of the Charlotte, should also be made known,' the man said.

Thomas Clarkson carried on for many minutes, outlining the trade and its evils. After a time, he reached to a large wooden box. On the upper shelf of the large box were artefacts made by Africans, fine clothes, beaded masks and other ornaments.

'Now let me show you what good the African's make,' said Clarkson.

'Good slaves is what they make!' yelled a wag near the back to a smattering of laughter.

'Ah, a Bristol man speaks,' Clarkson said.

'You have a problem with Bristol men?' the wag yelled.

'Only those that support the trafficking of their brothers so as to make greater comfort in their own lives. You sound like such a man as would stand and rejoice in this.' Clarkson pulled out a leg iron from the lower shelf of his box. 'Just one favour, dear sir, if you would indulge me, please place this iron around your leg and the other iron around that of a man next to you. Then you can make your way up here and give your rebuttal.'

Many in the crowd cheered.

Clarkson pulled out a small whip. 'You will not mind if while you speak, I whip you. If you are to defend slavery, you should do so in the same condition as a slave.' More cheers, louder this time. Then Clarkson pulled out two iron semi-circles, with two, foot-long prongs extending from each semi-circle.

'Halfway through your rebuttal, I will place this around your neck,' Clarkson said. He closed the two iron semi-circles together to form one complete ring and took out a lock and locked the two halves together. The room fell silent. 'You can then leave this on overnight and return it to me tomorrow and we shall then see if your opinion differs. If you have the stomach for it.

'For gentlemen, this is what the negro who takes umbrage at being sold into slavery is confronted with. Any man that speaks for the trade I welcome to share this stage but to truly defend this trade he must do so as a slave would do so. Anything less and that man cannot argue he is being authentic.

'Above all, I would welcome Captain George Tyler from the Charlotte, the opportunity to debate me. If any of you know this man, please extend to him my sincerest invitation to a future meeting.'

The roar from the crowd was now deafening. Calls of murderer were shouted when Tyler's name was mentioned.

Tyler and Pennington stared straight ahead, neither man willing to look around. It took all the courage Tyler had not to rise and walk out.

'Gentlemen,' Clarkson said, holding up his hands. It took almost a minute for silence to fall upon the room. 'When you leave here tonight, as you walk the streets of Bristol and see the grand buildings erected over the last few years, as you see men of wealth, remember on whose lives those things come, and ask yourself this. While I may be richer, others are in slavery to allow my riches. Remember that our Parliament, the House of Commons that is meant to represent us, still sanctions the trade in humans. Not slaves, humans who are forcibly enslaved, transported from their homes and worked to death on sugar plantations. So your tea and coffee taste a little sweeter.

'Then ask yourself, what have I done to end this? What have I done to stop this trade? Ask yourself, how I may become an instrument of good. For by opposing this trade, we may become instruments of good not only by rescuing thousands of our fellow creatures from wretched bondage but by bringing them by degrees to the privileges of the British Constitution and the light of the Christian religion.'

Thunderous applause rang out. Many of the men in the audience pushed forwards hoping to meet Clarkson, offering to sign or mount petitions.

*

Tyler and Pennington stood and headed for the exit.

'What did you think?' the man who had earlier spoken to Pennington said.

'He makes a strong case he does,' Pennington said.

'And you?' the man said to Tyler.

'Yes, he makes a good case,' Tyler said.

'Reckon I would like to meet that Tyler fellow, drag him to one of these meetings and have him stand up and justify what he did,' the man said.

'Me too,' Pennington said.

Tyler walked next to Pennington, the slave trader's final words at the meeting echoing in his ears. Did he need to justify himself to Pennington, he wondered.

The two men arrived back at Pennington's offices. 'Come in for a moment George,' Pennington said.

'So now you know just where things are at and why you will follow Taverners' instructions to the letter. If you are asked about this, you did what you did for the safety of your crew. Of course, we know different, but no one else needs to know that.

'For now, I suggest you stay on the Charlotte. I have had the carpenters change her name to the Emily for now, we will do the necessary paperwork over the next few weeks then get you out to sea again.'

'Thank you for standing by me, Charles,' Tyler said.

'George, I had no choice in the matter. If I do not what does that say? That I do not support your actions. How do I win a case against the underwriters if you are not seen to be my employee? How do I say slavery is good and legal if I do not stand by you? You created a storm out there with your actions, and it may pass over or it may yet ruin us all. Time will tell, but until then we are stuck together, whether I like it or not. Now get out of here and don't come back unless I call for you.'

Tyler stood and looked at Pennington who sat at this desk and took out some papers. Then he turned and left and wandered to the river and saw the Charlotte, the Emily as she now was sitting at anchor. He walked aboard and went down to his cabin and lay down.

That night, another meeting took place in Bristol, a meeting about George Tyler that would change everything Tyler knew.

'This is the worst massacre aboard a slave ship since the Zong,' Thomas Clarkson said.

'Another Zong is it,' Jeffery Kemp said. He was hosting this gathering at his townhouse in Bristol because he liked people knowing that he, the son of a Duke, knew Thomas Clarkson.

'Do you even know what that means?' Yorke Carrington said.

'Yes, another massacre like the Zong,' Kemp said.

Henry Mawson rolled his eyes. As secretary to Clarkson, he was tasked with organising meetings and resources. Unlike Kemp, he also knew almost every detail of the abolitionist cause. Some said he knew more about the trade than Clarkson himself. Together he and Clarkson had crisscrossed England over the past few years giving speech after speech condemning slavery.

'The Zong was a slave ship that dumped much of its black people overboard. The captain, a man named Collingwood was never brought to trial for murder as he died,' Mawson said.

'Yes, yes, that Zong, that is the massacre I meant,' Kemp said.

Mawson looked at Carrington who shook his head. Exactly why Clarkson chose to meet here, neither man knew. Later Clarkson would tell the two that Kemp was 'rich, connected and has a father in the House of Lords. And he hosts parties in town. He will tell everyone that he knows me and that will help further our cause. We cannot be righteous alone gentlemen, we must also be clever.'

For now, Carrington and Mawson continued to wish Kemp would go to a pub or party. 'Gentlemen, I propose that we bring Captain Tyler to trial for murder,' Clarkson said.

'I thought you just wanted to debate him, but this is much better,' Kemp said, smiling gleefully.

'I am sure you will enjoy the sport of it, Jeffery, but there are other reasons too. I have it on authority that Pennington, the owner of the Charlotte, intends to bring suit against the underwriters of the voyage for those lost slaves,' Clarkson said.

'Good God,' Kemp said, although precisely why even he couldn't be sure. It just seemed like the type of thing one said when meeting abolitionists who mentioned dead slaves.

'While such a trial will spark some minor outrage, it is low finance and of little interest,' Clarkson said.

'But a show trial for murdering 130 slaves, now that is guaranteed to garner attention in the press and elsewhere,' Carrington said.

'Bravo yes,' Kemp said.

'Precisely,' Clarkson said. 'And I want you to prosecute the case, Yorke.'

'I would be honoured,' Carrington said.

'Begin to build a case. Gather as much evidence as you can. I will have Henry here organise to get the transcripts of any suit against the underwriters. Jeffery here has a couple of men who know the wharves and the taverns nearby. They will help you see if you can find any of the men from the Charlotte.'

Carrington smiled. He could already see the challenge and began assembling the puzzle in his head, moving pieces here and there, identifying the missing pieces. Framing possible arguments.

'Oh, this calls for a toast,' Kemp said. Mawson shook his head and looked at Clarkson who smiled wanly at him.

*

The story of the Charlotte was the main topic of conversation in the pubs and taverns around the wharves. Drinks were to be had by men claiming to have sailed on her and most of the stories were fanciful at best.

'So that's when Cap'n Taylor said, be done with 'em, and he put out a plank and walked each slave down it,' the man said.

'Many thanks for your story,' Carrington said. He stood and looked around the room.

Another dead end. Each time Kemp's men, Harry and Frank as they preferred to be known, found a sailor who said he was on the Charlotte, Carrington would buy the man a drink and ask to hear the story.

And each time Carrington would listen to a tale of fiction, some fanciful, some dreadful but none of them resembling what was known about the Charlotte.

Frank waved Carrington over. 'That there's Gilbert Calum, some of the men here reckon he was an officer aboard the Charlotte.'

Carrington looked at the pale man sitting in the corner of the pub and fought the temptation to walk away. 'This should be good,' Harry said to Frank as they sat nearby. 'Wonder how much of the story he gets right.'

'Can I buy you a drink,' Carrington said.

'I'm not here for that,' Calum said.

Carrington looked puzzled. Frank and Harry laughed out loud. 'Thinks Carrington wants a rent boy,' Frank said smiling.

'I heard that you were on the Charlotte,' Carrington said.

'That's not true,' Calum said emptily. Then he stood to leave.

'It's just that every man here reckons they know what happened,' Carrington said.

'They don't,' Calum said coldly.

'How do you know that? Were you aboard the Charlotte?'

'No, now I need to go.'

'I'll buy you a drink.'

'There isn't enough grog in the world to wash that memory away.'

'So you were on the Charlotte?'

Calum stared blankly at Carrington.

'Mr Calum, I represent a group of abolitionists. The story of the Charlotte is contested by traders and abolitionists alike. All I want is the truth.'

Calum showed no reaction to Carrington knowing his name. 'Why?'

'I want to put the truth of what happened out there, in pamphlets. So the world knows.' Calum sat down and looked away. It was as if Carrington was no longer there.

'We dumped one hundred and twenty-nine of them into the Atlantic,' Calum said in a flat monotone. The hairs on Carrington's neck rose up and he shivered. He took out a pen and paper.

'Do you mind if I write this down,' Carrington said.

'We were becalmed for days following a storm. We lost a lot of our drinking water when some barrels shifted and smashed.'

'Do you know how many?'

'I counted them myself, I was first in the hold,' Calum said. He stopped and stared away and then shifted his gaze onto Carrington who had the impression that Calum was staring through him, not really seeing him.

'So Tyler called us together—'

'Who did he call?'

'The officers, himself, Miles, McDougal the surgeon, Franklin and me.' At the mention of Franklin's name, Carrington would have sworn Calum shivered.

'Then the captain said we did not have enough water to make Jamaica with a full ration for each man and slave. So he said if we dumped some slaves we would be alright. Mr Miles and McDougal argued against it but the captain wasn't hearing it.'

'What did they argue?'

'They just said that on rations we could make it and asked if it had come to that.'

'What about disease, was there disease?'

'McDougal, the surgeon said he couldn't rule it out entirely but he thought it was lack of water that was the problem. A couple of the slaves may have died from that but there was enough according to McDougal, and Mr Miles, for us to make it on half rations.'

'So why not do that?'

'We stood to lose money on the slaves being in poor condition. Better to dump some, rely on the rest getting a good price and the underwriters paying the owner for those dumped, Tyler put it,' Calum said. His voice was monotonous and without emotion, like a metronome.

'So we dumped some and then more, then it rained but we still dumped more slaves.'

'You dumped slaves because of lack of water even after it rained?'

'Yes. And after the wind came back.'

Carrington continued probing Calum for information but got little more. Then he asked about the whereabouts of the other officers and crew. Again Calum offered little.

'And Franklin?' Carrington said. 'Do you know where he is?'

A look of fear flashed across Calum's eyes, like prey seeing a predator jump out from cover nearby. Calum stood and left, resisting any further attempts from Carrington to ask for information.

'Frank, follow him and see where he's lodged please?' Carrington said.

'Right you be,' Frank said. He stood and followed Calum.

Then Carrington thought about the conversation with Calum and shivered until the goose bumps rose on his neck and forearms and he felt that odd cold flush of childhood nightmares. For the first time, he realised that a man could die inside and still continue on and he wondered if he had been talking to a man or ghost.

*

'What news of the case, Yorke?' Henry Mawson said.

'I was about to ask the same of you with the suit against the underwriters,' Carrington said.

'Pennington has had a loss. Here, have a read,' Mawson said, handing over a paper.

Bristol Daily Tribune
March 17th, 1805
Slaver's to go unpaid in Charlotte massacre

The Court of the Exchequer today, in hearing a case of the massacre of 129 slaves onboard the slave-ship Charlotte, has ruled that no insurance monies be paid. The case was brought by Mr Charles Pennington, a slave boat owner, to recoup what he claimed were costs lost in dumping slaves overboard.

This case was the result of an appeal by Arkwright, Knight and Jones underwriters, of London, appealing against an earlier finding by the King's Bench in favour of Pennington.

In hearing the case, questions were raised over the role of a captain in taking necessary steps against the perils encountered at sea and whether crew and slave cargo should be treated the same or differently.

The jury ruled that Captain Tyler of the Charlotte had not taken sufficient steps to protect his water supply, and by doing so endangered the crew and cargo alike and equally. Both being equal under the law should have the same rights to water.

Mr Pennington argued that a combination of storms and becalming left Captain Tyler with no other choice than to dump some of the cargo to ensure the safety of the crew. Yet the lawyers for the underwriters were able to demonstrate that such occurrences, while not normal at sea, were not unanticipated and therefore must be anticipated and preparations taken against such possibilities.

This is the obligation of all captains, whether to paid passengers, crew or slave cargoes, under the ruling by Lord Mansfield under the infamous Zong case.

Questions are now being raised as to what charges could or should be pressed upon the captain of the Charlotte. The actions of Captain Tyler must be now questioned for their legality, given a proven case of negligence offered here by the Court of Exchequer.

'This finding is a significant victory in the push to abolish slavery and must now bring pressure on those in the House of Commons who still defend the trade,' William Wilberforce said. 'Today's result confirms earlier legal precedents extended towards the right of slaves aboard English ships at sea.' When asked if he believed Captain Tyler had a case to answer Mr Wilberforce forcefully answered yes.

'Did you write this, Henry?' Carrington said.

'Yes, I'm quite proud of it.'

'Oh.'

'So it's not to your standards I see but it does convey the meaning.'

'Yes, I suppose so.'

'Thank you for such high praise.'

'Sorry, I did not mean to offend you, Henry.'

'Well, at least you didn't say that it was only published in the Tribune because it is against slavery, as Thomas did. We can't all be dazzling in our use of words now, can we? Here, these are for you,' Mawson said, handing over a bundle of papers. 'Transcripts from the two trials between Pennington and the underwriters.'

'I would like to see you organise something like that.' Mawson said quietly to himself.

Thomas Clarkson walked into the room. 'Is he still complaining about my lack of praise over his front page scoop?' Clarkson said.

'Afraid so,' Carrington said.

'Perhaps, Thomas, if I had more time to spend on it rather than organising you I might do better,' Mawson said sarcastically.

Clarkson laughed. 'See what I deal with, Yorke?'

'Everyone knows Thomas couldn't find his way to the next street without you, Henry. What you do is greatly appreciated,' Carrington said.

'Finally, a little praise, though not from Thomas,' said Mawson.

'Can we get down to talking about where we go from here,' Clarkson said.

'Out the door then left and then left again,' Mawson said.

'What?' Clarkson said.

'You're right, Yorke, he doesn't even know how to get to the next street,' Mawson said.

'Enough,' Clarkson said. 'Now Yorke, what of a trial against Tyler?'

'I think we are good, Thomas,' Carrington said. Then he, Clarkson and Mawson spent the next hour talking.

Four

Three weeks later, the bailiffs arrived at the Emily at 6 am with a warrant from the Admiralty Court for Tyler's arrest. The ship was moored at the riverside being readied for a voyage. A number of sailors stood nearby watching, wondering if this was the initial assault from a press gang to fill His Majesty's frigates.

'George Tyler, you are hereby detained and will be taken to London for trial for murder,' the larger of the two bailiffs said. 'You can resist if you wish, and we will quite enjoy that.' The bailiff made it sound like a limerick the way he said it.

'But you won't,' said the smaller of the two.

Tyler sat rooted to his bunk. Murder. He wanted to cry out it was a mistake but his mind raced back to the church hall meeting. 'Murderer!' they had cried when Tyler's name was mentioned. He offered no resistance as the bailiffs led Tyler off the Emily. As he was being led away, he saw young Jones. 'Boy, run and find Charles Pennington and tell him they have arrested me for murder.'

'Who'd you kill, cap'n?' Jones said.

'Slaves, boy, he killed a bunch of them,' the larger of the bailiffs said.

'What, the ones we dumped at the last voyage. That ain't killing, that's just sailing,' Jones said.

'We have the warrant, and we have our man,' the larger bailiff said.

'And that's that,' the smaller bailiff said.

'So, Mr Tyler, I assume you will come quietly then, no fuss and no bother,' the larger one said.

'I didn't do it,' Tyler said.

'Yep, they all say that,' the smaller bailiff said.

When they arrived in London, Tyler was taken to a private prison, little more than a few makeshift cells surrounded by a thick wall.

'Pleasure doing the trip with you, Mr Tyler,' the larger bailiff said.

'Hope it goes well for you,' the smaller said. 'Of course, we say that to everyone and well, sometimes it works out and sometimes it doesn't.'

Three days later, Tyler had a visitor.

'Captain Tyler, my name is Simon Rubin. Mr Pennington and a group of Bristol and Liverpool traders, which is a polite way of saying slave traders, have hired me to defend you.'

'I'd begun to think I was on my own.'

'Let us hold nothing back, shall we. You should know that Pennington and his fellows have appointed me in their interests, not yours. You have become the face of the slave trade. It's representative if you will. As such, your fate in this trial will likely determine the fate of the trade, at least in the short term.

'And of course, if Charles does not support you now then he may as well retire from the trade. It is a fine mess you have created just at a time when the abolitionists are edging close to a winning vote in the Commons. So lots to play for and best we get down to it.'

'I don't understand, the charge they say is murder. Of whom?'

'Did you not read the warrant?'

'No.'

'Is that because you didn't know you had the right or because you cannot read?'

'I didn't know I had the right.'

'So you can read?'

'Yes.'

'Good, should it come to it we can plead your clergy.'

'I am not a man of the cloth, Simon.'

'Call me, Mr Rubin. No, I mean that should you be found guilty and set to hang you plead your clergy, prove you can read and hopefully are let off with a brand on your thumb. That is so that you cannot plead again.'

Tyler remembered branding the slaves and shivered.

'It dates back to when we had church courts. No church court wanted to hang one of their own so they created a neat little legal loophole to get their own out of hanging,' Rubin said. 'Are you following?'

Tyler nodded vaguely.

'Right, we have a tremendous amount of work to get through preparing for the trial, so if you don't mind, we shall begin.'

Rubin opened a small bag, pulled out a pair of reading glasses and a bundle of papers. 'This case will be about intent. What did you intend in dumping those slaves,' Rubin said.

'How can they try me for murder? They are slaves, they are cargo,' Tyler said.

'Please, no matter what happens in court, never express that sentiment.'

'Why, does it offend you?'

'Personally, I have no strong feelings on the matter. But such sentiments expressed here in London will do more to get you hanged than a strong case. You may refer to them as slave cargo, but not cargo alone. Always with the qualifier, please.

'So where was I? Oh yes, intent. To convict you, the prosecutor, a fellow by the name of Carrington about whom I know nothing, will have to demonstrate some form of premeditation on your part or some form of enmity perhaps. Are you following?'

'No.'

'Let me put it another way, he will have to show that you had a motive for throwing those slaves overboard. A way to profit or some personal reason that meant you thought about what you did before you ordered it. I am assuming that you did not actually throw them over yourself?'

'No.'

'Good. Now I have perused the transcripts of the two cases Pennington brought against the underwriters and they are informative, perhaps even decisive. They leave little option in an Admiralty Court for arguing things like necessity and the like. Instead, the prosecution will have to prove intent of some sort. And I think we can bet they will not use recklessness as a reason. Your past record as a captain negates that, having barely lost a slave prior to this voyage.'

Tyler looked perplexed, struggling to follow.

'You make no mention in any type of log about why you did what you did?'

'No.'

'Good. Don't worry too much, Mr Tyler, this is all just my musing aloud on the issues we must begin to tease out. At the end of the day, we must think what avenues this Carrington fellow is going to take and anticipate against them.'

*

Yorke Carrington was also wrestling with the issue of intent. Short of finding an incriminating entry in Tyler's log or an eyewitness account proving intent was next to impossible. He had Calum's testimony but doubted that the man would be a strong witness. Nor was there a clear line or sentence that proved intent. And then who knows what other witnesses Tyler could call on to contradict Calum's version of events.

As he read through the transcripts of two cases between Pennington and the underwriters a line leapt out.

'...under the finding of Lord Mansfield a captain being responsible for every person aboard a ship, including slaves...'

'Including slaves,' Carrington said aloud. 'So if a captain is responsible for everyone...'

Carrington stood and walked over to his bookshelf and searched for a book on the legal career of Lord Mansfield. He hoped that this may cover the Zong ruling. Finding the book, he flicked through it until he saw the reference to the Zong.

'Yes,' Carrington said loudly. Mansfield's ruling on the Zong was included and specifically stated that captains must be responsible for all aboard a ship including slaves who could not be considered separate cargo.

An idea started to take shape, filling in the large blank at the centre of the jigsaw puzzle that was his case.

Quickly, he scribbled down a few lines.

Tyler's record is not his strength, it's his weakness!
An experienced captain who had barely lost a slave should know the perils of the sea and prepare for them, so why lose so much water in a storm?
Prove that Tyler had another option, just throw the slaves overboard and claim the insurance if things got difficult...criminal negligence???
How to prove it? Did Tyler know the slaves were insured, did this colour his judgement? How secure was the water supply?
Prove blatant disregard for the sanctity of life, including slaves, using Mansfield!!!

'But what did we put on the petition to the court?' Carrington said aloud.

He walked to his desk and searched through a pile of papers, hoping to find the petition to the Admiralty Court that authorised the case and the warrant for Tyler's arrest. His hand trembled as he found it and scanned it, waiting for something to jump out. Did it rule out criminal negligence? It wasn't in there. He scanned it again looking for the words criminal negligence. They weren't mentioned. So what did we say in the petition? Carrington calmed himself. *Sit down and read it through properly,* he said in his head.

An hour later, he leaned back and smiled. The petition mentioned nothing of criminal negligence, but nor did it mention intent alone as the reason for the trial. It simply said murder of 129 negroes taken for the purposes of slavery. *Thank goodness the court was more concerned about public pressure and perceptions it not be seen as pro-slavery, rather than legal arguments,* Carrington thought. His case now began to solidify in his head, locking the pieces into place, the puzzle now almost complete.

*

'Yorke, I want you to meet Father Albert,' Clarkson said.

'Father,' Carrington said, uncertain whether to shake the man's hand or bow or what to do.

'Albert is going to meet with our prisoner,' Clarkson said.

'You mean Tyler?'

'Yes, Captain Tyler,' Clarkson said.

'Why?'

'Tempting though it is to answer why not, the reason is simple. If we can convert this Tyler to our way of thinking what a coup that will be,' Clarkson said.

'I prefer to think of it as safeguarding his immortal soul,' Albert said.

'Well, as I always say, keep your options open,' Clarkson said. 'Come, Albert, I will have Henry organise a pass for you into the prison.' With that Clarkson and Father Albert walked out.

Henry Mawson looked up from the desk at which he was sitting. 'I have known Thomas for a decade, Yorke, and never once have I heard him say keep your options open. He is up to something.'

Carrington didn't appear to be listening. Instead, he got up and followed Clarkson and Albert out.

'That's the problem with great men wrestling with great affairs, they never listen,' Mawson said to the empty room. Then he began to do the paperwork for Albert's pass to the prison.

'Thomas, may I have a word in private?' Carrington said as he caught up with Clarkson and Albert.

'Can it wait, Yorke? Albert will be off soon and then we can talk.'

'No, it can't wait please, Thomas.'

'I will go and see if Henry has that pass ready,' Albert said. 'He is probably in need of someone to talk to.'

Carrington watched Albert walk back down the corridor with a sour look on his face. 'What do you mean he is going to see Tyler? Why? This will not do us any good.'

'I don't think I understand you, Yorke.'

'If you think Tyler will give up some information or incriminate himself, you are wrong. And even if he did, would it be admissible in court. I have this case in hand, Thomas,' Carrington said, finally coming to the point.

'Yorke, this is not about the case, it is about something more.'

'If you mean that wretch Tyler's soul I say send him to hell.'

'This is about what happens if we lose the case.'

'You mean if I lose. If you don't trust me, then tell me straight and get another lawyer,' Carrington said.

'Yorke, you are a brilliant lawyer and I am sure your case will be as strong and prudent as such a prosecution demands. But what if even that is not enough. We are taking on the establishment here, trying to change something at the very heart of this country that has delivered rivers of money. If we fail, not because of you, but because the powers of the day refuse to cede, then Tyler may still be useful. If he can see the folly of slavery and condemn it, imagine what a coup that would be.

'I am sorry to put it like that, Yorke, but this is everything right here. If we win, the Commons can no longer ignore the calls to end slavery. Even the most obtuse and uncaring of the politicians will face pressure like they never have. So we must be prepared for the trial and its result, either way. If not, if the court goes against us, then perhaps Tyler can still be useful. Do you understand, Yorke, this is about more than you or I?'

Carrington looked at Clarkson and nodded. He saw lines in Clarkson's face that betrayed stresses and a lack of sleep and wondered if he looked any different.

'I understand the pressure you are under, Yorke, I really do. And I would not choose another man for the task if I had my pick of any man in England. I believe you are the man best able to voice all that we desire said, and all that we need England to hear. That is why you are leading this case.'

'Thank you, Thomas,' Carrington said.

'Don't thank me yet. You can do that when the vote passes in the Commons. Now, do you need any help, anything at all?'

'No, I think I am ready.'

'Good, the trial begins soon, in the meantime, there is much work still to do.'

Then Clarkson put a hand on Carrington's shoulder. 'I am proud of you and always will be.'

*

'Slaver, you have a visitor,' the guard said.

Tyler sat up on the small cot in the corner of the cell. 'Come on, you ain't meeting him in here. You can walk out in the yard.'

Tyler walked into the light of the yard expecting to see Simon Rubin, instead, a priest stood watching him.

'You must be, George,' the priest said. 'I am Albert.'

'I think you have the wrong man, Father.'

'You are George Tyler are you not?'

'Yes,' Tyler said looking confused.

'I'm not a man who places a great deal in religion, Father.'

'That's fine. Perhaps you would simply like someone to talk to.'

'Maybe. Who sent you?'

'The Society for the Abolition of Slavery.'

'The people who have me locked up in here. Turn around and leave, Father, I'm not interested in whatever brings you here.'

'If you like I shall leave, but I promise you two things. Within moments of my leaving, you will be pining for someone to talk to, about your fears for the trial, about why you are innocent, about anything that takes you away from all this for a moment. And secondly, I promise you this, anything that is said here between us will stay between us. I swear that by all I hold sacred.'

Tyler stood staring at Albert, who turned and began walking away. 'No, wait,' Tyler said. Albert turned and faced Tyler, calmly watching.

'Please stay,' Tyler said. Tyler was uncertain what made him want to talk to the priest, perhaps the need for company or to state his case or simply to escape the boredom.

'As you wish,' Albert said. 'Are you happy to walk while we talk?'

'That's fine by me.'

'How are you going?'

'How do you think! I'm being tried for murder when I didn't do it.'

'How then do you see it?'

'What does that mean?'

'If it is not murder then what was it?'

'Dumping cargo, just as I would crates of cotton if they were too heavy and the ship was going to sink.'

Albert remained silent while they continued to circle around the yard.

'And I am not the first captain to have done that. Plenty of others have too.'

'So this is quite common on the seas then?'

'Yes. And the Atlantic is an ocean, not a sea,' Tyler said.

'Forgive my naivety, I am rather new to all this. While I think of it, is there anything I can bring you?'

'Some bread and cheese would be nice. It would make a nice change from the slop they serve up.'

'Slop?'

'All I get is a watery stew a few times a day, it reminds me of what we serve the slaves.'

'So you serve the slaves, how did you put it, slop?'

Tyler stopped and glared at Albert.

'Sorry,' Albert said, 'that was quite uncalled for.'

'Do you know anything more about—'

'About what, George?'

'About my trial. I am told nothing in here.'

'That must be dreadful. I have only heard rumours that it will be soon. I will try to find out for you. Are you coping with the waiting?'

'You ask some really stupid questions, Father.'

'Sorry, I am simply wondering how I can help you. Perhaps we can talk of something else?'

Tyler looked past Albert and spoke almost in abstract terms. 'I hardly sleep through the night. I wake and wonder what will happen when the trial will begin. Will it be fair? Do I deserve this? What injustice has brought this all upon me?'

Albert said nothing.

'It's so unfair my being here,' Tyler said.

'I can see why you would say that. You did nothing wrong, nothing that was illegal and what you did you did for the good of all aboard your ship.'

'Right, yes. Thank you!' An impulse to reach out and hug the priest jumped up in Tyler. He did his best to fight it, though why he was unsure.

The two walked on, talking about nothing in particular.

'George, I have to leave now. Would you like me to come back tomorrow?'

'Yes, absolutely,' Tyler said, surprising himself.

*

Tyler woke with a start. The dream was the same as always, hanging in the water and watching the slaves plunge in. But now, for the first time, he heard a slave, one of the women laughing.

Unlike the others, she did not sink. Like him, she was suspended in the water, her eyes watching him, laughing hysterically. The laugh of that hideous bit-like creature he had once seen in the port of Mombasa. A mangled and ghastly thing, dog-like and feline at once, with powerful snapping jaws and leering eyes and a strange call like a demented laugh of the old drunken sailors who roamed the ports. A hyena the men had called it, throwing it meat. Then it would call for more, that wild and broken laugh signalling the broken and lost of the world. Coming from her mouth as she hung suspended in the water, watching him, laughing at him.

Tyler was ushered outside by a guard and soon Albert arrived. 'George, you look tired,' Albert said.

'I have not been sleeping well.'

'Yes, I suppose it would be very difficult to get comfortable here, even without a trial looming. Speaking of which, I am reliably informed that the trial will begin in two weeks' time, perhaps a little sooner depending on the court.'

Tyler looked away. So near and yet a lifetime of waiting away.

'And here, fresh bread and cheese for you,' Albert said. 'You will have to break it apart with your hands. They confiscated my butter knife. As if I would scrape them into submission with it.'

Tyler smiled at the joke. 'I'll make do,' he said as he began to eat the bread and cheese. Albert watched him for a while, quiet.

'Do you want some?' Tyler said.

'No, it's just you look like a man who has not eaten in days.'

'It feels that way,' Tyler said between gulps.

'I will bring more tomorrow, and perhaps some ham if I can find it.'

Tyler finished and sat down on his cot bed. 'I feel better for the first time in weeks.'

'Good. Of course, you forgot to say grace before you ate.'

Tyler looked at Albert uncertainly. 'Did I? Father I am sorry. Can you forgive me?'

'I am afraid it is too late for that.' Albert laughed. 'George, such things are customs that matter very little. If we were always to keep to customs and traditions, the world would never change.'

'Alright,' Tyler said slowly.

'George, there are far more important things than saying grace. Things that define us and make us who and what we are. The decisions we make. Like you being a ship's captain. Tell me about that, about the sea and why you love it.'

Tyler spoke at length about his life, the oceans and the ports of the world. About his travels and adventures.

'You have lived an extraordinary life already, George,' Albert said once Tyler finished.

'And you, Father, what have you seen of the world?'

'I am happy for you to call me Albert. And I have seen Rome. I lived there as a child. My mother was Italian, my father English. I was educated by the Jesuits and chose the priesthood as my calling. Of course, the problem with that is I was raised by a Catholic and an Anglican, so I am the best and worst of both religions. God help me. That is why I was sent here to England. The Italians don't like how I think, and the English don't like what I preach. And of course, the Italians don't like my preaching nor the English like my thinking. So you see the problem. I am neither comfortable nor practical here or there. It was when I heard of the Abolitionist cause that I found my place. My people as it were. Much like you found your place and people at sea?'

'Yes,' Tyler said quietly.

'George, have I upset you?'

'You are an abolitionist and I am a slave boat captain. We are—'

'On opposite sides yes?'

'Yes. And yet here I find myself enjoying talking to you.'

'Shall I bring up slavery and we can change that, George?' Albert laughed.

'Father. Albert, what you said, about being neither here nor there. That is, that is what I feel. I find it hard not to doubt myself here. Hard not to think about…'

Albert was silent for a time. 'Whatever you say is between us alone, George.' Tyler nodded.

'Perhaps we can talk more later, or tomorrow?'

'I would like that, George. For now, I shall take my leave. We can talk again tomorrow if that suits you?'

'Thank you, Albert. And if you could find that ham.'

'I will see what I can do,' Albert said.

*

Albert knelt at the altar of the small Catholic Church near St Giles and crossed himself. As always, that gesture felt somehow hollow, more mechanical than heartfelt. He stood and looked at the iconography, Christ on the cross with his crown of thorns, Mary, an array of saints. It all meant less than it once did when he was in Rome surrounded by the splendour and wealth of the Church.

Here in England, the gaudiness felt like props on some elaborate stage rather than the tangible presence of God and his saints. Albert sighed and wandered out of the Church and into the street. He walked the short distance to Clarkson's house and knocked, to be greeted by Henry Mawson.

'Albert, good to see you,' Mawson said. 'Thomas and Yorke are inside. They are eager to hear from you about Tyler.'

Albert was ushered into the small drawing room that was the centre of the abolitionist cause in London. Papers were spread across tables and books lined the shelves.

'Albert, how is it going?' Clarkson said a little too eagerly.

'Good Thomas, and how are you? Yorke, good to see you too.'

'Tyler, Albert, how is Tyler? Can he be persuaded to recant his position?'

'We agreed that what Tyler and I discussed would remain between he and I. And I have no intention of betraying that confidence. All I will say is that there is a man behind the monster so many would have him be.'

'You sound as though you are coming to like him,' Carrington said angrily.

'And what of it, Yorke, if I do? Is a man now to be told who his friends are by those with whom he works. By those who think like him on issues like slavery.'

'Albert I don't think Yorke was—'

'But he is a monster, he murdered almost 130 people,' Carrington said.

'He doesn't see it that way.'

'Are you agreeing with him?' Carrington said.

'No, I am trying to walk a mile in his shoes. To understand him. Perhaps if I can do that, I will be better placed to reach him.'

'So you think you can reach him?' Clarkson said.

'I am not going to answer that,' Albert said.

'Nor it seems my question either,' Carrington said.

'I think I have answered that, Yorke,' Albert said.

'I beg to differ,' Carrington said.

'Gentlemen, please,' Mawson said. 'We have things to discuss. The timing of what we release when, and how that impacts on the trial.'

'That is mine to decide is it not?' Carrington said.

'Just as George Tyler is my responsibility?' Albert said.

Carrington and Albert looked at one another, the former looking ready for a fight, the latter smiling serenely.

'Are you done or would you like to wrestle?' Mawson said.

'Oh, I'm done with this nonsense,' Carrington said. 'Now can we get down to the important business of the case?'

'If you want, Yorke,' Clarkson said.

Carrington stared at Albert, not speaking. 'I am not about to share my case with him here. After all, who knows what he may share with his new friend George.'

'Yorke, that is hardly called for,' Clarkson said.

'No, Yorke is right, better I not know such things,' Albert said. 'Gentlemen, if there is nothing else I will bid you a good night.' And with that, Albert left.

Clarkson sat uncertain of what to do; follow Albert or stay and hear Carrington. The last thing he wanted was the people closest to him fighting, and yet that was exactly what was happening. He was still sitting when Carrington began talking.

*

'George, here is bread and cheese,' Albert said as he greeted Tyler. 'And some fresh ham.'

Tyler smiled and gratefully took the ham. He held it to his nose and took in the smell. Then he closed his eyes, as if in another place. A recollection of sharing ham with Royce in his cabin on the Elizabeth came to him. A recollection of words that he had dismissed but which now burned into him.

Tyler unwrapped the ham and saw it was sliced. Tears welled up in his eyes. 'I thought it best to cut it up,' Albert said.

Tyler took a slice and ate it, slowly at first but then greedily. Albert watched with a smile. 'I take it it's been a while,' Albert said.

'Yes, it has. I have not known hunger like I have since I have been in here. There is only gruel to eat most days.'

Albert then pulled out a newspaper. 'If you want to catch up on what is happening, though I should warn much of it is about slavery and the push to abolish the trade.'

Tyler took the paper and looked at it. 'Am I in it?'

'Yes, bottom of the front page it mentions your upcoming trial.'

'Maybe I will skip that part.'

'A wise idea.'

The two continued to circle around any talk of their discussion the previous day. Soon, the words dried up and Tyler looked away. Albert remained silent as did Tyler.

'Do you want to continue where we left off yesterday?' Albert said.

Tyler did not look at Albert. It took him a long time to speak. Twice he started and then stopped.

'I see the slaves in my dreams. I am in the water and they fall into the water and sink but I do not.'

Albert was silent.

'I think at times that perhaps…'

Albert waited.

'Could I have done things differently? When you have so much time alone and to think, well that is what I ask myself.'

'George, I think these doubts are normal. It is nothing unusual to think about going back to a time, to an event, and to question it. Are you familiar with John Locke, the philosopher?'

'No, is he a friend of yours?'

Albert laughed. 'Locke died a hundred years ago, and no, I am not that old. Locke wrote about being conscious to oneself, about understanding ourselves. One idea he wrote about is how we change over time. That the person I am today is different from the person I was when I was young.'

Tyler looked at Albert for the first time.

'What Locke is saying, George, is that over time we do change, we can come to view the world very differently if we are open to it. If we are willing to perhaps, revisit our past and examine it from a new perspective.'

'Something in the dream disturbs me. It's the faces of the slaves.'

'What of their faces?'

'They are frightened, they are fearful. I never…'

Albert was silent, willing Tyler to speak. Then, sensing Tyler was withdrawing into himself Albert spoke.

'You never, saw that before?'

'Yes. I never really looked for it so I never saw it.'

'It's surprisingly easy not to see things we don't want to see, including within ourselves. What did you see on their faces before?'

'We call it the African look, a sort of blankness really. Like the slack look on the face of an animal.'

There was a long silence.

'Sorry, Albert, I did not mean to offend you.'

'I am not offended, George. Confronted definitely but not offended. Please continue.'

'So it's fear on their faces and that…it makes them more human.'

'In a way that you can relate to?'

'Yes.'

The two of them sat for a time in silence.

'Thank you for sharing that, George. It means a great deal to me that you would share that.'

Tyler did not respond. He was away on the ocean, on the deck of the Charlotte, searching the faces of the slaves for the first time.

Five

Carrington was finalising his preparations when word came from Bristol.
'Yorke, Yorke, we got him!' Mawson said.
'Calum, he will testify?'
'Yes. Yes, he has agreed to come to London and testify at the trial.'
'That's wonderful news, Henry. Now we have the best chance possible of securing a conviction. Imagine what that will mean. It will condemn the whole trade.'
'What word of the other officers?'
'Our abolitionist friends in Bristol have been working to track them down. Miles, the second captain is at sea. His ship is due in port in the next few weeks. He may be willing to testify but no one really knows. Franklin, the lieutenant is at sea bound for India so he is a loss.'
'And the surgeon?' Carrington said hopefully.
'Sorry, Yorke, word has it he passed away a month ago.'
'Damn, I wanted him on the stand.'
'Yes, but we have Calum, his story is enough to show up Tyler is it not?'
'Yes, but having the surgeon admit that there was no disease, would really put Tyler in a bind. Well, we will just have to get Calum to say that that is what the surgeon said.'
Mawson looked at Carrington, seeing the lawyer putting the questions together in his head that he wanted to ask Calum and smiled.
'You're ready for this aren't you, Yorke?'
'Yes. Yes, I am.'
'Does this mean I can distribute the pamphlets through our networks?'
'I think it does. Let me see it again to make sure we are not showing our hand and then you can get them sent out.'

Mawson took a single sheet of paper off the top of a pile of papers. Each one was identical, printed on the new iron press that allowed a single person to print off dozens of pamphlets each hour. He handed the pamphlet to Carrington.

Abolitionist news
An eyewitness account as to the massacre of the Charlotte

The Charlotte abducted 300 Africans from the Guinea Coast of Africa, sold by barracoons and slavers into indentured servitude until they die.

Captain Tyler of the Charlotte then sailed across the Atlantic. After running through a storm where water was lost, the ship sailed on past several ports then became becalmed. This definitive account of what happened next comes from Hugh Smith a sailor aboard the Charlotte:

'We were still days with no wind and only some water, not enough for all of us the captain and officers said. Not that we were busy with sailing, we were just lazing about waiting on the wind.

'After several days of this, we got the order to dump the slaves over the side. The doctor on board chose 'em, we herded them like cattle to the side and forced 'em over.

'They sank quickly. The next day more got dumped and then more the next day despite there being rain fallen.

'None of us common sailors, the ones that do the dirty job of pushing 'em over the side dared ask why so many got dumped when we still had water to drink.

'The captain and officers watched us do all this, they did little to help. 'I feel sick to my stomach every day and night and when I sleep, I can see them sinking into the abyss. Don't think I will ever be free of it, but what choice did I have?'

So said Hugh Smith, a sailor aboard the cursed Charlotte.

It is a terrible crime that was done on the orders of the captain, George Tyler, who must face the consequences of his actions at a trial at the Admiralty Court beginning next Monday.

Abolish the slave trade before more massacres are done.

Next meeting of the Abolitionist Committee of London on July 9 at St Giles Church, 4 o'clock.

'The pamphlet will go out with the cartoon showing an image of the massacre,' Mawson said. 'It really brings it home to you doesn't it?'

'That is the point, Henry, to bring the evils of this trade into people's living rooms, into the coffee houses and drawing rooms so that people cannot pretend this doesn't happen.'

'So it's good to send out?'

'Yes, Henry it is. It should let the slave traders funding Tyler's defence know that we know what happened but it doesn't give up our hand either.'

'What about this Smith, will he testify?'

'No,' Carrington said. 'He is at sea and won't be back for months. And we are sure he was aboard?'

'Yes, Calum verified it, as did Smith.'

'Get this out there, Henry, get people talking. Well done.'

*

'George, how are you today?' Albert said.

'What I said yesterday, it was too much. I have thought about it and don't want to talk about it again,' Tyler said.

'It sounds like you spent a great deal of time thinking about it?'

'If you think that I have doubts about what I did then you are wrong. I am more certain of my actions than ever before.'

Albert looked at Tyler, saw the defiance on his face and sighed. 'Did you read the paper, George?'

'Some of it. Most of the stories about slavery don't know what they are talking about.'

'Why is that, George?'

'They don't, you can tell they have never been on a slave ship.'

'Oh, right,' Albert said.

'What would they know, what do you know? I'm the one who has lived this and now I have to face a trial from those who think they know. Well, they don't. Everyone thinks they know why I did what I did when they don't.'

'And why did you do what you did?' Tyler stared at Albert with fury.

'To save my crew and I would do it again, and again.' Albert looked away, uncertain of what to say.

'So no more talk of slavery from ignorant loudmouths who know nothing. Alright!'

'As you wish,' Albert said.

'I don't like that tone, Father. You make it sound like, like—'

'Like what, George?'

'You know what, I am done with this. Get out.'

Albert collected his bag and turned and walked out. As he left, Tyler muttered good riddance to himself and turned and lay down on his cot.

Tyler looked at the small prison yard. Then he rolled over and tried to sleep. The morning light was too bright and every time he heard a noise he looked hopefully into the yard, hoping to see Albert, yet unsure what he would say, what he could say if the priest came to visit today.

The need for the priest to visit, to talk and apologise and defend the slave trade and unburden himself of the doubts and turmoil inside felt palpable. And yet Tyler knew that if Albert did not come back that it was his own doing. Damn this prison and the waiting.

*

'Slaver, your priest is here,' the guard said. 'He asked if you want to see him?'

'Yes,' Tyler said, surprised at the speed and force of his response.

He waited while the guard left, pacing the cell, thinking of what to say to Albert. 'George, how are you this afternoon?'

Tyler spun around, still uncertain of what to say. 'Albert, I am better for seeing you.'

'Before we begin, I apologise for yesterday. I did not mean to pry.' Taken aback by Albert's apology Tyler looked at the priest who smiled. 'I have cheese and bread for you.'

'Thank you, Albert. I should…I should apologise.'

'George, it is done. There is nothing you need to apologise for. Now, are you doing as well as can be expected? Whatever that is?'

Tyler smiled and felt a weight lift. 'I am managing, Albert.'

'What shall we discuss?'

'I don't really know. There's not much to report on from in here.'

'I suppose that there is not. Well, I can tell you that Bonaparte is still up to his tricks on the continent. Other than that there is not much else.'

Tyler nodded, waiting for something more. 'How is the cheese today,' Albert said.

'It is good, do you want some?'

'No, I was just asking.'

The two were silent for a time. Albert bided his time, hoping the silence would invite Tyler to speak of more meaningful things occupying the sailor's mind.

'About yesterday, and the day before,' Tyler said. Albert sat quietly.

'It's difficult not to think of such things, and well I thought...could we talk again on, well you know.'

'George, it's natural that you defend the slave trade, as I would the church. Yet I have doubts about the church, about how it presents itself, its wealth and how it uses that wealth. When you are part of something for a long time, it becomes part of you, of how you think and how you see the world. Yet it is also worth questioning such things from time to time, as I do the church.'

'I have been thinking about the trade. And wondering what I might do if it's abolished.'

'What are you thinking of, George?'

'Perhaps sailing the route to India, I have sailed it before and well, that would be something I could do.'

Albert worked hard not to smile, seeing Tyler naively think he could just return to sea after this was over. 'Yes, you could do that. So you want to return to sailing?'

'It's what I do best, it makes me happy. Aren't we all entitled to some happiness in our lives?'

'Of course, I think that is something that all mankind has in common, don't you think?'

'Yes,' Tyler said enthusiastically. 'Everyone deserves a little happiness.'

'So going back to the sea that would make you happy?'

'Yes!'

'Why India, why not the Americas or somewhere else?'

'I don't really know.'

'What if slavery is not abolished, would you captain a slave ship again?' There was a long silence.

'Sorry George, I did not mean to offend you. Are you alright?'

'I don't think I would want that.'

'Well, I am sure India will be it, don't you, George?' Tyler turned away. Again.

Albert waited a few moments. 'Why not a slave ship, George?'

'If it happened again, being becalmed. I don't think I would want, that …responsibility…'

'For who lives and who dies?'

'Yes.'

'Such a burden is dreadful to contemplate,' Albert said. 'I cannot imagine what it must be to live through.'

Tyler sat in silence.

'It may help to talk about it, George, to get such things out of your head, if only for a time.'

'I ask why. Why me, why now? Why any of it happened? I have been a good man and it makes no sense.'

'Such things seldom do.'

'Do you know I had barely lost a slave before that voyage, barely a one. And you question why? Did I do something wrong in preparing? Did I make a mistake? I think about Calum and Jones one a Jonah, the other a fool. Was this their doing? In some ways that would be easier to bear. To know where things went wrong.'

'But things did go wrong.'

'Yes.'

Again Tyler was silent.

'I don't know, Albert, I don't know why?'

'George, this may be hard to hear, but perhaps there is a clear answer.'

'What?'

'Bad luck happens.'

'Wait, I thought you believed in God's will leading us?'

'I do, George, but look around. There is too much injustice in the world, too much misery and heartbreak. Too many good people have terrible things happen and more than a few awful people have too much luck. Are rewarded when that does not feel right. God is present, but not in the way that…he is not responsible for everything that men do.'

'So you believe in luck?'

'In a manner of speaking. Now you know that I have doubts, fears inside too. As I said I will defend the church but that does not mean I am without doubts. That I am the same man as I was when I took my vows. That is why I feel for you, George, I know that you are fighting inside to understand all of this. I cannot give you an answer, only you can find some meaning in this. If you choose to. Just as I have found meaning in my work, despite my doubts. But as Locke says, you must want to.'

'I don't know what I want anymore, Albert,' Tyler said in a quiet voice.

'And that is alright for now. Tomorrow, may I bring a friend, another lost soul to speak with us?'

Tyler nodded in agreement then studied the bricks on the wall, trying to find a pattern that he could identify in the brickwork. The two sat in silence for a while, Tyler grateful for the company.

*

Tyler had no deep spiritual connections even to the sea. He had not prayed since he went to sea, having witnessed too many men die regardless of who they prayed to or what god or superstition they followed. He thought for the first time of what that meant and it left him feeling hollow inside, but not enough to say in his head his darkest thoughts. Instead, he thought of Albert and the conversations the two had and it made him angry.

He thought of what he might do after this was all over and did not know. The sea, the one constant in his life was distant in his thoughts. He closed his eyes and rolled over to sleep, hoping for a peaceful night free of dreams.

*

Albert lay awake, replaying the conversation with Tyler in his head. He did not want to push Tyler any further, knowing that the man was broken. *Until Tyler knew that,* Albert thought, *there was little to do except visiting and talking.* He rolled over to sleep and started to say a prayer in his head for Tyler but it felt useless, more a gesture than real.

Then he lit a candle and pulled out his bible and opened it and started reading from James. 'But when he asks he must believe and not doubt, because he who doubts is like a wave on the sea, blown and tossed by the wind.'

Albert put the bible down and looked at the ceiling and wondered who was being blown and tossed about more, himself or Tyler. He was still trying to answer that when he fell asleep.

Six

'George, this is Micah,' Albert said, ushering in the black man who stood behind him. 'Micah is a friend of mine.' Tyler had never heard a man say that of a black man. He watched as Micah held out his hand. Tyler took the hand, uncertain what it would feel like and was surprised it felt like any other hand he had ever shaken. Then he realised that he had never touched a slave before, other than to use the occasional slave woman for his own gratification.

'George, are you alright?' Albert said.

'Yes,' Tyler said.

'You looked like you were miles away. Anyway, I thought Micah and you should meet. Micah is a freed slave, he was bequeathed to the church and now works ministering to the lost souls around St Giles Church.'

Micah stood quietly.

'Father, if you have brought him here to teach me something about slavery then I am not interested. I slept poorly last night and just want some peace today.'

'Micah, I apologise,' Albert said. 'Yesterday when George and I spoke he agreed that I should bring you along today.'

'No, I didn't,' Tyler said.

'George, as I recall you did agree.'

'And next, you'll be telling me I agreed that slavery is wrong.'

'Do you doubt slavery is wrong?' Micah said.

Tyler spun around and looked at Micah. 'You stay out of this.'

'If you had stayed out of my homeland we would not be here, either of us,' Micah said.

'So you bring this, this negro man here to lecture me, Father,' Tyler said. 'Get out both of you.'

'Is that what you want, George,' Albert said.

'Yes, go!'

'Come then, Micah, let us go,' Albert said. 'I will leave this bread and ham here for you, George.'

With that, Albert and Micah left.

Tyler thought about yelling something but nothing came to him. He looked at his hand and then at the bread and ham and opened the ham. It was cut up just like last time.

*

'So he is the one they want to hang,' Micah said.

'Yes Micah, he is the one. What did you think?'

'I thought you said he was having doubts about slavery, about what he did?'

'Perhaps that is why he does not want us to visit him, we make those doubts in his head real for him.'

'Well, I did not care for him.'

'He is having a bad day. What I found interesting is that he called you a man, not a slave or worse, a black man.'

'A negro man.'

'Yes, but a man. That is progress.'

'So, will you visit him again, Father? He does not seem worthy of it.'

'Those who seem least worthy are the ones who need love the most. And yes, we will visit him again.'

'Why would you drag me to see him again?'

'You both have things to learn from each other, Micah. Why slavery is wrong and why men like that have taken millions of Africans from their homes. When you each understand that in the other you will both be more complete.'

Micah looked at Albert. 'Am I free to decide that I do not want to see him, or must I do as you wish?'

'It is up to you, Micah, I am not your master. We are one and the same in that regard.'

'And yet I do not feel that.'

'Isn't that why you need to understand men like Tyler, so you can feel that you belong?'

'That is my curse, that I don't belong anywhere,' Micah said as he walked off.

Albert watched him go, feeling a great deal of sympathy for Micah.

*

'So that is, in essence, gentlemen, the nub of our case,' Carrington said.

The drawing room was quiet. Seven men sat on the crowded sofas and chairs in the book lined room. Eventually, Hall stood and walked and opened a window, letting air into the stuffy room. It was not possible to have the full committee for the abolitionist cause listen, and nor, said Clarkson, did he want so many to know.

When he had approached Samuel Hall about a meeting, Hall had been keen. 'Good, Thomas, good. I think a few of us should be a sounding board for young Carrington.'

'I agree, but if you see something that you don't like let me know, let us all know, Samuel. The rest of the men do not have the experience that you have. They do not have your connections in the Commons nor your skills in getting things done. That is why I want you there. But to just invite you, well you know how these men are. It will be fury and anger at me for being slighted rather than at the trade and those trying to keep it afloat.'

Hall laughed. 'I think it's more a social club for some of them. But tell me, Thomas, do you think Carrington is up to this?'

Clarkson looked at Hall for several moments without answering.

'Your silence tells me enough. Is it Carrington himself or his case that bothers you?'

'That is just it, I am uncertain on both fronts,' Clarkson said.

'Why now? You have always backed Carrington in the past?'

'I thought the case would be a straight murder trial, but Yorke is heading down a different direction, looking at negligence.'

'And you think that is not the way to go?'

'I don't know. Yorke is a brilliant lawyer, but my instincts say that he is on the wrong track.'

'Well then, let's hear what he is thinking and we can go from there.'

So Hall had sat and listened until Carrington was done.

Henry Kemp cleared his throat. 'Well, that sounds marvellous, young Mr Carrington, simply marvellous.'

Hall leaned on the wall near the window. 'I am trying to understand why criminal negligence and not just plain murder. After all, if I threw someone off a boat in the middle of the Atlantic in front of witnesses wouldn't I be charged with murder?'

'It's not that simple, Samuel,' Carrington said. 'The laws of the sea in regards to slavery are not the same as those here in England. Essentially, what we are saying is that Tyler did not adequately prepare for all eventualities and simply took a gamble that the insurers would pay if he dumped the slaves.'

'So why not murder?' Hall said.

'If you did throw someone off a boat, then yes I could prosecute you for murder easily. But for slaves, things are not so clear cut.'

'But didn't Mansfield clear all that up, saying slaves should be treated the same?'

'He did, but that all goes out the window if the crew of the ship are in danger. If it is a choice between crew and slaves, then the captain is obliged to act. He can argue that to save his crew he was left with no choice but to throw the slaves overboard.'

'Dear Lord,' Kemp said. 'How ghastly.'

'And that is what I am sure that Tyler's lawyer will say. But to negate that, I believe it is possible to prove that Tyler was negligent in not anticipating the perils of the sea, such as storms and becalming. In other words, he wasn't prepared and knew that he could just throw slaves overboard and claim the insurance later.'

'The scoundrel,' Kemp said.

'There is nothing that prevents us from undertaking this approach and it is one I believe that will get us closest to a conviction.'

'Are you saying that we might not get a conviction at all?' Clarkson said.

'We have discussed this, Thomas, nothing is certain in a case that appears clear cut and yet is not so, not even remotely,' Carrington said. He was beginning to grow tired of the second-guessing from Clarkson and the others. After all, he was the one who had taken the lead at each turn, writing petitions to the court and crafting a case and doing hours of research, often into the early hours of the morning. Carrington rubbed his eyes and fought hard against the wave of tiredness that rose up.

'So are you confident then, Yorke?' Hall said.

'As much as one can be. Our case is solid, it is grounded in the precedents around the slave trade and will present a clear argument. Or should I just restart the whole thing a few days before it begins?'

Hall looked at Clarkson searching for an answer. He knew Clarkson was not convinced and more that Carrington knew that too.

'I think we press ahead,' Hall said. 'After all, you are the expert here.' Clarkson nodded but said nothing.

'So we are to battle then,' Kemp said. 'I can hardly wait. Now, what is my role in all this?' No one answered him.

*

Albert walked into the drawing room. It was quiet for once. Henry Mawson was nowhere to be seen. Clarkson sat staring out the window.

'Thomas, you wished to see me?'

'Albert, yes, thank you for coming. How goes our project with Tyler?'

'So straight to the point then, Thomas. Are you worried about the case?'

'Why do you say that?'

'You look worried and why else would you call for me?'

'I am afraid that we may lose the case and with it the day. And that is unacceptable to me after all I have done.'

'I think you should trust in Yorke, he knows what he is doing.'

'I hope you are right,' Clarkson said and then looked out the window. 'This is my life's work, to end slavery. And I am so close. To have all that lost on the whim of a...that is why I need Tyler to recant, to turn on the trade. So tell me, can you turn him?'

'It is not for me to turn him. If I did and you lose this case and he goes back to sea, back to slaving, what good would his story do?'

'His story could tip things in the Commons, put ungodly pressure on those still holding out to finally vote against slavery.'

'But what good is his story if he doesn't really mean it? If he does not turn away from the trade so be it. But if he does without truly repenting of his sins then that too is meaningless.'

'I really don't care about Tyler and why he decides to tell his story, I just want him to tell it and say slavery is evil. Can't you deliver that? Whose side are you on? Who are you working for in this?'

'God, I am working for God in this, Thomas,' Albert said and walked out.

*

Tyler began to pity himself, refusing to get up except to relieve himself. He no longer walked around the yard, nor talked to the guards. When Albert arrived the next day, Tyler refused to see him. The priest left him some bread and cheese and a book.

Tyler ate the bread and cheese without enjoying it. It could have been anything but it tasted like nothing. Then Tyler started to cry, without knowing why. He was sorry for himself and picked up the old newspaper Albert had given him and read and reread the story about his trial. *No man has ever been so unjustly accused,* he told himself. *What did I do wrong*, he thought. How many other ship's captains had done the same. That is why owners buy insurance for the middle passage, precisely so the cargo can be disposable.

Tyler threw the paper against the wall and rolled over and tried to sleep, afraid of the dreams that he may dream.

Sometime later he woke, visions of slaves in the water filling his head. It took Tyler several moments to adjust to his cell. He stood and stretched and then sat down again. He looked at the paper on the far side of the cell and thought about picking it up, but he knew what it said.

Hungry, he rummaged in the small bag that Albert had left and found the book. On the cover was a picture of an African, dressed in a waistcoat and jacket. *Olaudah Equiano or GUSTAVUS VASSA* the African. Published March 1 1789 by G Vassa.

Tyler opened the book. The Interesting Narrative of the Life of Olaudah Equiano or Gustavus Vassa, the African. Seeing the title Tyler threw the book aside. What could an African teach him about anything?

He sat on the bunk and stared at the wall, counting the bricks. Then when he had finished, he counted them by pairs, then by threes. Bored he looked around and saw the paper and the book. He stooped down and picked them up and looked at them, one after the other. The paper he had read a dozen times. Quietly, he sat down and started reading about Olaudah or Gustavus.

*

Albert walked up to the cell, uncertain of what to expect from Tyler. 'Hello, George.'

Tyler looked at Albert. 'You alone then.'

'Yes, George.'

'You can come in then.'

The two exchanged greetings again and made small talk before that dried up. Albert sat quietly, Tyler fidgeted.

'I won't apologise again.'

'Nor do I expect you to,' Albert said.

'Good.'

'Good.'

More silence.

'Are you reading Olaudah's book?' Albert said.

'There's not much else to do,' Tyler said.

'What did you make of it?'

'It was interesting enough, I suppose.'

'George, are we going to talk or should I leave?' Albert said. Tyler looked at the priest and contemplated the hours ahead.

'Was it really such a boring story?' Albert said. 'That book tells a story of a man, an intelligent man sold into slavery. Olaudah was fortunate to have masters who educated him, who saw beyond the idea of a beast of burden to work the fields. That is what makes his story so fascinating, it tells of a man. Don't you think?'

'And if I agree with you?'

'Then you agree with me, that's all,' Albert said smiling. 'Is that such a hard thing to do, George?'

'Alright, it's fascinating in its own way. The stories of his childhood, of the Eboe people, of his journey to the coast, they—' Tyler stopped.

Albert stared at Tyler, willing him on. 'Damnit, I never understood…' Tyler said.

'It's hard to miss the humanity that Olaudah brings to his story. And the tale of his friend, John Annis, a fellow African abducted from a ship here in England and forced to work the fields in St Kitts.'

Tyler started to cry. He looked away and then back at Albert. 'George, why are you crying?'

Tyler didn't answer. He turned away from Albert, who left soon after. As he did, he placed a hand on Tyler's shoulder and quietly said, 'I will come back tomorrow.'

*

Simon Rubin read the note summoning him to the Bristol Club and sighed. He hated that kind of ceremony filled with fussiness and men nodding to others in quiet rooms reeking of cigar smoke. A world where hierarchy mattered as much as, if not more than anything else. He gathered his coat and walked the half mile to the club, with its dark-panelled door and stuffy facade.

Rubin ducked between carriages crossing the road and presented himself to the doorman.

After a moment, the doorman opened the door and Rubin walked into the club and was ushered into a private room. Charles Pennington sat along with several other slavers. A waiter brought in coffee and then retreated over the plush carpet and pulled the heavy door to.

'So Simon, are we set?' Pennington said.

'Yes, I have all that I need and have drawn up a number of possible prosecutions, and then defences against each.'

'Good,' Pennington said. 'And Tyler, is he ready?'

'As well as can be expected.'

'Now we wanted to talk to you about your commission. If you win, we will double the fee for you. That is only fair don't you think?'

Rubin nodded. *Just how much was riding on this case*? he thought. He had charged a king's ransom to represent Tyler and now these slavers were prepared to double it. If he won, he would never need to defend another man again.

'We need this, Simon,' Pennington said.

Rubin remained quiet, wondering if the other owners were to speak or were there only for display, or solidarity, or both.

'Our men in the Commons are under increasing pressure to justify their stand. Time and again petitions are delivered and votes to end the trade threatened. The public mood is turning and we need a victory, a scalp to show that we can carry on'.

Pennington stopped and Rubin waited. He knew what was at stake as much as the next man. Then he reached over and poured a coffee and sipped it. The coffee was strong and bitter, the way he liked it. He pretended not to notice the looks that passed between the slavers when he did not take sugar and drop it in his coffee.

*

Albert and Micah walked across the yard to Tyler's cell. Micah looked at the thick walls and the cell and shivered, reminded of another time, another world that ended when he was imprisoned on the shores of Africa.

He had been in that no man's land between a boy and man, forming muscles on his boy's body, ready for initiation and yet forced to wait when his sister had fallen ill one morning. And that was the misfortune that defined his life. The slavers had come over the wall into his parents' house hard and fast, like a winter wind.

Instead of the initiation into his tribe, Micah was bound and yoked, forced into a line of other men and boys. A cloth was stuffed into his mouth the taste of it foul, a taste he could still remember. He was recast, not as a person, the boy emerging into manhood but as a slave.

He remembered the weariness from walking. To this day, Micah had never experienced tiredness like that, from shuffling along in chains. For the first few days, he and others would look back, hoping to see someone pursuing them, a friendly face, a rescuer. They never came.

Then one day, beside the road the coffle stopped before an array of statues and idols.

Slaves muttered prayers. Some who spoke his language asked to be forgotten and when Micah asked why they said it was better for those left behind. It was not proper to leave your home and homeland knowing you would not return. That is why they asked to be forgotten, to have those ties broken.

Micah could not bring himself to do it. To forget. Somehow, he knew that his old life would not leave him as easily as he had been forced from it. And yet he recanted, said the dreadful prayers of forgetting.

The last memory of his home was seeing his sister dragged off to a different line of slaves, all girls and young women, her face twisted back towards his, mouth open, screaming his name.

What he remembered, had never forgotten is the speed with which the slavers moved him and the others beyond their world, beyond all that they knew. As they moved, the coffle joined others and linked together, only being unchained to cross rivers. Then they would join up again like some monstrous snake that can survive being cut in two and re-join itself. Something unholy.

In those days, Micah learnt a new language, the words slave and slaver, the sting of the whip and the faces of fear.

He tried to remember his parents, his sister. Their faces and names. The more he sought them, tried to remember, the further away they drifted. As he was moved further from them.

Then they reached the ocean and a new type of terror. The land disappeared into waters that were so vast they were like another world, rolling and moving. Always moving. That is what he remembered most about the ocean and the voyage, beyond the dread and sickness and terror, the constant movement. There was no place to find stillness, inside or out.

While they were marching, there were those in the coffle who would say what was coming next. Always there is someone in a group who says they know such things, even if they don't. But none of them were prepared for that vast blue land that never stopped moving. None of them.

At the end of the march, they reached a huge building of brick and stone, unlike anything he had imagined or seen. Here they were put into cells, fed and taunted by the guards. Until one day, they were marched out and put into canoes, rowed across the angry surging edge of the blue moving world to ships and pushed down into holds, chained laying down beside others, with no room even to roll over.

That was a new horror, piled on top of the march. Laying in the rolling dark, with cries of pity and terror and men relieving themselves and throwing up, all of it rolling under them, splashing them and covering them.

Then each morning they were herded out, chained to a long chain running down the side of the ship. The dead bodies thrown overboard into the vast blue. Forced to eat and dance and then back into the belly of the ship. Sometimes the movement was gentle, sapping the energy, sometimes it was violent and pitching with noise and wind howling outside. It was difficult to breathe and the air was rancid and stank of death and decay.

Micah shivered again. He heard Albert say good morning to Tyler and the priest ask if he could sit down and talk too.

'Yes,' Tyler said.

'So how are you today, George?'

'Well enough, Albert. They tell me the trial will begin in a day or two,' Tyler said. He looked down at the ground.

'At least you will not have to wait any longer,' Albert said.

'I suppose so.'

'Have you finished Olaudah's book?'

'I did,' Tyler said. Then he looked at Micah and looked away.

'Do you want to talk about it?'

'I get it, why you gave me that. So the slaves are not savages, just people like us.'

'Yes, George. Olaudah's book was widely praised for humanising Africans, like Micah here.' Albert tensed up, waiting for Tyler to push back. Instead, Tyler smiled.

'Alright then, so that is why you brought Micah, to make that point.'

'Yes, I suppose so.'

'Well, consider it made. But answer me this, who brings the slaves out of the interior and to the coast? Who helps sell the slaves? Africans is who. Like Micah here.'

'That is true, Albert,' Micah said.

'So we agree. Well…' Tyler said.

'But it is the English and other civilised nations that take us across the Atlantic to work in the fields,' Micah said. 'That forces us to give up our lives, to ask our gods at roadside idols to forget us, to help our families forget us. Who have us in the fields working.'

'And yet you are here, not working in the fields.'

'As I said, George, Micah was bequeathed to the church,' Albert said.

'Micah is happy enough to speak up, Albert, so let him speak. Or are you going to speak on his behalf?'

'I did work in the fields, once the master of the plantation got sick of me,' Micah said.

'What do you mean sick of you?' Tyler said.

'I was bought by a man who liked…' Micah said. Then he looked down and a tear ran down his cheek. 'He used the boys he bought for his…Well, you get the idea. Either humiliating us or violating us or beating us.'

Tyler recoiled, uncertain of what to say. 'I'm sorry,' Tyler said.

'Then I got sent to the fields. Soon after, the master got sick and his nephew arrived and ran the plantation. When he died, I was taken from the fields along with a few other boys he had used and we were given to the church. Some of us got sent back here to England. So I worked the fields for a time, but I wish it had been for the whole time.' Micah looked at some distant point, back into his past.

Albert looked at Tyler who could not meet the priest's eyes.

'There was peace before you Europeans started taking slaves from Africa. There were empires like the Ashanti and some fighting, but not much. The elders used to talk about it, about tribes that were matched evenly so none could destroy others.

'Our chiefs had learned that war and fighting was a last resort that diminished us all. Which didn't mean that it never happened, it did. But then came the slavers and the guns and tribes had to make choices, work with the slavers or be enslaved. That is why Africans are involved in the trade.

'And on it went until the Dahomey and Ashanti traded slaves for guns and found a way to make another type of war, where they always won. They knew we couldn't stand up to them so that gave them the right to wage war, for slaves and riches and land. And so instead of making lives and crafts and clothing and farming and hunting, men built defences and schemed to get their own guns.

'The elders changed too. They went from being happy and asking if we were happy and ensuring peace to fearing war. There is a big difference in how you live between the first and second. And so no man thought of building his Timbuktu or things to make his village better.

'That is what the Europeans brought and still I don't know why, why they see us differently, not as men but as something to be exploited. Because other than the colour of my skin I am the same as you.'

Tyler looked away from Micah. The whole time that Micah had spoken his eyes had never left Tyler's. Now Tyler could not look at Micah nor Albert, sure that both men would be able to see what lay inside him.

'Have you heard of Gomes Eanes de Zurara?' Albert said.

'I was talking to him just the other day, Father, he is two cells over,' Tyler said hoping to deflect the priest's gaze.

'He was a Portuguese chronicler. When I was in Rome a Jesuit priest told me his story.'

'And I suppose you are going to tell us now,' Tyler said.

'Yes, I am. Zurara wrote about the Portuguese discovery of Guinea, on the African coast.'

'I know where that is, Albert, I've been there,' Tyler said.

'As have I, though I think in different circumstances,' Micah said.

'Are you two listening?' Albert said. 'So Zurara became the head of the Royal Library and was commissioned by the King of Portugal to write some histories, of people and places. His history of Guinea suggested Africa as a place of barbarians, of warring, illiterate and godless people in need of saving. He did so to justify the slave trade, to suggest that the trade would bring these heathens of Africa to God.'

'And yet there is no attempt to introduce God to Africa, only to extract Africans and use them as slaves to save their souls,' Micah said.

'Precisely. If we are to believe Zurara, and for that matter the Jesuit who told me this, then the justification for slavery is made up. As is the idea of white men being superior to black men. It does make one think,' Albert said. 'For as you said, Micah, that is not the Africa you remember the elders of your village talking about.'

'Even in my memories, people made beautiful things, clothing and containers and pottery and art. We had music and performances to remind us of our traditions. We were in so many ways rich without money and guns and rum and slavery.'

The three were quiet, each with his own thoughts.

*

'Is that true, Father, about Zurara and what he wrote?' Micah said as he and Albert walked towards St Giles.

'I tried to find a copy of Zurara's work while I was in Rome and could not. What I did find out is that during the Roman Empire there was no distinguishing between men on the basis of their skin colour. That does seem to be a more modern, um, invention as it were.'

'So why would Zurara do it?'

'If you were Portuguese in the fifteenth century and wanting to take slaves from Africa sooner or later, you would have to justify that to the Pope and the Vatican. And once you see Africans as heathens, you have a justification for intervening. Then it is a short step to seeing them as lesser in other ways. As inferior to white Christians in whatever manner you choose, if you will pardon the term. And so what better way to justify all of that than to say you are doing God's work in Africa.'

'But they were taking slaves,' Micah said.

'Of course, and I don't doubt that the Pope and others knew that, but as with many things, it was less about the good of those poor taken from Africa and more about money. The money that would come to the Church from slavery. And of course, once the Americas were opened up and the riches from the New World flowed back here, what Pope would argue against slavery?'

'But the Church, they have looked after me. Are you telling me that they have allowed slavery?'

'Micah, what the Church does and what some in the Church do is not always the same as God's work. I know how much the Church means to you, that it has given you a good life here and allowed you to minister to some of your fellow Africans, believe in that. Do not think too much about the whole, focus on your small part and the people who have done right by you.'

Micah nodded. He thought about the lost souls, his African brothers who gathered around St Giles and about what the Church did to help them. And for a brief moment, he thought that this was the least it could do, that like Christ, they were being betrayed by those in power, and for money alone. Then he drifted off into the gathering evening gloom.

The following day, Albert and Micah visited Tyler again.

'George, this is for you, a new shirt and coat. I have guessed your size. I thought it best to look good at your trial.'

'Albert, thank you.' Tyler held the shirt to his nose and smelt it. It smelt fresh, new, unlike anything in the prison. Carefully, he folded the shirt and coat and took the newspaper that Albert offered and placed them on top of it, with a handkerchief between the paper and clothing.

'You like them,' Micah said.

'Yes, I do. This is the first time I have felt anything like happiness in some time,' Tyler said smiling.

'It is good to see you smiling, George,' Albert said.

'I'd almost forgotten what it feels like.'

'Smiling?' Albert said.

'And feeling happy,' Tyler said.

'When was the last time, George,' Albert said. Tyler looked blankly at Albert then looked away.

'Probably at sea, Albert, that is where I always felt happiest.'

'When you speak of the sea, George, you look different, lighter perhaps.'

Tyler smiled. 'Sometimes at sea on an evening, the slaves would sing. We would have them on deck and well, it is probably awful to say, but I did love those times.'

Tyler hummed a few notes to mimic the tune. At that moment, Micah stiffened and then closed his eyes. A memory, distant and painful, washed over him. And without fully realising it Micah began to sing.

Tyler looked astonished. The words he could not be sure of but the tune, the sound of it transported him back to the deck of slave ships, listening to the song as the sun disappeared into the horizon ahead. He closed his eyes and listened then opened them and playfully slapped Albert on the shoulder.

'That's what it sounded like,' Tyler said elatedly.

Micah stopped singing and Albert and Tyler looked at him. Tears streamed down his cheeks.

'It is a death song that is sung to farewell the dead. If slaves sang that on a boat it was to mourn their deaths, their removal from their homes and lives. For the deaths, they probably knew were ahead of them,' Micah said.

Tyler trembled. He looked at Micah searching for something but what he did not know. He felt Albert's hand on his shoulder, steadying him and for a moment hated Albert for it. He pushed Albert's hand away and immediately regretted it, realising he needed a connection to another person now more than ever. He had taken that song, of death and mourning and celebrated it, usurped its meaning to make him happy. Something that they would never know again. *That is what I took from them, from those slaves, from those men,* Tyler thought.

He looked at Micah who still had tears running down his cheeks. The African looked distant, as though he had retreated into his memories, an array of emotions running across his face. Tyler did not know it, but a flood of memories were pouring out in Micah, of his past and those dreadful days on the march and the boat and his master naming him Micah. Of days in the fields, men calling the lazy slaves Foin, after the tribe they all hated and laughing at this slur. Of Micah calling lazy slaves Foin and laughing viciously. Of wiping dirt across his face and body before statues and idols while in chains. Of his grandmother and mother quietly dismissing his initiation, the one he never had, as men being men all the while knowing the deceit behind its mysticism. Learning English in the room at the back of the plantation house. Of his sister having a tantrum over something and his father telling him of working in the fields. Of the plantation house's bedroom and crying under the weight of the master as he penetrated Micah for the first time. He remembered the smell of his mother's cooking and the breath of the master, of his time on the boat and the awful smell of death that never really left him. Of encounters in the alleys behind St Giles, of being the abused and the abuser depending on his mood. And still, the tears flowed.

Seven

'Get up slaver, today is your big day,' the guard said. 'You need to be ready in an hour.' The guard placed a bucket of lukewarm water, a dirty towel and a razor on the ground outside the cell. 'Do what you need to look decent and put the bucket and towel on the ground outside the cell when you are done. And if that razor ain't sitting in an empty bucket we will come in there in force so you won't look so pretty for court, you clear?'

Tyler nodded.

The guard left and Tyler picked up the bucket and towel and razor. He found a small piece of soap in the towel and worked up a lather and carefully shaved his face as best as he could.

Then he stripped and washed and poured the water over himself. It was cold and dank but it was more than he had had to wash with in days. He dried himself as best he could and put his trousers back on and took the clean shirt and smelt it again. He pulled it over his head and fastened the buttons and pulled the braces over his shoulders and put on the coat. Carefully, he placed the razor in the empty bucket and put it and the towel outside the cell and sat on the bed and waited.

Soon the guard returned with three more guards behind him, all holding batons. 'So let's see if slaver here can follow instructions?'

He walked over carefully and quickly glanced in the bucket and then at Tyler sitting on his bed.

'No fun this morning, boys, seems Mr Tyler here is a good boy,' the guard said. 'Mr Tyler, your carriage awaits.'

Four constables stood outside the strong door of the prison and took Tyler from the guards and sat with Tyler in the carriage, one on each side of him and two more opposite. The carriage rumbled and clattered off and within ten minutes Tyler was at the court.

Outside a large crowd was gathered, with gawpers and those just wanting to see the infamous slave boat captain along with abolitionists and those paid by the slavers to cheer when Tyler arrived.

The carriage stopped. 'Bloody hell it's a rabble out there,' one of the constables said. 'Mr Tyler, if you cooperate with us we can get you in that courtroom quickly. Or it can go hard, so which is it?'

'I'll cooperate,' Tyler said.

The first constable opened the door and stepped out, followed by two more constables. 'Right, Mr Tyler, with me,' the lead constable said. With that, Tyler and the constable stepped out.

'There he is' and 'that's him,' were shouted. Someone screamed and the pro-slavers cheered and the abolitionists booed. The noise was overwhelming after the silence of the prison. Tyler put a hand on the shoulder of the constable in front and shuffled and walked as best he could. He tried to focus on his feet and put one foot in front of the other while not tripping on the feet in front. *That seemed harder than it should have been,* he thought.

Five minutes later Tyler was seated in the courtroom, behind a heavy railing, two of the constables behind him, and with a constable on each side of him. Simon Rubin turned and waved and walked over.

'George, so this is it. Now stay calm, try not to show too much emotion and do as the judge asks, is that clear?'

Tyler nodded. He had barely remembered what Rubin looked like. Then he looked over and saw a tall skinny man dressed in good clothing sitting at the table opposite to Rubin. The man looked over at Tyler with a distasteful expression on his face.

A bailiff walked into the courtroom. 'All rise.'

Everyone stood up and the hubbub of noise and speculation died as the judge walked into the chamber. His face was impassive, an expression that he would keep for most of the trial.

Tyler expected the judge to speak, to outline the charges or the rules or to say something, instead, he simply nodded to the tall skinny well-dressed man opposite Rubin.

Yorke Carrington took a deep breath and rose to his feet.

'Slavery is the evil of our times,' Carrington said. A raucous cheer went up in the courtroom.

The judge banged his gavel down hard. 'Order,' he said once and loudly, staring down the crowd. Then he nodded at Carrington.

'Slavery has consumed the hearts of men, it has tainted one of the great bastions of English freedom, our sailors. Many of the sailors that have helped make England great, from those who faced down the Armada to our men of today have suffered through this evil trade. They are sometimes pressed, other times unwitting in their knowledge of how evil this trade is. They hew these poor Africans from their—'

'Mr Carrington,' the judge said in a booming voice, 'I do hope that you are going to get on with things very quickly. If you want to grandstand go buy a soapbox and find a street corner like every other lout and time waster. You are straining my patience. Now let us have your case or be done with it now.'

Carrington swallowed hard. His hands that were gripping his coat dropped and he quickly walked to the table and hands trembling took a paper off the pile.

'My apologies. This trial is about murder,' Carrington said. He shot a quick look at the judge hoping for some kind of acknowledgement but was met with the judge's impassive face.

'It is about the responsibilities of a captain at sea in preparing for and managing all the known eventualities that may occur. That captain carries a duty of care to all aboard. He must pay attention to the vital matters that ensure survival.

'To neglect these duties is an offence, for all captains at sea are bound by these duties. Even the captain of slave ships,' Carrington said, realising his grammar was wrong but ploughing on, 'are bound to look after all aboard, under the findings of Lord Mansfield in the case of the Zong.

'George Tyler, captain of the Charlotte, did not sufficiently undertake these duties. Instead, his actions were negligent. He did not act reasonably as a captain should.

'I will prove that the actions taken by George Tyler aboard the Charlotte, by Captain Tyler, set in train a series of events that led to the murder of 129 slaves. Principally, Tyler did not take sufficient care of the duties to be expected of a captain and instead relied on dumping cargo, as he calls it, and recouping losses through insurers.

'Captain Tyler is a captain of many years of experience of the sea and slave boats and it is in this light that his actions must be considered. This experience demands a deeper and harsher assessment of his decisions and actions.

'The events, becalming and storms, are not new nor unprecedented. Rather, they are known hazards of the sea. They must be considered and actions taken to ameliorate against such risks, to anticipate and insure against. Instead, Tyler's lack of foresight together with a desire to recover inevitable trade losses, inevitable because of his poor preparations, created a mindset that saw murdering slaves as the best way to ensure a return for his ship's owner. The slaves aboard came to be viewed as expendable, because Tyler was left with no other choice.

'So let me now outline the legal precedents that dictate our case,' Carrington said.

Carrington spent the next hour outlining precedents from Mansfield, the Zong and a range of other cases. At the end, he sat down, already exhausted. The judge declared a recess then he looked at Carrington. The young lawyer fancied that for a moment the judge had offered the merest of nods, but in his exhaustion, Carrington couldn't be sure it was real or imagined.

The constables stood and motioned Tyler to follow them out a side door and down a short corridor into a room that doubled as a cell. 'This is where you stay during the day if the court is adjourned, and each day after proceedings we take you back to the prison. Clear?' the lead constable said.

Tyler nodded. At least it was a different cell to the one he had spent the last few weeks in.

There was a knock on the door and one of the constables opened it a short way, said something and fully opened the door.

Simon Rubin walked in and sat down. 'I am fine alone with my client please constables.'

With that, the constables left. 'Just knock on the door when you are ready to leave,' the lead constable said to Rubin.

'So what did you make of that?' Rubin said.

'I am not sure I really understand it all.'

'Mr Carrington is saying that because you did not account for storms and becalming and loss of water, you decided the easiest way out was to murder the slaves.'

'That's ridiculous, I made a decision to save my crew.'

'Be that as it may, it is a good avenue to prosecute. So it will likely come down to your thinking and state of mind at the time, did you think about it as murder.'

'I didn't and even if I did, they can't prove that.'

'To secure a conviction Mr Carrington does not need to offer absolute proof, such as you saying let's murder the negroes or something similar.'

'I don't understand, how can he prove murder otherwise?'

'When prosecuting a criminal case such as murder it is necessary to prove two things. The first is *actus reus,* which is Latin meaning a guilty act. This must be accompanied by a guilty mind, in Latin *men's rea.*

'So Mr Carrington will try to link gross or criminal negligence to murder and that requires he satisfy the court on at least one of three tests. And that will need proof that you displayed a disregard for human life, against what a reasonable person would have done in the circumstances,' Rubin said.

'Now, of course, from my perspective, no reasonable person would ever put to sea, but in this case, a reasonable person would be another captain of some considerable experience. What would they have done? So he is trying to prove that you either knew the water supplies may be lost or simply didn't care.

'So then, Mr Tyler, let us imagine for a moment how Mr Carrington will proceed,' Rubin said.

Tyler shook his head. 'I am tired and just want to rest.'

'Let us imagine this for a moment please, Mr Tyler. It is important. So the guilty act will be dumping the slaves, or at least the order to do so. Right then? So what is the intent, the guilty mind?' Rubin sat and looked into space for several moments.

'Because a guilty act is not enough. It may prove criminal negligence if Mr Carrington can convince the judge that the water was not properly secured, but that is not all of it.'

Another long pause ensued.

'The guilty mind could be, could it be…you took the easy way out in throwing the slaves overboard. Would that do it?' Again Rubin sat and thought. Tyler watched not knowing what to say.

'That could be the guilty mind, that you owed a duty of care to the slaves and ignored it. Yes, that could be it indeed.'

'I owed no duty of care to the slaves. The only person I owed any duty to was Mr Pennington.'

'Please don't say that in court or anywhere else for that matter, Mr Tyler. Even if you were not aware of it you did owe a duty of care to all aboard including the slaves. That is the law of the sea. At the least, it shows a shocking ignorance, at worst such statements may just get you hung.

'So where was I?' Rubin closed his eyes and paused for so long Tyler wondered if he had fallen asleep.

'It's a hybrid case,' Rubin said. 'So he will argue that you dumped the slaves to protect the crew. Having been negligent in securing the water you placed everyone in that position. Had you done better such actions would not have been necessary. It is a narrow window but if finely argued it is a very clear case.

'So there you go, Mr Tyler, do you see it now?'

'No, but you sound like you have a defence figured already. Is that why you are smiling?'

'I am smiling because it is a very good case and presents a difficult challenge to defend. But then I like a challenge,' Rubin said.

*

Yorke Carrington had just finished outlining the voyage of the Charlotte. It sounded so mundane, like any other voyage. Carrington described the storm, the loss of water and the becalming in a flat monotone, careful to present these events as run of the mill.

'So I call Captain Paul Drummond to the stand,' Carrington said.

A middle-aged man stood and walked to the stand and swore an oath over the bible.

Drummond had retired from the slave trade and settled in Bristol with his Irish wife. Having bought his own boat he ran a trade route between Bristol and Dublin, using the connections of his wife's family in Ireland.

'Mr Drummond,' Carrington said.

'Captain Drummond, it's Captain,' Drummond said nodding to the judge. 'It's a naval court so that matters, being called captain.'

Carrington smiled. 'I beg your pardon, Captain Drummond. You have sailed as captain on seven voyages to Africa to pick up slaves and transport them across the Atlantic?'

'Aye.'

'So you are familiar with preparing for a voyage?'

'Aye.'

'Can you please indulge my ignorance and tell us all what that involves.'

'Aye. So it depends on the ship and its owners as to how they do that. Some employ a person in their company, some contract an outfitter, others leave it to the captain.'

'I see. How do they decide on basic supplies, food and water, for instance?'

'There are rules that we all followed. Basically, it's worked out on the number of the crew by the number of days of the voyage. So for example, enough flour to bake bread every third day and biscuits the other two days.'

'And water?'

'Same thing, the rules are based on those of the navy, three quarts of water each day each man aboard.'

'I see,' Carrington said. 'Oh but excuse me, one thing is actually not clear. How do you know how many days it takes? I mean depending on the wind and tides it cannot be the same for each ship?'

'Aye. So we work on the worst case possible, to ensure that there is a margin for error.'

'And what is the worst case possible?'

'You add days on to a good voyage, say a week or two.'

'Oh, I see. And that allows for the margin of error?'

'Aye.'

'So how is the water stored?'

'The water is stored in barrels below deck and tapped as needed.'

'And how are the barrels secured?'

'Very carefully. I always had the barrels stacked, roped and netted and then squeezed.'

'Squeezed?'

'Aye, that is putting other cargo in between the barrels, filling the spaces up.'

'Why when you have roped and netted the barrels?'

'That makes it less likely the barrels will move around. There is nothing more important than water aboard a ship.'

'So, did you ever lose water barrels?'

'Only once. We got hit with a monster wave out of the blue. They happen sometimes. We lost most of our water.'

'What did you do then?'

'We turned around and sailed to the nearest port and got more.'

'So when this wave hit, did it rock the ship or?'

'Rock the ship, more like picked it up and dumped it down again. We had a right mess on our hands that day, cargo every which way.'

'So your experience is that it takes a large force to move all the cargo?'

'Aye.'

'So, is it possible for a storm or wave to move only a small amount of cargo?'

'Possible, but that would mainly be due to the cargo not being properly secured.'

'So you are suggesting, as a captain of seven slave voyages across the Atlantic, that if only a small portion of the cargo broke free and was smashed, that is because of poor preparations in securing that cargo?'

'Aye, that's the nub of it.'

'Now, before I let you go, could you help out on one other matter?'

'Aye.'

'You have sailed seven Atlantic crossings with slave cargo?'

'That's right.'

'How did you treat the slaves?'

'I'm not sure what you mean. Is that something about slavery being wrong?'

The judge stared hard at Carrington. 'What I mean is did you ensure enough food and water for them, was it three quarts of water a day for each slave?'

'Oh, I see. Well, I made sure they had enough food and water, at that rate you said. You gotta treat the slaves like any other live cargo, fed, watered, cleaned so it gets to the destination in good condition.'

'Why in good condition?'

'So it sells well,' Drummond said, looking at Carrington as if he were a simpleton.

'Of course. Now Captain Drummond I take it you profit from that, from slaves being sold?'

'Yes, I did. You don't have a problem with that?'

'No,' Carrington said lying. 'What I am asking is you have the incentive to get the slaves across the Atlantic in good condition?'

'Yes, the better the price, the better the outcome for the owners of the ship, and me and the crew with a share.'

'Finally, did you ever dump slaves?'

'Aye, only once and only a handful who had disease. The doc on board thought it best so that is what we did.'

'Did you get any money for those slaves?'

Again Drummond looked at Carrington like he were a simpleton. 'Son, you don't get paid for what is not delivered.'

'So the owners you sailed for never told you it was alright to dump slaves?'

'No.'

'So to sum up, you agree that the better treated the slaves are, the better the price on delivery?'

'Aye.'

'And that means looking after them, including food and water?'

'Aye.'

'Thank you, Captain Drummond.'

The judge nodded to Rubin. 'Do you want to cross-examine Captain Drummond?'

'Thank you, your honour,' Rubin said. He sat and looked at Drummond for a few moments then slowly stood.

'So it was seven voyages carrying slaves was it?'

'Aye,' said Drummond.

'If I may I would like to take up on two points of your testimony? You said you aimed to keep the slaves healthy?'

'Aye, to the best that we could.'

'So did this involve making choices. For example, you said you once threw slaves overboard?'

'Aye.'

'Why was that again?'

'They were sick and likely to either spread disease or die anyway.'

'How did you know they would die anyway?'

'The ship's doctor said so.'

'But ultimately, you made the decision?'

'Aye.'

'And to squeezing the barrels as you called it. Is one reason to ensure barrels don't roll?'

'Aye, a rolling barrel can cause all sorts of mischief.'

'So you have seen a barrel roll?'

'On several occasions yes.'

'And this despite securing the cargo?'

'I suppose so.'

'And you said that even with the best preparation a wave or storm could make it possible, I think that was the word you used, make it possible for cargo to shift?'

'Aye.'

'Or perhaps even cause a barrel to roll, as you said you saw on several occasions?'

'Aye.'

'So it happened to you, having cargo shift?'

'It happens at sea.'

'Thank you, Captain Drumond.'

*

'Mr Weldon, you are the man contracted to outfit the Charlotte for her voyage?' Carrington said to his next witness.

'That's right,' Weldon said.

'Why you?'

'I'm the best at it and Pennington likes having the best do work for him.'

'I don't doubt that, however, why use you or another outfitter, why not have Captain Tyler here or one of his own people do the outfitting?'

'You mean other than I'm the best at it?'

'Yes, Mr Weldon, other than that?'

'You should probably ask Pennington that, it's his choice after all.'

'But it wasn't because Mr Pennington say, doubted, Captain Tyler?'

'He never said that to me.'

'So moving on, how much water would you supply for the whole voyage?'

'I don't know that.'

'Mr Weldon, are you saying you don't know?'

'For the whole voyage yes, my job is to get the ship to Africa with the right goods to trade for slaves.'

'I see,' Carrington said. 'Did you ever discuss water supplies with Captain Tyler?'

'No, I don't really have much to do with the captain of the ship, I just get it ready for sailing.'

'So you never ever spoke to Captain Tyler about water supplies?'

'Not ever.'

'In your outfitting did you follow the three quarts rule for water?'

'Yes.'

'Do you think Captain Tyler was aware of that rule?'

'I suppose so, I couldn't really tell you.'

'And finally, if you outfit the ship to Africa who outfits it for the voyage across the Atlantic?'

'That is up to the captain of each ship.'

'So the captain of each ship does that?'

'That's what I said.'

Carrington sat down and the judge nodded to Rubin, who slowly rose, walked to the front of the table and leaned back against it, closing his eyes for a moment.

'Do you outfit all of Charles Pennington's ships?'

'Only those that go to Africa.'

'Right. So…there are other ships that you don't outfit if that is the correct term?'

'That's right, Pennington has a couple of ships that do runs to parts of Europe. That is less complex than a slaver.'

'Fascinating,' Rubin said. Then he carefully removed his spectacles and absent-mindedly chewed on one arm, staring at the wall above Weldon. After a time, Weldon looked at the judge and made to stand up.

'Just one thing, Captain Royce of the High Glen had trouble selling some bafts of cotton on his last voyage, bafts that you supplied? Did you know those bafts were out of fashion?'

Weldon looked angrily at Rubin. 'No, I did not!'

'You strike me as a thorough and well-organised man, Mr Weldon. The best I think you said. Certainly, one that commands enough respect that a trader as successful as Charles Pennington would contract out to you. It was, in the case of the bafts, just bad luck that the tastes in fashion were as fickle in Africa as here?'

'That's correct. What's your point?'

'I should explain a little something and tell me if I'm wrong? The High Glen is one of Pennington's ships, trading directly to Africa and India for peppers and the like. One of those trade goods was bafts or rolls of fabric. The crew had to dye the fabric so as to sell it. All that is correct?'

'Yes. But why make something of that?'

'Only that even for the best, as you call yourself, it is nearly impossible to predict everything that happens on voyages of this length.'

*

That evening, Simon Rubin called on Charles Pennington at the Bristol club.

'So Simon, what do you make of this Carrington and his case?' Pennington said.

'I think we have our hands full, Charles. This Carrington knows his law. A lesser man would have charged off down a murder prosecution, seeking to portray Tyler as mad or something other, but not our Carrington. No, he is smarter than that.' Rubin looked off at the books lining the room. 'Is there a chance that he has a witness who was on the Charlotte?'

'What makes you say that?'

'His case is going to place the onus on Tyler to have done the right thing in securing the water. I feel that in my bones. But how would he know, how would he prove that unless he has someone who was aboard?'

'Would that hurt our case?'

'If this Carrington fellow can link the loss of water to the dumping of slaves, then yes.'

'So he could win?'

'We are a long way from that, Charles, a long way. But yes, if he executes the case well enough then he could win. And Tyler could hang.'

'A guilty verdict would be a terrible blow to the slave trade.'

'And to Tyler, one would think?'

'Yes, of course,' Pennington said.

'He seems an odd fellow this Tyler, a bit lost if you ask me.'

'Tyler is a first-rate captain. He's always a little uncertain on land. He belongs on the sea, which is why he's such a damn fine captain. I have no doubt he did what he did because he saw no other option.'

'No, there is something more there. I wonder if he is beginning to doubt himself.'

'Well, in the current climate one can hardly be surprised. It seems that slavery is now the great issue of the day, the great evil of our times. And the problem with that, Simon, is that there is no room for nuance, for dealing with the complexities of the issue.'

'I'm not sure the complexities to which you refer?'

'Well, either you agree with the abolitionists or you are condemned. That is no way to live, to expect people to have to take a side, but only one side of course. All that does is drive people to say what is expected, not deal with what is in their heart.'

Pennington looked at Rubin, waiting for an answer. Instead, Rubin stared off into space. 'Charles, I need to go. I need to do some research.' Rubin stood. 'By the way, you are on the witness list for tomorrow. This Carrington fellow seems to want to question you.'

'About what?'

'I expect about any instructions you gave, Tyler. And you need to be honest. If they have a witness and he was privy to any instructions you gave, perhaps a letter of commission or other, and he contradicts you, then you look dishonest.'

'Why would it be me who looks dishonest? Why not the other witness?'

'You are the owner of slave boats, hardly a reputable profession these days. Besides, in court, it is always the rich man who looks dishonest. Trust me on that.' Then Rubin quietly made his way out of the room, leaving Pennington alone with no one to hear him rail against the abolitionists.

*

'George, how are you, now that the big day has been and gone,' Albert said.

'Bone-tired, Albert,' Tyler said.

'There is ham and bread and cheese in the bag,' Albert said, handing the bag over. 'And a bottle of ale.'

Tyler opened the bag and took out a slice of ham, then cheese and put them between two slices of bread. He ate slowly, more out of tiredness than any other reason.

'It's odd,' Tyler said between mouthfuls. 'I have dreaded this day for so long, waited for it, hoped it would be over and now, nothing but tiredness.'

'Because there are many more of these days ahead?'

'I think so.' Tyler took a long drink of the ale then burped. He stared at Albert who smiled.

'Are you intending to share that ale or have it all for yourself?'

'I didn't think you would drink beer.'

'Why not, I like a beer as much as the next man, and if he would kindly share, then I could prove that.'

Tyler handed over the beer and Albert took a long pull from the bottle and burped contentedly.

Tyler laughed, not knowing what else to do. 'Do you really see me so differently, George?'

'You are a priest.'

'That doesn't mean I don't like beer. Why on earth would you think that?'

'I don't actually know. It's just an idea that I had in my head. I mean the robes and all.'

'It's funny how people see us, priests. Put on a robe and somehow people get permission to see us as totally different. To play out all sorts of odd ideas.'

'Sorry. It's just I never really thought about. I just thought that is the way of it, you know?'

'Yes, I do, George. Like a great many things, we see what we want to see.'

'I guess we do,' Tyler said.

'Now I can't guarantee that I can bring you such fine dining every evening after the trial, but I shall endeavour to try.'

'Just do your best and I'll be happy,' Tyler said.

'It's good to see you smile, George,' Albert said.

'I do feel good.'

*

Carrington stood slowly from the table and looked at the witness box. Charles Pennington sat confidently. *Almost eagerly*, Carrington thought, watching the slave boat owner carefully.

'Mr Pennington, could you please tell the court how long Captain Tyler has worked for you?'

'The best part of fourteen years.'

'And during that time, how many voyages has he undertaken for you?'

'At least eight, perhaps ten or even more.'

'Could you be more precise?'

'I would have to consult with my secretary on that.'

'Well, we know it is definitely eight, can we agree on that?'

'I think we can,' Pennington said smiling.

'All to Africa?'

'What all the voyages or the eight we have agreed upon?' Pennington said. He saw Rubin frown at him but ignored it. Always control the engagement he reminded himself, before smiling at Carrington again.

'I think it is safe to say, given the unreliability of your memory on such matters, that we should stick to the eight voyages,' Carrington said.

Pennington's smile disappeared, replaced by a scowl. 'Yes, eight to Africa.'

'Good, now we are getting somewhere. And before this last voyage, had Captain Tyler lost many slaves?'

'A handful, I would say.'

'You would say or you would know?'

'I would know, a handful.'

'On each voyage or in total?'

'In total, less than ten before this voyage.'

'In your expert opinion, given your knowledge of the trade, would you say that is normal, or a high or low number?'

Pennington smiled, knowing that Carrington was fully aware of the numbers that were usually lost on the middle passage. 'It is an extraordinarily low number. Few men have recorded lower numbers.'

'Few men? You mean few captains. It's not men who routinely sail across the Atlantic with a hold full of slaves.'

'Yes captains then if you wish to be pedantic,' Pennington said.

'For a moment I wondered if Captain Tyler was still in your employ?' Pennington sat quietly, not wanting to respond.

'Could you clarify for the court, is Captain Tyler in your employment?'

'Yes, he is.'

'So you are backing him?'

'Yes, I am.'

'Even after this last voyage? How many slaves did he lose?'

Pennington looked at Carrington then to the judge, uncertain how to answer.

'Oh no, I am not expecting you to answer that Mr Pennington, although you were precise and pedantic in your claim to the insurers on the numbers. No, I would rather you let the court know what went wrong on the voyage.'

Pennington had sat through too many negotiations and meetings to fall into such a trap. 'Misfortune, it happens at sea.'

'Still, the losses were very high. Did it surprise you, to lose so many slaves?'

Pennington paused, smiled then answered. 'No, that is what happens when misfortune occurs at sea. Sail long enough and such misfortune is inevitable.'

'Are you suggesting that it is inevitable that more than one hundred slaves had to be thrown overboard?'

Pennington smiled wolfishly. He had goaded Carrington into asking the question he most wanted to address.

'Yes! Trade long enough in slaves or any cargo for that matter, and you will experience storms, becalming, lost or broken cargo, sometimes all on the same voyage. This is not unprecedented by any—'

'Thank you,' Carrington said. Pennington looked at Rubin whose frown bore into the slave boat owner.

'So given that these perils are well known, are inevitable to use your words, they should also be anticipated. Given that what instructions did you give Captain Tyler?'

Pennington looked at Rubin again, saw the anger and frustration on the defence lawyer's face. Then he looked at Carrington, expecting the man to be smiling, having won that concession from him. Instead, Carrington looked at Pennington with eyebrows raised, wanting an answer.

'Mr Pennington, do I need to repeat the question?'

'The-the usual terms for such a voyage. The number of slaves the ship is licensed to carry, the letter of commission outlining shares, that type of thing.'

'The usual terms. Did that include anything about insurance arrangements for the slave cargo?'

'Yes, but—'

'So there is a value set for each slave covered by insurance?'

'Yes.'

'Do you recall the value?'

'Not…er…specifically.'

'But would it at least match the price in Jamaica for a healthy slave?'

'That's the point of it.'

'Anything else in the instructions for Captain Tyler?'

'Yes, I told him not to endanger the ship, or the bulk of the cargo,' Pennington said. Then he smiled in an odd way, the smile becoming a smirk that remained fixed on his face. This was the line he had agreed with Rubin to say during the questioning.

'How noble of you. To worry about the welfare of slaves.'

'Sensible. Slaves in poor condition don't sell well.'

'Certainly, when they sell for less than they are insured, would you say?' Pennington's smirk vanished.

'Could it be that Captain Tyler felt that a better return was on offer for dead slaves dumped overboard, via an insurance claim, rather than for underfed and thirsty slaves? Slaves delivered in poor condition?'

'You would need to ask him that.'

'So you are still backing him then? Sorry, I shall move on,' Carrington said. 'So knowing the perils of the sea, and experiencing them firsthand in such a way that water was in short supply a captain could dump slaves knowing they would get a higher price on insurance than at market?'

Pennington looked at the judge, then at Rubin then at Carrington.

'No need to answer that, Mr Pennington, I think here we will let your silence and the actions of Captain Tyler answer that question.'

Then Carrington turned and sat down. He looked back at the gallery and saw the nods and quiet words from the public.

Rubin took his glasses from his face and sat and twirled the glasses by one arm. Then he leaned back in the chair.

'Mr Pennington,' Rubin said. 'Could you please reiterate who was in command of the Charlotte on this voyage?'

'Mr, I mean Captain Tyler.'

'And he bore full responsibility for the welfare of the slaves?'

'That is correct.'

'You never instructed him to dump slaves, rather than sell them, should their condition be poor?'

'No, I did not. It took two court cases to try to claim against the insurance. I would be damn well broke if I had to do that after each voyage.'

Rubin then tilted his head to the left, started into space for several moments and put his glasses back on. 'Thank you.'

*

Simon Rubin poured a large brandy and walked over and sat down in the chair in the corner of his flat. He stared out the window looking at the Thames, swirling the brandy, alone with his thoughts.

Pennington had almost instinctively taken his lead, throwing Tyler under the carriage. Rubin had had seconds to make his decision following Carrington's excoriation of Pennington. Like so many rich men, Pennington had been convinced of his argument, certain that his standing was enough to enforce that argument and had allowed himself to underestimate the prosecution.

Rubin had seen it time and again, the arrogance and contempt, the smirks and smiles, even while the words being said undermined his case.

All Pennington had to do was answer simple questions, Rubin thought. Instead, Pennington had decided to be useful. 'How many smart men think they can be useful in court and say things that they shouldn't,' he said as his cat wandered into the room. The cat, used to such conversations, crawled up and sat in Rubin's lap.

'And of course, he wasn't even close to useful,' Rubin said to the cat. 'No, instead he gave that Carrington fellow exactly what he wanted. And daddy had to make a decision, whether to back the man I was defending or to get another rich fool out of the trouble of his own making.'

The cat stared at Rubin with big eyes, knowing that once Rubin was done speaking dinner would be served. 'If this Tyler is found guilty and Mr Charles, I know it all, Pennington isn't clearly delineated in terms of legal responsibility, then he could be next on the chopping block.' Rubin patted the cat then stroked its belly as the cat rolled over.

'So daddy got him out of that by ensuring that it is all on Tyler. I did the right thing,' Rubin said before staring out at the Thames and the night sky for a long time. 'After all, you don't get to where Pennington has got to in life without being ruthless, without not caring for your fellow man. He is after all a slaver, Saul?'

Saul the cat stared at Rubin waiting for his dinner. Rubin carefully lifted the cat, found some food for it and then went and poured another drink. He knew that it would not wash away the guilt. He just wondered if Tyler had understood what had happened.

Eight

The next morning, Rubin sat with Tyler trying to outline how the case was going. Tyler, like many defendants Rubin had known, was not interested in the legal intricacies.

'So what are my chances?' Tyler said.

'It's still too early to tell,' Rubin said. He waited for the questions about yesterday, about responsibility and Pennington and Tyler and the distance that now stood between the two, but they did not come.

Rubin wondered what was worse; throwing an unknowing man like Tyler under the carriage or dealing with a man fully aware of what was happening. He was still pondering on that when the first witness of the day was called.

John Syndon was gaunt, coughed frequently and shook and trembled as though cold throughout his testimony.

'Mr Syndon, you were a factor, working at the British settlement on the Slave Coast of Africa?'

'That's right,' Syndon said followed by a bout of coughing.

Carrington had then led Syndon through a series of questions about slave trading on the coast, how ships operated and the decisions captains made in relation to water.

'So in your estimation, the amount of water a captain takes on board is not set, there is no precise measure per crew and slaves?'

'It all depends on the captain and how confident they are.'

'Confident of what?'

Syndon shook.

'Are you alright?' the judge said.

'It's from an ailment, I got it in Africa,' Syndon said. 'It's how confident the captain is of the tides and winds. Some expect them to go their way, others are more cautious.'

'And that is the main determinant of how much water is taken aboard?'

'That and the supply of slaves and the comings and goings of ships.'

'What do you mean by the comings and goings?'

'Well, see if no ships have left in a few months then there will be a shortage of slaves in Jamaica and elsewhere in the Americas. So if you get sailing first then you get into port first and get a premium on the sale of slaves, because there have been none sold for some time. Under those circumstances, well, it's a race isn't it?'

'So how does that affect water supplies on board?'

'Two ways really. The first are the cautious ones, who take on enough water for the whole crossing and don't make stops, like at Sao Tome or the Canaries. The second are those that take on the bare minimum in the hopes of a lighter boat and faster times to those stops. The risk takers as it were.'

'Had you ever met Captain Tyler?'

'No, he always traded with Nagle, another factor.'

'Did you know of him by reputation?'

'You get to know all the regulars.'

'You make it sound like a pub, all the regulars.'

'But they are regulars, and they know their stuff. Tyler here, he was considered more of a cautious captain.'

'Thank you.'

Rubin spun his glasses around and then leaned back in his chair. 'So you never met the man here,' Rubin said pointing to Tyler.

'No,' Syndon said.

'You only knew him by reputation?'

'Yes.'

'And that reputation was good?'

'Yes.'

'Thank you. I don't think I will ask you to clarify what makes a slave captain have a good reputation, though it may console Mr Tyler to know that at least somewhere in the world people think good of him.'

*

The trip from the court to the jail was uneventful, which meant quick. Tyler hated that, the idea that within minutes of leaving the court, he would be back in the cell. The routine of cell to court to cell was crushing. Tyler paced up and down in his cell. He felt angry and frustrated now the trial was underway, worried that too much was happening that he did not understand. Where previously the wait and uncertainty was enervating, now he found himself irritated at the smallest things.

He had refrained from asking Rubin where exactly he stood with Pennington. Yet, the words between Pennington and Rubin cut deeply.

'Could you please reiterate who was in command of the Charlotte on this voyage?'

'Mr, I mean Captain Tyler.'

'And he bore full responsibility for the welfare of the slaves?'

'That is correct.'

Tyler replayed that exchange in his head time and again. *'Mr, I mean Captain…full responsibility for the welfare of the slaves…that is correct'.*

Tyler couldn't shake the idea that Pennington was ready to cut him loose, throw him overboard like a used slave. And that irritated him. Yet Pennington was paying for his defence. Around and around he went, uncertain who he was angry at, Pennington and Rubin or the world or himself. Deep down, he suspected himself but couldn't tell why.

'Slaver, looks like your dinner is here,' a guard said.

Tyler saw Albert walking across the yard with Micah beside him. He took a deep breath hoping it would still the powder keg inside.

After pleasantries, Tyler opened the bag and saw ham and a bottle of ale. He was tempted to skip to the ale and down the lot in one go.

'So, George, you are the only thing anyone wants to talk about at the minute. How does it feel to be famous?' Albert said with a wry smile.

'Like being in a prison,' Tyler said. 'So what, is the trial being reported?'

'Every word,' Micah said.

Tyler opened the bottle and took a long draught of the ale before handing the bottle to Albert who did the same. Then he handed it back to Tyler.

Tyler looked at Micah eyeing off the bottle. He paused, unsure of what to do. 'May I?' Micah said looking at the bottle.

Tyler looked at Albert who simply smiled then reluctantly handed the bottle over to Micah who drank a long pull. Then Micah handed the bottle back to Tyler, who looked at the opening of the bottle and wondered for too long if he should wipe it with his sleeve. Micah had not done so nor Albert.

'And do the papers say what my chances are?' Tyler said as he put the bottle aside, conscious that he had not drank from it since taking it back from Micah.

'It depends on the paper, George. Funnily enough, the pro-slavery papers have you getting off while the abolitionist papers say you are for it.'

'The abolitionists have organised a boycott of sugar and coffee while the trial is underway,' Micah said. 'For some, it is seen as a waste of time, but for many, taking sugar is now considered wrong.'

'So some are not getting involved. How many would you say?'

'Everyone I know is supporting the boycott,' Micah said.

'I think George is talking more broadly. There are some who are ignoring it, for others it does not matter one way or another,' Albert said. 'But it is the vocal groups who have drawn the attention of the papers and the politicians. And they are gaining support.'

'You make it sound as if slavery's days are numbered,' Tyler said punctuating his words with a savage laugh.

'I would not laugh, the day is coming,' Micah said.

'I didn't ask you,' Tyler said. Then he picked up the bottle and made an elaborate display of wiping the top of the bottle before he took a drink and then handed it to Albert. Tyler waited for Albert to drink before he held his hand out to take the bottle back. Then he drank a long pull from the bottle.

'It doesn't matter who you ask, the day when slavery is abolished is coming soon,' Micah said.

'Don't think it will change things for you, even if it does happen,' Tyler said.

'I don't think this is helping,' Albert said.

'Do you think that people are just going to forget that you negroes were once slaves, that suddenly they will say, "Oh, let's give them everything we have?"'

'George!' Albert said.

'What, Father, you think you can overturn the order of the world in a day or a week. There is a reason Africa is rich picking for slaves. Even the locals get involved, trading their fellow Africans.'

'You are no better than a Foin,' Micah said. 'Speaking of hatred and being a slave trader.'

'We all gotta hate someone don't we,' Tyler said. 'And we all gotta be better than someone. See that is what you don't understand. If slavery doesn't exist, it won't make you equal, because we all have to be better than someone else, or else we know just how miserable we are.'

'I am free, you are in prison, so how are you better than me?'

'Get out of here now!' Tyler yelled.

Micah stood up and walked out of the cell into the yard. 'See me walking, I will keep going right out that door. You stay here and wonder if you are gunna get hanged.'

'You fucking black bastard!' Tyler yelled.

'Micah, go now, go!' Albert yelled. It was the first time Tyler had heard the priest raise his voice.

'You best be going too and don't bring that thing back here!' Tyler screamed.

Three guards appeared and pulled Albert out of the cell and closed the cell door. Then they grabbed Albert and pushed him away and out the door of the prison.

Micah was waiting outside, pacing back and forth.

'He fights against this change even though he knows that it's right!'

'Yes, Micah, but when you believe in something your whole life, it is hard to turn from that. In fact, in many ways, it is extraordinary even to think of doing so. If he turns his back on slavery for any reason other than he realises it is wrong, what has he learnt. That is what we want for him, and nothing less.'

'That is why you want me to forgive him because only then will I be free,' Micah said. Albert smiled.

Micah looked at the priest and frowned. Inside he felt empty, knowing Albert was right and yet unable to see the way to change his own life. He had begun to like Tyler and now that too was gone, swallowed up by his hatred of slavery, by the desires that lurked inside.

That night, Micah drifted to St Giles, to the alleyways behind the church where the other lost souls, those like him consumed by a life stolen from them and abused for most of that life went to find solace or comfort or to fuel the fire of hatred.

He drifted along, searching for the one, for a man who knew how he felt and knew what he wanted. Every time he got angry it consumed him, his broken past welling up to destroy anything new and good. He needed to be used, to hate his abuser all over again, until that anger turned and spilled out in tears of rage and self-hatred, until he could reverse it and become strong by taking another, by taking a boy or young man and channelling his own anger outwards.

He felt revolted, at himself, his past, Tyler and the church.

A man looked at him, a predatory look that Micah needed and Micah stared at the man and nodded. Then he walked into an alleyway and the man followed. Micah turned and faced the wall and felt the man push his elbow against his own head and felt the man's breath on his neck. Then the man pulled roughly at Micah's pants, forcing them down and Micah closed his eyes and felt the tears falling down his cheeks and gave himself up to his loathing.

*

Simon Rubin sat in his chair staring at Carrington, his respect for his opponent growing. Carrington, for his part, knew better than to expect a reaction from Rubin, even as he called the next witness.

Gilbert Calum stood and walked to the chair beside and below where the judge sat. He quietly swore to tell the truth. Rubin looked at Calum trying to assess the man, yet only gained the impression of a man without a life force, a soul, without any form of animation. Then Rubin turned to the gallery and found Charles Pennington and with a polite nod said to the slave owner, *I told you so*.

Pennington looked at Rubin, resented the fact the lawyer had correctly predicted Carrington had a member of the Charlotte's crew and hoped that this was not the death knell for Tyler, or more accurately, for his lucrative empire trading in slaves.

'Mr Calum, could you please tell the court what role you played on board the Charlotte?' There were gasps and whispers in the public gallery at the mention of the Charlotte.

Scribes working for the papers leaned forwards, men speculated on what was to follow. It took the gallery several moments to realise that Calum was already speaking, oblivious to the reaction he had caused.

'I was a mate aboard the Charlotte,' Calum said mechanically.

'Where does the mate sit on the pecking order of ship's officers?'

'I was the most junior of the officers.'

'But an officer nonetheless?'

'Yes,' Calum said.

'And was this your first voyage with Captain Tyler?'

'Yes.'

'How was he as a captain?'

Calum stared blankly at Carrington.

'Was he, did he ensure the crew were treated well?'

'Yes.'

'And the slaves?'

Again Calum stared at Carrington.

'Did he treat the slaves decently, were they fed and exercised?'

'Yes.'

Carrington sighed. 'Let me lay out the circumstances leading up to the slaves being thrown overboard. If I get something wrong, please tell me. The ship was becalmed.' Carrington looked at Calum who nodded. 'That was after a storm hit and much of the water supply was lost. Yes.'

'Yes.'

'How much of the water supply would you estimate was lost?'

'More than half, maybe.'

'Could you be more precise?'

'More than half.'

'When the water was first loaded, did Captain Tyler take an interest in that?'

'No.'

'Why not?'

'That was not his job aboard.'

'Did he, Captain Tyler, ever inspect the water supplies or other parts of the ship?'

'No.'

'From your experience did other captains you have sailed under ever inspect the ship, say its water supplies or cargo hold?'

'Yes.'

Carrington worked hard to hide his frustration. *This was like talking to a child*, he thought. 'Before the storm and the loss of the water, do you think there was enough water to make Jamaica, even with a few days of becalming.'

'I assume so.'

'You assume so. Why assume so?'

'That was someone else's job, so I assume they would have done it right.' Carrington rubbed his eyes gently, sighed and tried to refocus.

'So you assume there was enough water. Can you please say yes or no?'

'Yes.'

'And given how many barrels were smashed during the storm, do you believe the water was properly secured?'

'I guess not.'

'So you believe the water was not, I repeat, was not properly secured?'

'I guess not.'

'Again, Mr Calum, yes or no please?'

'No, then.'

'Why was the water not properly secured?'

'The ropes were snapped in one place and barrels had moved everywhere.'

'You were the first person in the hold immediately after this occurred?'

'Yes.'

'Was anything else used to secure the water barrels?'

'No.'

'So no netting or other devices were used to hold the water in place?'

'No.'

'Just ropes?'

'Yes.'

'So to summarise, Captain Tyler did not inspect the water supplies, and only rope was used to secure it?'

'Yes.'

'But more could have been done to secure the water supply?'

'Yes.'

Carrington looked at Calum, searching for some humanity, a spark, anything. He found nothing, and they had yet to get to the heart of the matter.

'So let us move to the becalming. This is not unknown amongst sailors is it?'

'No.'

'Have you experienced it before?'

'Yes, but not for a few days.'

'It is more common in tropical waters, would you say?'

'Yes.'

'How far from Jamaica were you when the Charlotte was becalmed?'

'Three weeks sailing.'

'And how much water was left after the storm?'

'Twelve days' worth.'

'So potentially you were short of eight days water?'

'Yes.'

'Could you...were there ports where the Charlotte could have resupplied with water prior to reaching Jamaica?'

'Yes.'

'Once it became certain you were becalmed did Captain Tyler order the water be rationed?'

'No, we had scooped up some water from the hold and gave that to the slaves.'

'What happened next?'

'Captain Tyler asked us to meet and said we should start dumping slaves.'

'Without rationing the water aboard?'

'No.'

'Did he say why?'

'He said if we dumped them we could claim it back via the underwriters.'

The gallery erupted. The Judge hit his gavel down hard several times. 'Silence or I will have the room cleared,' the judge said.

'Carry on, Mr Calum,' Carrington said.

'That is what Captain Tyler said the letter of commission told him to do.'

'What letter of commission is that?'

'The one from Mr Pennington to the Captain,' Calum said.

Most of the gallery turned or craned their necks, searching out Pennington. Muttering and whispers could be heard. The judge banged his gavel twice and silence returned. Carrington tried to keep his mind focused, fighting the excitement of knowing he had what he needed from Calum and measuring that against what he still wanted to hear. He paused for several moments and tried to think.

'So Captain Tyler clearly said that if slaves were dumped the underwriters would pay the costs for those lost slaves?'

'Yes.'

'Alright...were those slaves well?'

'Maybe?'

'Yes or no please?'

'I don't know. Some did not get up and Mr McDougal the surgeon thought it best to throw them overboard rather than find out if they were sick.'

'Were some of the slaves thrown overboard, did they stand, or were they laying down too?'

'Some of the slaves rose up, certainly as the days went on they did.'

'So all the slaves weren't thrown overboard at once?'

'No, there were groups thrown overboard, even after it rained.'

'It rained? You are saying that slaves were thrown overboard, then it rained, and after that still more slaves were thrown overboard?'

'Yes.'

'When it rained were attempts made to capture some of the water?'

'Yes.'

'How much was captured, stored?'

'Maybe two barrels.'

'And what about sailing to another port before Jamaica, was that discussed?'

'Yes.'

'Why was that not done?'

'The captain said we had nothing to trade.'

'What about slaves, why not sell a few and get water?'

'He said they weren't ours to sell, they were Pennington's.'

'But the captain could order them thrown overboard?'

'Yes.'

'But not trade a couple of slaves for water?'

'No.'

'Did he say why?'

'That would mean lesser shares for each officer.'

'Lesser shares?'

'Each officer gets a share of the sales of slaves. So by throwing them overboard, some of the officers argued, they got more money.'

'How so, why more money?'

'The insurers would pay more for dead slaves than would buyers for poorly presented slaves.'

'Did you all agree or did some argue against it?'

'Mr Miles argued against it, and I tried but what was the point of that?'

'Could you explain?'

'By then I didn't care.'

Carrington was unsure how to proceed and paused for several moments. 'You didn't care because of the lack of water?'

'The slave trade is not one I like.'

Carrington noticed Rubin take a note of that and silently cursed Calum for saying that. 'You don't like it but still you signed on to a slaver?'

'I didn't know what I was getting myself in for.'

'So during this time was Captain Tyler rational?'

'You mean like normal or?'

'Was he emotional, or did he act as he usually did on the voyage?'

'He was normal. He thanked us after we agreed to dump slaves.'

'He thanked you! And then did he issue the orders right away or wait?'

'Right away.'

'And he seemed in control, as though he had thought about what he was doing?'

'Yes.'

'Did Mr McDougal ever say the slaves should be thrown overboard because of disease?'

'He mentioned the possibility.'

'But he did not specifically ever say that disease was present?'

'No.'

'Nor did he say that there was an outbreak of disease aboard the Charlotte?'

'No.'

'Thank you. Can I ask how all of this affected you?'

Calum just stared blankly at Carrington, unable to elaborate on feelings that were no longer there. His silence and demeanour said more than any words.

'I apologise, Mr Calum, you need not answer that. I think you have suffered enough.' The judge ordered a recess for lunch, with Calum to return to the stand for cross-examination.

Nine

Rubin sat and stared off into space as the gallery shuffled out. He looked at the note that he had scrawled and wondered how to use it to defend a client who now appeared very guilty. So Calum hated the slave trade. *Who wouldn't after that experience,* he said to himself. All Carrington had to do was not drop the ball and he had his case. It was clear that Tyler had made a commercial decision to ensure the best return. *That was intent as clear as day,* Rubin thought.

Calum had all but sealed the noose around Tyler's neck.

Rubin thought about how to unpick those words, *'He said if we dumped them we could claim it back via the underwriters'*.

The only recourse was using the letter of commission as a clear instruction, but that would mean implicating Pennington. *How on earth do I get Tyler off without using Pennington,* Rubin thought to himself. *How?*

Rubin was still pondering that dilemma when the guards ushered him into the small room where Tyler sat.

'It's bad isn't it?' Tyler said.

'Yes, it is. But I am confident we can find a way out of this mess. This Calum, was he a good officer, reliable?'

Tyler simply nodded.

'Damn. And it would be hard then to prove otherwise. Mind he does seem rather wan, as though he is, how can I say this, dead inside.'

'I think I know how he feels,' Tyler said.

'Well, don't go saying that in court. Now we need to refute his allegation that you threw those slaves overboard knowing you could get the money back from the underwriters. Did you raise the lack of water being a problem?'

'Yes, that was the crux of it really.'

'Good, so why?'

'I believed that it was a threat to the Charlotte, both because of thirst and also the possibility of disease.'

'Excellent. We are still in this fight my good man. What alternatives to throwing those men overboard did you raise?'

'I didn't.'

'Oh dear. Well, did anyone else?'

'Mr Miles did. I had gone through it in my head a dozen times. We had nothing to trade for water so we had to ration it and wait it out. When that wasn't going to happen, well, we had to dump, to throw the slaves over…'

'Good. Calum mentioned the meeting so we will reinforce the idea, that things were discussed but the result inevitable. And one other thing, my dear Tyler, don't say "I believed". Say I believe.'

'What did I say?'

'You said you believed. I do not need the judge thinking that you are second-guessing your decisions by changing your mind. Is that clear?'

Tyler nodded, unsure exactly what he believed then or now.

Rubin's cross-examination of Calum began after the lunch adjournment. The lawyer had considered the best way forward, eager to break down the effectiveness of Calum's testimony without reinforcing it. The defence lawyer's art, Rubin called it.

'Mr Calum, thank you for your earlier testimony. It was most interesting, your recollection of events. Let us start with the water. Have you ever sailed on a voyage where the water was secured by rope alone?'

'Yes.'

'Would you say that was common on the voyages you have sailed?'

'Yes.'

'And you have experienced other storms at sea?'

'Yes.'

'And cargo has shifted or fallen about in these storms?'

'Yes.'

'Now as to the Captain inspecting the water supply, did he inspect the rigging?'

'No.'

'Did he inspect the hull or every watch?'

'No.'

'And is that because he has officers, like you, to do that?'

'Yes.'

'Yes, he has officers for that. And did he, being Captain Tyler, discuss with the officers the decision to throw slaves overboard?'

'Yes.'

'Were you aware, for instance, during that discussion or at other times that it was Surgeon McDougal, the ship's doctor, who was the first to raise throwing slaves overboard?'

'No.'

'No, you weren't, were you? Now, during the discussion, you said that Captain Tyler raised the issue of seeking a return on the cargo. As you put it, "He said, if we dumped them, we could claim it back via the underwriters." Is that correct?'

'Yes.'

'Why did he want to dump slaves? Was it to save the ship and crew?'

'Yes, that is also what he said.'

'Did Captain Tyler say that the lack of water and the possible presence of disease was a threat to the Charlotte?'

'Yes.'

'Did Captain Tyler say or suggest that such action of dumping the cargo was to save the crew and the cargo?'

'I think so.'

'You were able to precisely say what Captain Tyler said when Mr Carrington was asking you questions. You either need to be precise and accurate again or let us know that what you said earlier was your best recollection and not a precise recollection?'

'He said the crew first and then the cargo.'

'Now during that discussion of the officers you said Mr Miles, the second captain suggested buying or trading water in other nearby ports?'

'Yes.'

'Why did the captain say that was not possible?'

'We had nothing to trade.'

'So the Charlotte would have needed to trade for water?'

'Yes.'

'And at that time, the ship was becalmed?'

'Yes.'

'So how could Captain Tyler have relied on sailing to nearby ports without wind?'

'I suppose he couldn't have.'

'He could not have done so without the wind, which was not present. So Mr Miles was suggesting a strategy that was only effective with a sailing wind?'

'I suppose so. After the wind came back up, we sailed on dumping slaves.'

Rubin thought quickly. 'Because the Charlotte was still short of water, that is why slaves were thrown overboard despite the wind.'

'Yes.'

'And there was no guarantee the wind would hold?'

'I guess not.'

'And the Charlotte would still be short of two or more days of water before reaching Jamaica?'

'Yes.'

'And if there was a wind but still not enough water there was peril for the ship and crew?'

'I suppose so.'

'Did it seem as though Captain Tyler was surprised by Mr Miles's suggestion, or did it appear that he had already considered it?'

'I don't think he was surprised.'

'Did he stop and think about it for a time?'

'No.'

'Is it possible that Captain Tyler had thought about that already, had, perhaps, agonised over all the possibilities?'

'It's possible.'

'I can tell you that he did. He would have answered to all the suggestions raised because he had already gone over them, as a captain should. Would you agree?'

'I suppose so.'

'One final question, where was Captain Tyler when the slaves were dumped?'

'He was in his cabin.'

'Did he watch any of the slaves being dumped overboard?'

'No.'

'Did he seem happy about the decision?'

'No, he seemed as though he had a lot on his mind.'

'A lot on his mind, a mind going through the options, realising that the only decision, the decision all the officers agreed to, was to dump slaves to save the crew and ship. Thank you, Mr Calum.'

Calum stood and quietly walked away from the stand, then into the gallery. A few moments later, he was gone.

*

At the end of the day, instead of being taken to the carriage by the constables, Tyler was ushered into the small room where he spent breaks. He sat on the chair and waited, more uncertain than he had felt for days. The only comfort was in the routine, of waking and dressing and then the constables and the carriage ride. As stifling as it was, there was comfort too.

He tried to follow what was going on and for the first time had sensed, more than understood, that perhaps there was a chance he might get off. Calum's testimony had been muddied, which was the best way he could put it, by Rubin's cross-examination. Yet that hope had been replaced now by the uncertainty of what was about to happen. He wanted to be in the carriage with the constables, listening to their ribald jokes, feeling a connection, slight though it may be, to someone.

The door opened and Simon Rubin walked in.

'My dear Tyler, we have a real crack at it now,' Rubin said.

'Does that mean I might get off?'

'Yes, it does, but I am going to need your help. I need you to take responsibility for your actions. You see this Carrington fellow is going to call you to testify. I feel it in my bones. And when he does you need to take responsibility for your decisions and actions. If this plays out the way I think it will, we have two chances to get you off, as you put it. I won't worry you with the technicalities now unless, of course, you wish to be walked through them?'

Tyler looked at Rubin uncertainly.

'Best you know this, my dear Tyler, if you try to hide from what you did, if you prevaricate on your thinking and decisions I cannot help you. This Carrington fellow has done a remarkable thing to date, and if he continues, then we are likely to have only one card left to play. But all of that depends on tomorrow. So for now, remember this, I accept responsibility, alright?'

Rubin gently put his hand on Tyler's shoulder and held it there for a moment. Then he turned and left, unable to shake the idea that Tyler was completely lost, and not just in terms of the legalities of the case.

*

Tyler lay in his cot in the cell, the words of Calum going through his head. The mate had appeared supportive of the actions of Tyler, at least when Rubin was questioning him. Drawing out a tale that supported Tyler. But tomorrow it would be Tyler in the stand answering questions, about his state of mind at the time, what options he had considered, and why he chose to dump the slaves.

Did I give sufficient thought to all the options? Tyler asked himself. *Could I have ordered the water rationed? What about the other ports, I never thought of trading slaves for water. I never considered it. Did I give so little thought to that decision? Did I condemn so many people to death with such little thought?*

And then there was Calum. Seeing him in court had resurfaced a doubt about the man that he long held. Something in Calum suggested a boy playing at being a man, a lost soul. That was never clearer than watching him drift into the gallery and in a moment just disappear. And what was the tension between Calum and Franklin? That now shone through like a shaft of light into deep water.

Had Calum been distracted by Franklin, by searching for something in the older man and had that led to Calum not securing the water properly? But then was that even Calum's watch? Tyler could not remember. 'Should I have checked that myself?' Tyler said aloud.

Was my trust in the crew misplaced? It had always been his way as captain, place trust in the crew and let them grow into trust. The more he trusted them the better he came to know a crew, to understand them and manage them. To anticipate problems and manage against them. Had he got things so wrong or was it bad luck alone that led to the Charlotte being becalmed and short of water, he wondered.

And was the throwing overboard of people the easy way out of a hard situation?

As he drifted into the fluky currents of sleep, the questions circled in his mind. And beyond them all, he heard Rubin's voice. *So for now, remember this, I accept responsibility, alright?*

*

Yorke Carrington sat at his desk, the lamp still burning late into the night. The prosecution was going well, but he knew he had fumbled some of the questions to Calum. Some of the more educated and thoughtful abolitionists who sat each day in the gallery had sent messages to him, and to Clarkson and others, hailing the questioning of Calum. It was clear that Tyler had taken no responsibility for the water supply and had forced the officers into agreeing with him.

One had even approached him as he left the court saying, 'Congratulations, you have won the case already'.

But Carrington knew these were the true believers who filtered everything through the lens of the evils of slavery. Refracting the evils of the trade into the obvious guilt they attached to any involved in slavery.

Carrington's own assessment was far less flattering. He felt he had missed the chance to drive the point home, and that the trial was less a triumph than a botched protest against slavery. He had hoped for a recess after his questioning of Calum and had not forced the point. He wanted the judge and the gallery to have a night to sleep on Calum's testimony, before any cross-examination. Instead, he had finished with Calum too early, had given time to Rubin to break down the worst of Calum's revelations, to introduce doubt.

Doubts that he now felt keenly.

He had wanted to leave that idea, of Tyler's guilt hanging in the minds of observers, then have Rubin start his defence. In that way, he could cross-examine Tyler and have the last word. But to do so now would leave too much hanging, leave too much doubt around how much responsibility Tyler held.

There was only one option now and Carrington worked deep into the night, teasing out ideas, putting defences to these, preparing questions for tomorrow. For when he would call George Tyler to testify and try to pin the man down, to prove Tyler was a murderer. *Do that, Yorke*, he told himself, *and you win*. He dared not contemplate the alternative.

*

Tyler woke early. The questions of the previous night swirled and spun through his head like a tidal eddy, constantly moving without beginning or end. And today those questions would be put to him by a man wanting him to hang. He was afraid more than he had been at any time since the trial began. Afraid of what he might say, what he wanted to say, and how far that may stray from what Rubin wanted him to say. To accept responsibility in court. Afraid of where that might lead.

The constables came and took him to the carriage but the camaraderie was absent. The journey seemed to pass in a blur. Then he found himself in the waiting room. He looked around and noticed the small watercolour painting on the wall. *Had that always been there or was it new?* he wondered.

A small painting showing a merchant vessel loading its cargo. Barrels and crates, an array of trade goods being packed into an unseen hold. *What else may be in there?* Tyler wondered. A flurry of activity, but all with a purpose. Commerce, the lifeblood of England's growing empire. *But more too,* thought Tyler. A meaning to life, adding worth to so many others simply because they valued those goods. Never asking where those goods came from, only seeking the solace of owning that which they desired. He was asking those questions when he nodded off to sleep.

Tyler woke a time later, as the bailiff and constables came into the room.

'Looks like you get your chance on the stand then, George old boy,' the bailiff said. 'At least it should be more interesting than hearing lawyers drone on about legal precedents. That's how we spent the morning, not dozing off contentedly,' one of the guards said.

Tyler resented that. He had barely slept the night before and finally, he had slept the sleep of the dead, without dreams. That was about the best he could hope for.

Tyler emerged into the courtroom from a side door, flanked by the constables. When it became clear that he was walking to the seat to testify, excitement almost overwhelmed the gallery.

Tyler swore to tell the truth. His truth, new in its creation, righteous in its beliefs.

Then Yorke Carrington stood and silence fell over the courtroom, many in the gallery wondering if this was the moment when the trial would be decided.

'Mr Tyler, can you please tell the court how many slaving voyages you have captained?'

'Nine.'

'And before that, have you captained any other voyages?'

'No.'

Carrington questioned Tyler about his life at sea for some time, from the roles he had played to the locations he had sailed to.

Finally, Carrington finished circling around Tyler.

'How many slaves did you lose in the nine voyages you captained?'

'Seven, perhaps eight in total.'

'That few? And did you dump those seven or eight souls overboard while alive or dead?'

'They were all dead.'

'So on those voyages there was sufficient water?'

'Yes.'

'Did you check the security of the water on any of those voyages?'

'No, I trusted the officers to organise that.'

'But you accept that ultimately that is your responsibility?' Tyler glanced at Rubin.

'Yes.'

'And on those voyages, you got a share of the profits?'

'Yes.'

'And you are aware that the profits on selling people, slaves, is underwritten by insurance?'

'Yes.'

'If a slave dies of natural causes does that attract an insurance claim?'

'No.'

'So you are aware of what constitutes a death that can be claimed under insurance?'

'Yes.'

'And that involves the death of a slave where the cause is not natural?'

'Yes.'

'So is running short of water a natural or unnatural death?'

'If they die of dehydration that is unnatural.'

'Are you sure? For if that is the case, why bother to dump them overboard while still alive? Why not just let them die?'

Tyler stared at Carrington, thinking about how to answer the question. He went to answer but Carrington cut him off.

'So before this voyage, did you ever run short of water?'

'No.'

'But you know that lack of water constitutes an unnatural death for a slave?'

'All captains are familiar with what can and cannot be claimed.'

'Really, all captains. How do you know this for a fact?' Again, Tyler stared at Carrington.

'You seem confused, is dehydration a natural or unnatural death?'

'I answered that.'

'Did you. What did you say?'

'It is an unnatural death.'

'So it is possible to claim against this death when the living person is thrown overboard dying from dehydration?'

'Yes, I think—'

'You think! You think or you know? Which is it, Captain Tyler?'

'If they were going to die, it is necessary to dump them for insurance.'

'For insurance. Necessary for insurance. You seem well-versed in what can and cannot be claimed. Now, had you been becalmed before?'

'What, I missed that?'

'Missed the question or the becalming?' There were chuckles from the gallery.

'You are aware of becalming, the dangers of it?'

'Yes.'

'So you knew it was, at the least, a possibility. What is the best way to ensure that becalming is survived?'

'I don't follow you,' Tyler said. He was still trying to work out what he had just said.

'Would you say that having sufficient supplies of food and especially water is the best way to ensure all aboard survive becalming?'

'If there is wind—'

'If there is wind Captain Tyler there is no becalming. Try to keep up. So you ordered the water supplies to be secured and that is enough?'

'I think…yes.'

'But you didn't inspect it?'

'No, the officers do that.'

'Do other captains do that?'

'I don't know.'

'But you do know that all other captains are aware of what can and cannot be claimed under insurance in the death of a slave. It is amazing what you prioritise, Captain Tyler. So you just trust the officers?'

'Yes.'

Something in the tone of Tyler's voice did not ring true for Carrington. He was unsure if he imagined it or if the doubt was there. He was momentarily thrown and was searching for a way to exploit the opening.

'Maybe I did doubt, Mr Calum,' Tyler said. Carrington paused for a moment. Thought quickly.

'Did Mr Calum secure the water supply?' Carrington said.

'I think so.'

'You think so!' Carrington stared at Tyler, thinking of the next question.

'I don't entirely recall,' Tyler said.

'The water is vital to the survival of the ship, and you don't recall who you ordered to secure it?'

'I—'

'And despite not knowing this you did not inspect the water yourself?' There was a long pause.

'No,' Tyler said and dropped his head.

'So you don't recall who secured the water, or even who had that responsibility, and did not check to see that the most vital resource on the ship was secure. And this despite admitting you had doubts over at least one of your officers who may or may not have secured the water?'

Carrington stared quietly at Tyler who struggled to look the lawyer in the eyes. Carrington waited, playing a hunch. He quietly counted the seconds in his head ...*five...six...sev—*

'I-I trusted the officers to do that.'

'But you didn't really trust at least one of them, did you? I put it to you that those are opposing positions, not trusting an officer but trusting the officers to do their jobs. That is unlikely to give any man in command peace of mind is it?'

Again Carrington paused, and again Tyler broke. 'No, I suppose not,' Tyler said wearily.

'So it would be fair to say that you should have acted on those doubts?'

'Yes.'

'What else did you not act on? When the water was low and the Charlotte becalmed did you consider all the options?'

'There weren't other options.'

'But Mr Calum said your second captain, Mr Miles, suggested sailing to nearby ports and trading for water?'

'That was…we would have…there was nothing else to trade?'

'What was in the hold, Captain Tyler?'

'Slaves.'

'So are they trade goods, these slaves, or are they not?' Tyler was quiet.

'Let me put it another way. What did you intend to trade for sugar in Jamaica?'

Tyler looked away from Carrington, convinced the man had seen into his soul. 'What, Mr Tyler!'

'Slaves, we were going to trade slaves.'

'So you had a hold full of slaves that could be traded, you were within sailing distance of other ports where you could have traded a few slaves for sufficient water, and yet you decided it was easier to throw live people overboard?'

'It's not that simple.'

'Why is it not that simple?'

'It just wasn't.'

'That is not a satisfactory answer, Captain Tyler.' Carrington stared hard at Tyler, counting the seconds in his head.

'I was, I was not authorised by Mr Pennington to do so.'

'Did the letter of commission empower you to trade goods?'

'Yes.'

'And the slaves, the people, were trade goods?'

'Yes.'

'So why not trade a few, a handful for water to ensure the rest lived?'

'Mr Pennington—'

'I am sure Mr Pennington would prefer you trade a handful of slaves for water than dump more than a hundred overboard and then have to battle insurers for that money?'

'It did not seem, practical, we were becalmed, it was difficult.'

'Practical, difficult. This was the lives of people, Captain Tyler, and you speak as though you are considering if it was practical to keep an appointment. As though going out in the cold is difficult. These were people.'

Carrington let the words hang in the air for several seconds.

'So did Mr Pennington instruct you about such a situation?' Carrington said.

'No.'

'Did he ever say if becalmed just dump slaves overboard and we can recoup our losses via the insurers?'

'No.'

'Did he expect you to make those decisions?' Tyler merely nodded.

'Answer please.'

'I received no specific instructions. I was…' Tyler paused for a long time. 'I was responsible.'

Tyler stared downwards. All that he had hidden so long came tumbling out. The world he had known was gone. All that he had wanted and lived for since first seeing the ships at the docks as a boy was discarded. Thrown out, tossed overboard. And all his efforts to hide it were now for nothing.

Tyler felt someone staring hard at him and looked up and saw Rubin. Tyler looked at Rubin, remembered what was at stake, and focussed. Trying to remember the new truth he was tasked with creating, but unable to find it. And still, the questions came. *Just answer them,* Tyler said to himself, *get this over and done with while you find some truth, real or imagined.*

'Why not divert to another port, as Mr Calum suggested?'

'We would have lost time.'

Even Carrington was momentarily stunned.

'I am sorry, can you repeat that,' Carrington said.

'We would have lost time.'

'And why was that so important?'

'We were ahead of the other boats, we would have been the first into Jamaica.'

'Why is being the first boat into Jamaica important?'

'No other boats had left the slave coast bound for Jamaica for a few months when we were there. Being the first boat into Jamaica after a few months without slave auctions, well it's worth a premium.'

'You mean getting a higher price for the slaves? That is what you mean by a premium?'

'Yes.'

'And of course, a greater share of the profits for yourself?'

'Yes.'

'So then, if there was a premium on offer why dump so much of the cargo?'

'They would have died or been in a poor—'

'Poor condition?'

'Yes.'

'So there goes the premium? And that was because of a lack of water?'

'Yes.'

'And who bears that responsibility, who is ultimately responsible aboard a ship for that?'

'The captain.'

'And you were that captain?'

'Yes.'

'And it was your decision to dump the slaves, the people overboard?'

'The officers agreed.'

'Mr Calum said that you dismissed their concerns almost immediately. You made sure you got the decision you wanted?'

'I, yes, that is fair.'

Simon Rubin stood and stepped forward. 'Your honour, may we take a break at this time, my client is tired and—'

'Sit down, Mr Rubin, this is just getting interesting,' the judge said.

'So you admit, Captain Tyler, that you dismissed the other options, sailing to another port, rationing the water for all. Why?'

'They did not seem practical.'

Rubin glared at Tyler, trying to get his attention, but Tyler continued to look at Carrington. 'Why not?'

'It was easier to… some of the slaves were sick.'

'But not all?'

'No, not all.'

'Did Mr McDougal the ship's surgeon, did he raise concerns about a disease spreading?'

'Not that it should harm the crew.'

'Was disease present?'

'McDougal couldn't be sure.'

'So if no disease it could not spread?'

'Some were ill.'

'Because of disease or because of lack of water in the tropical heat?'

'The illnesses were due to lack of water and heat.'

'So you took the easy option, the practical option. It was easier to dismiss any suggestions as to alternatives to dumping the slaves? It was better to get a premium on some slaves and rely on the insurers for the remaining profit?'

'It was…I—'

'So it was better to protect Mr Pennington's investment and your share of the profits than it was to ensure the welfare of all aboard?'

'I was protecting the crew.'

'You were protecting Mr Pennington's investment and his and your share of the profits. Surely, being becalmed you had plenty of time to think of alternatives?'

'Yes, but—'

'So you had time to think?'

'Yes.'

'To think of the other options?'

'There were none that were practical.'

'But before you said there were no other options, now there were none that were practical. So let me make this clear for you, did you consider the other options during the discussions with the officers?'

'No.'

'Did you consider them before that? In your own thinking?'

'A little.'

'A little, but not in full?'

'They were not practical.'

'So you thought only a little about other options and dismissed them and on that basis, you dumped 129 people to drown in the ocean?'

Tyler did not speak.

'So, Captain Tyler, you did not foresee the possibilities of storms, losing water and becalming despite captaining nine previous voyages. You doubted at least one of your officers, cannot be certain if that officer or another oversaw the securing of the water and despite this, did not check on the water supplies. Water supplies that were lost in a storm.

'Then when the Charlotte was becalmed you fixed on a solution to the problem of losing the premium on offer in Jamaica. You decided, by your own admission, and with little thought, to dump slaves, to throw people overboard to their deaths. This despite having enough water to sail to a port only a day or two's sail away and trade a handful of slaves for sufficient water for the rest of the slaves, the rest of the people aboard.

'You dismissed the suggestions and concerns of your officers to ensure your choice was carried out. And in doing so, you maximised the profit available to yourself and Mr Pennington. A return that would in all likelihood be higher than you could have delivered any other way. To justify this, you said the crew were in peril when water was a day's sail away and there was more than enough for a week, enough to reach nearby ports. There was no threat of disease, confirmed by the ship's surgeon. So the only peril to the crew was a detour or a water rationing.

'Ultimately you admit, you admit here openly, that the responsibility for this decision was yours and yours alone. As captain, you bore that responsibility. You were reckless and negligent and unwilling to compromise or seek other solutions. You instead wanted to get the most return possible in the circumstances. You took the practical option, those are your words. The easy option, again your words, Captain Tyler.

'That easy option, dumping the slaves to ensure profits, is an act of murder, Captain Tyler. Murder bought by profit, by reckless and negligent actions in failing to draw on your experience as a slave boat captain, and replacing your duty of care with a concern for profit. Only by murdering those people could you recover from your negligence and recklessness, only by murder could you ensure the profit that defines this trade was delivered to slave traders.'

Carrington stared at Tyler, who in turn looked down at the floor.

'Your honour, I would now like to agree with Mr Rubin's suggestion of a break. Mr Tyler has obviously had a difficult time of it and I would feel it in his best interests to grant an adjournment for the day.'

Rubin jumped to his feet and started to say something which was lost as the gallery started talking.

'I agree, we shall recommence tomorrow,' the judge said. Then he stood and walked out before Rubin could say anything else.

Carrington turned and looked at the gallery. He tried to find Charles Pennington but the slaver had already gone. Then he looked at the abolitionists seated in one group and saw the smiles and hoped that they had read it right, that a conviction was now a real probability.

Ten

Rubin sat and looked at Carrington, wondering what to do now. He sensed eyes on him and looked up and saw Tyler, still sitting in the chair below the judge's bench. Rubin stood and walked over.

'I know, dear Tyler, I said to take responsibility but really. We shall have our work cut out for us now just so you know.'

Tyler looked at Rubin blankly then stared right through him, his eyes distant, his mind thousands of miles away and months ago, on a ship at sea. Tyler closed his eyes and saw slaves hitting the surface of the water above him, while he drifted below.

Slowly he returned to the present, looked at Rubin and wondered if the lawyer had been speaking.

'For now, get some rest, dear Tyler, and we will see what tomorrow brings.'

Then Rubin turned and saw Carrington looking at him, and nodded the barest of nods to say well played to his opponent.

Tyler went through the motions as the constables came and took him to the carriage and then to the prison. He registered nothing as he walked into his cell and saw Albert sitting, a bag of food beside him. It was the first time he had seen the priest since the confrontation with Micah and now he wondered what would happen.

'George, you seem very tired,' Albert said, unable to find words to describe what he saw in Tyler. Tired yes, but much more too. It was as though Tyler had changed since their last meeting.

'It was a tough day. I had to answer questions.'

'And it did not go as well as hoped, I take it?'

'You could say that,' Tyler said.

'I should apologise but I have bad news. It is Micah, he is…he was found dead two days ago, outside St Giles church.'

Tyler sat and opened the bag of food and rummaged through it. 'Did you hear me, George? It's Micah.'

'I heard you,' Tyler said between mouthfuls of cheese.

'I have thought that perhaps that might have, it may have affected you more?'

'Why?'

'I know you fought with him, but perhaps there was also something of a friendship between you both?'

'Maybe.' Tyler opened the beer that was in the bag and drank from the bottle.

'That is all you have to say on the matter?'

Tyler shrugged his shoulders, continuing to eat.

'I did not think you so callous and uncaring. Perhaps you are suited to slaving?' Tyler stopped chewing and looked at Albert.

'Perhaps I am.'

'Have you not thought of turning from this trade, of recanting your past?'

'No, I haven't thought of it.'

'And if I were to say I do not believe you?'

'Fine.'

'I do not believe you, George. I have seen you start to wrestle with this. Tell me you have not and I will leave you in peace.'

Tyler turned and looked Albert in the eye for the first time. 'What do you know about being at peace! That is just a lie made up by men to-to—'

'To what, George? It is at the heart of us, peace, and contentment. That is the experience of God or of spiritualism or whatever religions call it. I think that is what you want and yet you are far from it.'

'I did no wrong, I must believe that or…'

Albert waited but Tyler took the beer and drank slowly. 'Or what, George?'

'Nothing.'

'Do you truly believe that, George?'

'Yes,' Tyler said looking past Albert. 'I do.'

Albert left soon afterwards, walking slowly through the streets towards St Giles. He stopped and waited for a carriage to pass before he crossed and walked into the church. He looked around, saw a handful of people sitting and praying and wondered what to do now.

Tyler was close, he knew that. Devoid of emotion, fearing it and what it could unleash. His lifeless desperation to believe he did no wrong felt like the final efforts of a drowning man to reach the surface before the waves finally washed over him. Tyler was so very close to letting go, close to breaking and when he did, he would need someone there. Albert sat and closed his eyes and started to say the Lord's prayer, then stopped.

Damn it, Father, either let me be free of this man, Tyler or have him break, for both our sakes, he mouthed silently. Then he stood and left.

*

It was rainy when Tyler woke, which seemed to suit his mood. He didn't bother to shave or dress well, instead, he sat and waited for the carriage and the constables. Then he was back in the court, ushered into the small waiting room.

Simon Rubin walked into the waiting room and sat opposite Tyler. He ignored Tyler's unkempt appearance. 'So I will be blunt with you, my dear Tyler, yesterday did us no favours. We are left with only a single option and that involves you accepting responsibility for your actions. Totally and unequivocally.'

'Do I have any other choices?'

'Realistically, I think not. This Carrington fellow has, in eliciting such testimony from you yesterday all but sealed his case. There is no profit in refuting his arguments, for that will only reinforce his case. Do you understand?'

Tyler nodded.

'That, of course, does not mean there is no way forward. There is one possibility. It is a risk but that is all we are left with and it means that no matter what you must accept responsibility for your actions. Are you clear?'

Tyler swallowed hard and nodded. The more he heard that the more he hated himself, and the more he opened himself to the doubts inside.

Rubin then slowly outlined the way ahead, pausing often as he stared into space figuring out the questions he would ask.

'So you are clear then?' Tyler nodded.

'And one other thing, try to clean yourself up a bit before you come into the court. You are likely to look less guilty,' Rubin said. Then he left.

I must believe that or… The words leapt unprompted into Tyler's head, his own words to Albert. '*…you must accept responsibility for your actions'*, he heard Rubin say in his mind. Then he thought of Micah.

Would you do it, would you throw him overboard? he said to himself.

The bailiff came for him before he had any idea of how to answer that question.

Simon Rubin took his glasses off and leaned back in his chair, spinning his glasses by one arm of their frames.

'On board a ship, authority and discipline are essential. These are the lifeblood of any ship.

'The great skill of captaincy is knowing how to do this in a way that does not push a crew to breaking point. The responsibility for the course the ship steers, the decisions made regarding dangers and perils on that course, whether to take them on or sail around them, belong to one man, the captain of that vessel.

'That does not mean that the captain is consulted on every decision, for that would make sailing all but impossible. Do any of us here expect to be asked about each action that impacts on our days? Should a judge be asked where the man on trial is held at which prison or does the judge delegate that decision to others?

'Such everyday actions, be they running a court or running a ship, involve a whole range of people, from bailiffs and lawyers here to officers and sailors on a ship. On a ship, the captain lays out the course and sets the rules. Each man knows these and is expected to follow these. Each man knows the decisions that this leaves for him. But then there are hard decisions that need to be made, like deciding on a verdict in a trial or pushing ahead into a storm.

'It is these decisions, the decisions of leadership, that we are ultimately discussing in this case here today. Now the prosecutor, the redoubtable Mr Carrington has made a good case, that George Tyler got it wrong, that he was negligent and reckless and got the Charlotte in a right mess and the only way out of that mess, the only way, was to dump cargo overboard, and he did that to ensure a profit.

'Now, I don't know about you, but if I were becalmed on the ocean with limited water supplies, a profitable voyage would not be my first priority. I think it is fair to say that the priority would be the crew first and then any cargo.

'For this is the reality that Captain Tyler faced. He was responsible for the welfare of 22 crew first, and then 300 slaves second. It is as simple as that. No more, no less.

'From afar, thousands of miles away and months later, it is easy to complicate such matters. From the comfort of full tummies and slaked thirst, it is difficult to understand such matters. And those matters are this, that Captain Tyler owed a duty of care to his crew first.

'Did Captain Tyler think of the profit involved, only he knows that. Did he think of the investment of Charles Pennington, again only Captain Tyler knows that. But here is the crux of this matter, does that make him a murderer? Was he trying to protect his crew, to ensure their welfare, or was he motivated by greed to murder slaves?

'And if you believe something so fanciful, that this man who on nine voyages had lost eight slaves in total, was a man prone to murdering slaves, why so few losses until now. If one was a slave boat captain with an appetite for the murder of slaves, surely those losses would be greater.

'Instead, the reality is this, Captain Tyler was a good captain, a man who looked after crew and, I repeat this for it is important, and slaves alike.

'But these are not mutual interests, they are competing duties and only one, crew or slaves can rank the highest of priorities. This is why the insurance of cargoes exists. Not insurance of crews, but of cargoes. For in times of peril, the highest priority is the safety of the crew. That overrides all other concerns on the ocean.

'We don't have to like it and I confess that I do not like it. But this trial is about the law, not what we like, nor what is popular or fashionable amongst the chattering classes. This trial is about the moment that the perils of the sea and the need to protect a crew collided against one another. It is about the investment of a ship's owner and protecting that. Again, we may not like that, but this is commerce and we must recognise that.

'So we must ask hard questions here. What should a captain do when his crew faces peril, what should he do by way of action? And should he act, even in the most extreme of cases, to protect his crew, or should he put them in further peril, in harm's way?

'In the Charlotte's moments of peril, a firm hand was required on the till, a resolute and strong captain was needed, so the crew were not imperilled and as a result, the ship was not left to drift to its doom. George Tyler was that captain, and he did not shy away from his responsibility as captain, and for that, the crew of the Charlotte remain grateful.

'I call to the stand George Tyler.'

The gasps and astonished words of the gallery filled the courtroom. Tyler stood and walked to the stand as the judge banged his gavel down.

'I remind you, Captain Tyler, you remain under oath following your testimony of yesterday,' the judge said.

Simon Rubin stood and ambled across the space between his seat and the seat on which Tyler sat.

'Captain Tyler, during your testimony yesterday you were asked who is the ultimate authority aboard a ship. Could you please remind the court of your answer?'

'The captain of the ship.'

'So on the Charlotte that was you?'

'Yes.'

'You fully accepted that role then and hold to that belief today?'

'Yes.'

'So that means that any action or decision is ultimately yours to own?'

'Yes.'

'Even if a crewman or officer is the one taking that action or making a decision?'

'Yes.'

'Even if that action or decision is poor or wrong?'

'Yes.'

'So if an officer makes a mistake you are responsible?'

'Yes, they are too.'

'Sorry I am a little confused,' said Rubin scratching his head in a mock display. 'Could you tell us what that means?'

'The officer is responsible for the mistake, but the captain takes responsibility for that mistake and works to correct it.'

'So the captain must rectify the mistake and that begins by accepting that as his responsibility?'

'Yes.'

'Does that include punishment of the officer, or crew for that matter, if warranted?'

'That is part of a captain's duty.'

'Ahh yes, duty. That is what this all comes down to is it not, that a captain has a duty to his crew?'

'Yes, that is something that is easily forgotten by many.'

'Would I be presumptuous in asking if a duty is also owed to the men financing the voyage, including the owners of a ship?'

'That is a fair statement. The duty is slightly different but it is there nonetheless.'

'What about slaves, is there a duty owed them too?'

'A captain owes them a duty too.'

'For their welfare and safety?'

'Within reason, yes.'

'What do you mean by within reason?'

'There are times when choices have to be made. If we are talking about paid passengers, they are like crew, perhaps even above the crew. But slaves are a commodity, a cargo.'

'Forgive me if this offends anyone, but dare I say, slaves are a live cargo, like sheep, or cattle?'

'Yes.'

'So they are the equal of beasts of burden, farm animals?'

Several members of the gallery yelled out and a group of abolitionists stamped their feet loudly.

'Order or I will have you removed,' the judge said.

'Yes, all slave boat captains would agree with that,' Tyler said.

'All captains, would that not be an exaggeration on your behalf?'

'If you saw slaves as the same as the crew how could you be a slave boat captain?'

'Fair enough,' Rubin said.

'So slave boat captains, and I presume crews, make a clear distinction between crew and slaves?'

'Yes.'

'What would happen if a captain treated crew and slaves alike?'

'Mutiny I expect. The crew sail the boat and the slaves are in the hold. To treat the two groups as equal, well it would be a disaster.'

'Now let us turn to the question of laws in this matter. Is slavery still legal on the high seas?'

'Yes.'

'And is it legal in Africa?'

'Yes.'

'And the Caribbean?'

'Yes.'

'So in captaining a slave boat you have broken no laws?'

'No, I have not.'

'What of dumping live cargo? Is that illegal?'

'No, but such cargoes are not usually dumped.'

'Why not? I would argue that if they are insured why not just dump them?'

'It would be odd to sail to Africa, pick up a cargo and then dump it for the insurance. Why would you do that?'

'And the same goes for animals?'

'Yes. Cargoes are only ever dumped out of necessity.'

'Out of necessity. What necessitates dumping cargo?'

'Necessity is a direct threat to the vessel or to the crew or both.'

'Could you provide an example of each of these?'

'If a cargo shifts and the ship is listing and being threatened with sinking, or disease or perhaps both.'

'So lack of water, particularly in the tropics, could be a threat to the crew?'

'Yes.'

'So humour me, if some of the crew died who would sail the ship?'

'The remaining crew.'

'What if there were not enough crew? Would that threaten the ship?'

'Absolutely, it is possible all aboard could die.'

'So turning to the Charlotte, becalmed...' Rubin paused for several moments. 'Limited water.' Another pause followed. 'Could you have rationed the water for the crew?'

'Not without letting them know that they were the same as the slaves.'

'A dangerous idea in your opinion?'

'Where does it end, with the crew knowing they are the same as the slaves? Probably in mutiny, in lives lost.'

'So you made sure the crew were looked after?'

'Yes.'

'What of disease?'

'We did not know if some of the slaves were sick from lack of water or disease.'

'What did Mr McDougal, the surgeon, recommend?'

'He could not be sure either, and as those slaves were dead or dying, it is better to be safe than sorry. So he recommended they be thrown overboard.'

'And you made a decision to do so, for the welfare of the crew?'

'And for the welfare of those slaves, not exhibiting possible illness.'

'So the lack of water and possibility of disease, these were the reasons you ordered slaves dumped overboard?'

'Yes.'

'To ensure the welfare of the crew and, this is important I think, and the welfare of those slaves still aboard?'

'Yes.'

'Do you accept that the lost water was, ultimately, your responsibility?'

'Yes.'

'But what if Mr Calum loaded the water? Did you not say you had doubts about him?'

'Doubts about his temperament but not his skills.'

'And what of the idea you should have anticipated the storm? The becalming.'

'Those things are always in the back of your mind, but if we as sailors waited until we thought it safe to sail, well no one would sail anywhere.'

'So risks are part and parcel of sailing?'

'Yes, and you manage those as best you can, but even then, well, sometimes accidents happen.'

'And you accept that?'

'Yes I do, as I said you accept responsibility for what happens, man-made or accident and you do your best to manage what happens next.'

'Finally, and this is vital, did you overrule the officers, even after some of them had suggested alternatives to dumping slaves?'

'Yes.'

'Why?'

'The decision on how to proceed was mine alone. I had thought of the options already. Nothing suggested was a surprise to me. But ultimately you cannot hope that the wind comes back, you must anticipate that it will not. You cannot hope to trade slaves in a nearby port, without knowing what water supplies are available. A captain that hopes and waits kills his crew.'

'And did you considerer Mr Pennington's investment and a return on that investment in your considerations?'

'Yes, that is what he expects of me. The reality is that the two considerations, the welfare of the crew and the return on investment were aligned, and as such should not be ignored. That is part of the reason insurance exists.'

'You said yesterday you thought about these decisions a little?'

'Only because I knew what was needed and that the options were not practical.'

'Practical, an interesting word, why that one?'

'At sea, a practical approach, drawing on your experience and being aware of what can happen, is vital. There is no room for hope. There is only what is before you and what can be done.'

'Do you regret the action you took?'

Tyler looked at Rubin and then down at the floor. He knew the answer Rubin wanted, but doubted he could say it sincerely. Tyler looked up and fixed his eyes on Rubin.

'No, no, I do not. My crew are alive because of it.' Tyler looked away from Rubin, saw Carrington's eyes questioning him, looked at the ceiling and then the floor.

'So, Captain Tyler, you acted to ensure that your crew and the slaves aboard the Charlotte would be safe. When no other options were available, you sought to maximise the number of slaves that would live, something was that compatible with a return on investment for the financiers of the voyage. It was, in effect and reality, the only option to maintain and discharge the duty you owed to your crew and your backers. I thank you for this.'

Rubin walked over to his seat and sat down. He had taken his gamble. Now it was up to the judge.

*

Tyler sat in the carriage and listened to the banter of the guards, feeling more distant from them than ever.

'So is he done for?' the largest of the guards said.

'Who?' said the bald guard.

'Georgie here, is he done for?'

'How would I know?'

'You sat in the room listening to all that talk didn't you?'

'Doesn't mean I understood any of it, it's all legal mumbo jumbo.'

'Fancy getting hung though 'cause you threw a few slaves overboard, I mean that is why they use 'em on plantations ain't it, 'cause they die soon enough anyway,' said the guard known as Tony.

'Yeah, a few less blacks in the world ain't gunna hurt anyone now is it?' said the largest.

The guards laughed at that.

'Besides, if I don't get my tobacco and sugar for my coffee, well that's really what matters here ain't it,' said Tony.

'Right you be, Tony, right you be.'

Tyler sat in silence listening to the guards, growing angrier by the minute. He wanted to tell them to shut up, to scream in anger at the world and the injustice of it. By the time he reached the prison, he was fuming.

One of the guards put a hand on his shoulder and said, 'good luck.' And Tyler shoved the hand away violently.

'Steady Georgie,' said Tony.

'Fuck you,' Tyler said.

Tony hit Tyler hard in the stomach, doubling Tyler over. 'You fucking piece of shit,' Tyler said between breaths.

Tony kicked Tyler hard in the side, but it only made Tyler angrier. He lashed out at Tony from the ground and received another kick.

'Stop it, he's had enough,' the largest of the guards said.

The guards grabbed Tyler's legs and dragged him screaming into his cell. Then they stood to leave. Tony put a knee into Tyler's groin and leaned in close. 'Enjoy the noose, murderer.'

Tyler spat at Tony who went berserk raining down blows on Tyler. It took the other three guards and two from the prison to drag Tony off Tyler.

'I will fucking kill you myself!' Tony yelled. 'You fucking don't disrespect me by spitting on me.' Tony lunged forward at Tyler again, who had dragged himself into a corner of the cell.

'You can kill me for all I care,' Tyler said.

The largest of the guards felt his stomach turn, hearing a man have so little value for his own life. He pushed Tony away and left him with the other guards, then went into the cell to see Tyler.

'You'll live,' he said after looking at Tyler.

Tyler stared back at him, and the guard turned away, sickened not by the injuries to Tyler, but by a despair that he saw in the eyes of a man he thought he knew.

Tyler sat and screamed, then tore the straw mattress from the cot and tried to rip it up, but couldn't. That only made him angrier and he swore violently at the world, kicked the cot over and threw the mattress. Two guards came over and watched him. Tyler swore at them, at Carrington and Rubin and Pennington and the world.

He hit his head with his hands until stars appeared before his eyes dancing a merry jig, then he slumped to the ground. He hit his head again and then started crying, sobbing loudly. 'I am responsible,' he said aloud.

Slowly, over the next hour, he started to calm down, crying and occasionally hitting his head until he had nothing left inside, no anger, no hatred or fear. Just emptiness.

Suddenly, he thought of Micah and knew that he could not throw him overboard. He thought of Albert and longed to see the priest. There was so much he wanted to pour out, to tell the priest.

Then his mind settled on Carrington and he knew deep inside that the lawyer had won, that Tyler had lost his case and would hang and the thought of it did not disturb him. He closed his eyes and saw the slaves falling into the water. He saw a woman holding a baby, crying in the water and knew that she cried for him, for his lost humanity.

He wondered if a guilty verdict may indeed be right and what he would do if that resulted. It was as though he were contemplating a report in the paper of someone else and not himself.

Then finally, he closed his eyes and fell asleep. He woke to the dream, of slaves in the water, only now he was sinking with them, into darkness, into the abyss.

*

Two days later, Albert visited. At first, Tyler sat quietly, refusing to answer questions about the bruises on his face, or talk of Micah or the trial. Inside, Tyler tried to find the courage to say what he wanted to say.

'Father, I…'

Albert sat quietly, sensing the need in Tyler.

'I have been having…' A deep sigh followed. 'I have been having a dream, it is—'

'I would be grateful if you shared it with me,' Albert said. 'Between us.'

'I am in the water, under the water and see slaves above me, being…being thrown into the water. They sink but I do not, until now, the last few nights I have sunk with them. I…'

Albert was quiet wondering if there was more. Tyler did not speak, he looked away. 'Is that it, George?'

'Yes.'

'Dreams can mean many things. Do you recognise any of these slaves?'

'No. They are strangers. They were all strangers to me.' Then Tyler started crying. Albert stood and walked over and sat next to Tyler and put an arm around his shoulders. Tyler leaned into the priest, sobbing.

'It is alright, George.'

Tyler sat for a long time leaning into Albert. Then eventually, he stopped crying and sat up. 'I don't know what to do now, Albert. The trial, the verdict, none of it seems to matter much.'

The two sat in silence for a time longer.

'Perhaps we should take things as they come for now. We wait and see what happens at the trial and then work out what comes next, don't you think?' Tyler nodded. He had no idea what else to do.

Eleven

'George, it's the day,' the large guard said as he walked up to the cell. 'We'll give you some time to get ready, there's no rush. And for what it's worth Tony ain't here today. We thought that better for all.'

Tyler nodded and slowly washed and got dressed. The mention of Tony's name brought back his words from the carriage. 'Fancy getting hung though 'cause you threw a few slaves overboard.'

In that moment, Tyler knew he was guilty, before the judge and before himself. It wasn't a few slaves, it was one hundred and twenty-nine. But that was just the beginning of it. How many had he transported? A couple of thousand, at least. And many of those would have died, worked to death on the plantations. And for those still living, what hell did they face? Like Micah, their lives stolen from them, replaced with something reduced, lesser. Broken and violated in so many ways.

They were people, like him. The only difference a skin colour and an idea that made them lesser. Made them viable for the taking.

'Right, George, we need to start on our way,' the large guard said.

Soon they were in the carriage, London passing in a blur. Outside the court, people milled about with a strange sense of expectation, of fear and relief. The day was here but the result uncertain.

Tyler was hustled from the carriage into the court and into the waiting room where he was left on his own for what felt like an eternity. Then he was ushered into the courtroom and sat down, a bailiff on one side and the large guard on the other.

Tyler turned and looked at the gallery. Around the edges of the benches in the gallery a number of sailors in uniform stood in groups of three or four. The abolitionists sat in their usual spot, Pennington and a group of slave owners opposite them. Several men sat near the front of the gallery with paper and pencils in hand, ready to capture the judgement in all its detail. Some worked for abolitionist papers, others for pro-slave papers. For the past few days, both sides had been publishing pamphlets and papers describing the case and speculating, as far as they dared, on what a judgement may look like. All of that conjecture now meant nothing as the judge walked in and everyone stood and then sat down.

'Let me begin by asking for silence,' the judge said. 'If you wish to speak, to speculate or to interject, then you can do so on the street. The sailors here today will be more than happy to show you the way if you speak up and let them know.'

Tyler looked up. It took him several seconds to realise the judge was speaking.

'Moral clarity,' the judge began, 'is not a position that has found its home in the debate surrounding slavery. Both sides claim it, yet neither side is able to win the day. There is, therefore, no clear understanding, legally or as a country, of where we stand, other than the precedents and laws already in place. Those laws are what this trial is about, those laws are what this decision is based upon.

'There will be those tempted to use this finding to bring clarity and understanding to these moral arguments. Should they wish to do so, that is their prerogative. This I leave for each of you, and after today I shall not comment on this judgement, nor this trade. Some will seek to read today's verdict as a reproach to views that diverge from their own or to reinforce that view. That again is the right of each of you.

'The legality of your actions Mr Tyler will be revealed in moments, but regardless of this the true sentence you must bear is the moral indictment brought upon yourself by your actions.'

As he said this, the judge looked at Tyler and Tyler knew that he could see inside, see the confusion and anger and guilt that he tried each day to push down. That only made it harder to bear, to fight the feeling of guilt.

'For the rest of us, the vexed reality of the slave trade creates a number of conundrums. We no longer have the time or comfort as a nation of debating these topics, it is necessary we answer these questions. My hope is today's verdict will not further cloud the moral dimensions of slavery coming from the perspective of that part of our nation most actively engaged in the trading of slaves, our sailors.

'I am obliged to deal in the law, finding the outcome that reflects not these moral or social conundrums and arguments but the tests applied by the law to the specifics of this case.

'Mr Carrington has made an elegant and eloquent argument and should we have given him the command to range farther, I have no doubt that he would convince us of the evils of this trade. We are not, however, here to do that.

'This was a trial to determine the charge of murder, made by way of criminal negligence and recklessness. I commend you Mr Carrington on your presentation of this case, for it carries great weight.

'I will not sum up the proceedings in detail here, those will be published in my summation. Turning now to the verdict, I would remind you of what Mr Lee, Solicitor General said at the time of the Zong case. "A master can drown slaves with a surmise of impropriety."

'This case turns on that simple point of law. So is there impropriety in choosing the lives and welfare of the crew over the lives and welfare of slaves. To accept your side, Mr Carrington, would be to accept that there would be no wrong, no impropriety if Captain Tyler had chosen to let the crew of the Charlotte suffer. To perhaps die. No captain would, nor could, accept this course of action and remain a captain. No captain would voluntarily choose this path and not expect to find himself here, charged by his crew, for neglect.

'Slaves are still property under the law, and in this case, were the lawful property of Mr Pennington. He in turn ceded a duty of care for that property, to Captain Tyler, who was by the terms of commission to "ensure that property was not ill-treated" and in doing so, "not to endanger the ship or the bulk of the cargo". In legal terms, this made Captain Tyler the master of the vessel and the defacto owner of the slaves.

'In the course of the voyage, the Charlotte found itself, for reasons beyond the control of the captain of the ship, becalmed and having lost water. I cannot find sufficient evidence for a negligent or reckless loss of the water supply, without condemning centuries of practice at sea. Nor can I definitively assess whether the loss of water was more than an accident or accident only. I do accept that under acceptable maritime practice care was taken in the matter of securing the water, but that despite this care accidents may still occur.

'So legally we are left with the options, discharged under letters of commission, to a captain, not to endanger the ship when that ship is becalmed and lacking water. A ship is nothing more than a collection of timber and ropes and canvas. Without a crew that is all a ship is. It is the crew that breathe life into a ship, that sail and pilot and steer her.

'It is my considered opinion that a crew is part of the ship, and constitutes by its presence, the heart of the ship. It is the crew, officers and men alike, that make this collection of materials, wood, canvas, rope, into a vessel that is capable of navigating the seas. The owner of the ship, the employer of captain and crew alike, made it clear in the letters of commission that the ship, crew included, should not be endangered.

'Likewise, but not overriding this concern was the commission to ensure the wellbeing of the cargo. Given that instruction, one held and enshrined in maritime law, does then a cargo constitute the same respect as a crew. This is the crux of this case. The simple answer is no, but this is not a case relating to simple cargo. This case pertains to live cargo, to slaves.

'Mr Carrington, you are correct in citing the Mansfield precedent that a slave cargo is not like other live cargoes. As such live cargoes require a greater duty of care. I do not debate that. What I do dispute is that a crew and its live cargo, be it slave or cattle or horse or other beasts of burden, are equal, both at sea and under the eyes of the law. Can it be said, under maritime law and under common law, that slave cargo is equal to that of a ship's crew? The crew are free men, having no master nor commercial transactions binding them as commercial entities to another. They submit to officers, but do so by choice, upon entering into a contract to serve aboard a vessel. Slaves are not the same. They are not free men, have not freely entered into a contractual agreement to serve. Instead, they are mastered. They have, in effect, a master. So the question is are such, free men and mastered slaves, equal?

'The answer is obvious, both under the law and here to any man, a slave is not the equal of a Christian British man, be he sailor or otherwise. Legally, outside this nation, slaves have never been considered equal under our laws. And to delineate, I remind all that since the Somerset case slavery has effectively been outlawed in Britain, so the slavery and slaves of which this case touches upon are those of the slave trade outside Britain. This is an important difference and not to be considered or confused under laws pertinent only here in Britain.

'To all intents and purposes of the laws of this land slavery is still legal on the high seas. A slave under these laws can be mastered, a sailor cannot.

'The laws surrounding slavery outside Britain may, in all likelihood, change soon but as they stand here and now today, slave trading outside of Britain is legal and so must be considered from this legal viewpoint alone, for the purposes of this case. Maritime law extends to all British ships on the oceans and seas and does not always concur with common law. But in this case, it is clear that the law that covers the events on the Charlotte is most clearly maritime law, on the high seas where slavery is still legal.

'It is my opinion that the Mansfield precedent, that slave cargoes must be treated with a higher duty of care than other cargoes holds. It is not sustainable, nor practical, to hold this precedent up when a captain faces a choice between the welfare of that cargo, as opposed to the safety of crew and officers. Welfare and safety are not the same. The safety of free British men trumps that of the welfare of mastered slaves, on the seas.

'A captain that chose to consider the safety of his crew as the same, as equal to, the welfare of slaves would so place his crew in the unenviable position of needing to rebel against his authority, to commit what would amount to an act of mutiny, to ensure that the law applies. To drive a crew to this point over water would constitute reckless behaviour. That Captain Tyler did not place his crew in this terrible position suggests that he understood his duty of care to ensure the safety of his crew outweighed the welfare of slaves.

'The greater negligence and recklessness on Captain Tyler's behalf would have been to place his crew in a position that would have likely ended in mutiny, and left Captain Tyler open to charges himself from his crew.

'This court does not accept the jurisdiction of common law that would place all aboard a vessel, including what amounts to live cargo in the form of slaves, as equal in terms of safety, nor that welfare to live cargo can or should amount to the equivalent of safety to a crew. This court will accept the principle and precedent set by Lord Mansfield holds, that a captain owes a duty of care to slaves, only so long as the ship is not imperilled or in danger. Upon that eventuality, the duty of care owed slaves is a secondary consideration to the safety of the crew, or indeed paying passengers. This is a more than adequate description of the circumstances which prevailed upon the Charlotte and her crew.

'Based on this law the actions taken by Captain Tyler, though distasteful to many, including some of us here, were taken not as a means to murder, but as a necessity to protect, both crew and the bulk of the cargo. By doing so, Captain Tyler ensured the crew were able to perform their functions, ensuring that their part as a ship, continued and the said ship was not endangered.

'As a captain, such choices, though difficult, must be taken in reference to the duty of care owed to the crew first, and only after that to any live cargo and then as a secondary consideration. The clear delineation between crew and slave, between the safety of that crew and the welfare of slave cargo, frees us from having to make a further distinction that strays beyond the law and into the realms of morality and public opinion.

'Given that, I find that Captain Tyler has no case to answer.'

As one the abolitionists stood and started jeering and stamping their feet. Whoops and hollers of joy competed as Pennington and his fellow slavers cheered. Scribes worked frantically trying to capture the moment.

Tyler slumped in his seat, a mixture of relief and revulsion coursing through him. Both were corrosive, sapping his energy and his will to fight his feelings. It took him several moments to realise that Rubin was holding out his hand to Tyler. What did he do now? Did he go back to the Charlotte and the sea? To slaving? To something else? And beneath it all, as he took Rubin's hand and shook it, as he looked around, as he saw Albert nodding to him, as he smiled and mechanically returned the nod, he could not shake the feeling of revulsion inside. Of hatred and guilt.

He felt split in two, one half acting out the motions, shaking hands, nodding to the gallery, the other half hunting down the feelings inside. He cornered the feelings, realised at that moment that this was a beast he feared and backed away from it, letting the celebrations of the slavers carry him away. The judge's words echoing in his ears, '*...the true sentence you will carry is the moral indictment brought upon yourself by your actions*'.

*

Yorke Carrington looked at Tyler and saw him slump down. He stood as the judge left, failing to notice the nod of respect from the judge, lost in his anger at the decision. He packed up a few papers, piling them loosely into his bag, rather than carefully aligning them as was his practice. Then he shoved and pushed past the men in the gallery and walked outside, lost in his anger.

'Yorke, my boy are you alright?' Thomas Clarkson said.

'Why didn't someone tell me the Admiralty court was the wrong court? You should have warned me, Thomas.'

'There was no other option. Come on, you are disappointed as is to be expected.'

'You expected me to lose didn't you?'

'No, I thought you should have won, and I can tell you so does most of the gallery. Not just the abolitionists, most of the people watching disagree with the verdict.'

'Well, it doesn't matter now, I let them down, and you and myself.'

'Yorke, we will talk later, but believe this, you should have won. Your case was exceptional. The fact is the Admiralty Court is never going to convict an English sailor.'

'What does that matter now,' Carrington said. Then he looked hard at Clarkson. 'I never stood a chance did I?'

'No, and that is the beauty of it.'

'What do you mean, was I set up to fail?'

'No, but it is clear now that the Admiralty is still for slavery. And that puts it out of touch with the people. Don't you see, Yorke, if we had won people would say that's justice. But now people are angry, they are outraged. Already people are spilling from the court speaking about a great injustice. It just fuels everything they hate about the government and life, but it channels that anger, Yorke. It channels it into wanting justice and now that means ending this trade. Oh, we are so close, Yorke, so close, don't you see. This is the match that lights the fire of indignation, of outrage. People will be asking how the Government and the Courts can be so out of touch with their own sentiments. It is astonishing that the powers that be cannot acknowledge what is plain, that true liberty must encompass all men or it cannot be said to truly exist.'

Clarkson's words did little to suppress the anger rising in Carrington. In feeling used, in losing.

'I know that you can't see this now.' Clarkson said. 'But rest assured, you have probably done more than any man since Wilberforce to further a hatred of this trade and through that bring about its demise. In a short time, when you feel that wave of anger wash over you, you will know that you have done an extraordinary thing here today.'

A group of abolitionists came up to the two men, eager to vent their anger at the result. Clarkson shot Carrington a cheeky wink and smile and then turned to the abolitionists, a look of anger on his face.

Carrington heard a man say to Clarkson, 'How dare they let him off!' Then he turned and walked towards home. The long walk did little for his anger but it helped him focus. And in his head, Carrington thought of Tyler, of his slumped shoulders, of the lost look on his face, of how quickly he turned away from

Pennington and the other slavers, as though Tyler was embarrassed or angry at them. As though he somehow did not believe the verdict himself. He wondered if Tyler perhaps thought himself guilty and dismissed the idea. But again and again, the thought came up. Carrington wondered if he was imagining it, seeking some sense of solace from losing. It was the look in Tyler's eyes, a look that he had only seen in men clearly guilty. Maybe, just maybe, there was hope yet.

Carrington turned and headed for Clarkson's home, hoping to find Albert there.

*

The group of slavers pushed through the crowds in the court, seeking out Tyler. 'George, we are victorious,' Pennington said. 'C'mon, let's get out of here and celebrate.'

Tyler looked around for Simon Rubin but the lawyer was nowhere to be seen amongst the throng of slave traders. Men he did not know slapped him on the back. One put his arm around Tyler. 'By Jove, George, we sure showed them.' Exactly who 'them' was remained unclear.

Soon the group swept Tyler from the court, stopping only for one to stand upon a bollard and say loudly to the crowd, 'slavery is vindicated'. This brought about a loud chorus of booing.

Then before Tyler knew what was happening, he was in a carriage with Pennington and other men who talked too loudly and was at the Bristol Club. The group entered to jubilant cries of 'we won' and soon most of the members were listening to Pennington sum up the judgment and read it as a bright future for the slave trade. Then the drinks started flowing and men who knew better couldn't help themselves, drunk on victory and soon hard liquor.

Tyler desperately wanted some quiet and time to confront what the verdict really meant. Hours later as men lay snoring in chairs, Tyler found a quiet corner and a few cushions and lay down to sleep. He closed his eyes and soon sleep fell upon him. He woke hours later cold and with the remnants of a new dream circling in his head.

He was aboard the Charlotte, with slaves being loaded. A woman holding a baby was amongst the slaves. She was crying. And Tyler knew it was not for the baby but for him. Then the baby started giggling and laughing, the harsh cackling laugh of the caged hyena he had seen in Mombasa many years before.

She crying and the baby laughing.

He went and found a bathroom and splashed some water on his face and looked into the polished mirror. Looked at his own hollowed-out face. He had seen that hunted, haunting look on the faces of so many slaves. He shivered inside, not from the cold water.

Why do I feel guilty? When I have been found innocent, he wondered. *I am innocent.*

He repeated the mantra to himself, then looked at himself again in the mirror.

He could no longer repeat those words, words that carried no meaning for him. Words that he no longer believed, as hollow and empty as the face staring back at him.

*

Simon Rubin listened to the judgment and nodded. He scarcely believed that the gamble had paid off. In any other courtroom, Tyler would have been sentenced to hang, but this was the Court of Admiralty and for all the faults of the Admiralty one was not hanging their own.

Rubin looked at Carrington and nodded to him, unsure if his opponent even registered his presence. Carrington was staring at Tyler. *Tyler*, Rubin thought, *having all but forgotten the man he was defending.* Then Rubin turned and looked at Tyler, the slumped shoulders, the broken look and the lost gaze on his face. The look of a man found guilty.

'We won, my dear Tyler, we won,' Rubin said, uncertain if Tyler had not understood the verdict or was simply overwhelmed by relief.

Then Rubin packed up his bag and turned and saw Pennington and his fellow traders swarming down towards him and Tyler and decided he wanted no part of it. He quickly ducked behind some men standing near Carrington and then found the bailiff.

'When will the judge publish his decision in full?' Rubin said.

'Friday, it will be out then,' the bailiff said.

Rubin nodded a thank you and used another group of men as cover and exited the side door that led to the waiting room and to other courts. Then he went and sat in the waiting room for a time and closed his eyes and relaxed. He waited a good twenty minutes and then stood and opened the door and found the corridor empty. Rubin retraced his steps and walked back into the courtroom that was now deserted. He walked to the table where he had sat during the trial and sat down in his chair and enjoyed the silence, the thrill of a victory against the odds. He stood and looked around and then patted the table before walking out into the street.

It could have been any mid-summer day in London, the air was pleasant and warm, people were pushing past each other going about their business, carriages filled the streets and Rubin fancied he smelt a tang of pie on the air.

That sounded good, he thought to himself. He found a pie shop, bought a pie for himself and a sausage for Saul and then walked home. Not once did he think again of Tyler, nor of the case, until that Friday when he walked to the courts and took a copy of the judgement and found a coffee shop and ordered himself a cup. Then he sat and read the judgement savouring the bitter taste of the coffee, a smile on his face.

The Bristol Daily Tribune
August 2nd, 1805
A Judgement for Common Sense

Captain of the Charlotte found NOT guilty. Yesterday in London the Court of Admiralty ruling in the case of the Charlotte found Captain George Tyler not guilty of the murder of 129 slaves, thrown overboard due to the deprivations of the sea.

In his summation, Judge Wilson exonerated Tyler who, the judge ruled, acted appropriately given that it is not possible to 'see all aboard a vessel, including what amounts to cargo in the form of slaves, as equal'.

Judge Wilson went so far as to say there is no law that prevents slavery outside Britain, even disputing laws that hold here in Britain should apply on British ships.

The judgement is a blow for the cause of abolition, founded on principles that now no longer apply to British ships. Tyler was charged with murder by abolitionists seeking to make a political and legal point now discredited by yesterday's ruling.

The noted Bristol merchant Mr Charles Pennington, owner of the Charlotte, and a man renowned for his charity said that 'justice has shown itself to be both fair and understanding of the trade'.

Yesterday's verdict will be hailed as a turning point in the misguided and dangerous push to abolish slavery. The campaign to end slavery ignores the fundamentals of commerce and history, including the large numbers employed in the trade, the wealth the trade brings and the benefits to everyday English men and women.

The Admiralty Court has acted in accordance with the law of the land and the seas. Perhaps now the abolitionists will acknowledge that their campaign has foundered on the laws of our great nation.

The Bristol Examiner August 2nd, 1805
Murder is murder
Abolitionists criticise verdict

Yesterday's decision by the Court of Admiralty to reject the case of murder against the captain of the Charlotte, infamous for murdering 129 slaves by throwing them overboard, has been widely criticised by leading abolitionists.

The charge of murder was brought against the captain of the Charlotte, George Tyler, after 129 slaves were dumped into the ocean to drown. This has become known as the massacre of the Charlotte.

Thomas Clarkson of the Committee for the Abolition of Slavery said the judgement of the Admiralty Court was a miscarriage of justice delivered by a court seeking to legitimise and continue the trade in slaves.

Mr Clarkson also said the prosecution case, delivered by Yorke Carrington, was overwhelming, based on a number of legal precedents, notably that arising from a similar massacre aboard the Zong some years before. These precedents had seemingly been 'ignored in the not guilty verdict'.

One of the main precedents on which the judge refused to acknowledge was from Lord Mansfield's ruling on the case of the Zong, who said that slave cargoes are owed a duty of care. In ruling yesterday, the court found that this precedent, established in law, was not a duty of care owed when a ship is in peril. This provides all slave boat captains with an excuse to dump slaves at even the suggestion of peril.

This allows a captain and crew to murder slaves with a simple story of peril, said Mr Clarkson. 'Murder is murder, unless you are a slave boat captain on the high seas with a cooperative crew. The laws of England now no longer apply equally to all men but now serve the whims of slavers'.

One can only wonder at the damages and distresses this now places in the way of slave boat crews. An officer of the Charlotte who testified at the trial was a broken man, saying under oath that the crew have no choice but to follow the captain.

Despite yesterday's verdict, it is the lasting testimony of this man, and so many former sailors like him, drunk, destitute or deceased by their own hand, that cannot be ignored any further by the legislators of our city and nation. Legislators who purport to represent the views of so many opposed to this trade yet who pass no laws to end it.

Twelve

Yorke Carrington had failed to find Albert the previous evening at Clarkson's residence. When he had arrived, men clearly less important than they believed themselves to be all vied for Clarkson's time, musing on what the judgement meant for the trade.

One man had even asked Carrington if he had seen the trial and what role he played in the abolitionist cause before lecturing Carrington on what the man himself had done. Which was four-fifths of nothing, but it sounded very important nonetheless.

And so Carrington had gone home.

'I heard you lost,' Sophie said once Carrington had put his hat and coat away.

'Yes.'

'I do suspect that given the outcry already about an unfair verdict you will come out of this alright. You always do Yorke.'

'That sounds a lot like Thomas.'

'It's not just me, after the verdict, I walked in the street a little and it was all anyone was talking about. People said you are a hero for taking this case on. My husband, the hero.'

'I just feel like I have let everyone down.'

'You could never let me down, Yorke. You should be proud, you have shown how unjust this trade is.'

'So a hero then?'

'Yes, just don't let it go to your head.'

'So does the hero get given a drink or should I pour my own.'

Sophie laughed. 'I am your wife, not your slave…' She stopped and looked at Carrington. 'Oh, what a poor choice of words.'

Then she and Carrington laughed together.

'You should rest, you have barely slept during this trial. I will fetch you a drink, this one time only, and then dinner.'

Sophie left and came back into the room a minute later with brandy. Carrington was already asleep in the chair.

'The hero at work,' Sophie said quietly to herself. Then she covered her husband with a blanket and ate alone.

The next day, Carrington had gone to visit Clarkson, finding him with Mawson and Albert. 'Here he is gentlemen, the man of the hour,' Clarkson said.

'The sooner the hour passes the better,' Carrington said. 'I need some advice please.'

'I will organise some tea,' Mawson said.

'No Henry, please stay, I think you should be here too for this. Yesterday did any of you see Tyler when the verdict was given, and afterwards?'

'No, why?' Clarkson said.

'I have been involved in more than a few trials and I know a guilty man when I see one. And I would wager my last pound that Tyler thinks himself guilty.' There was silence in the room.

'Do you see what I am saying? I think he thinks himself guilty. And I was thinking, could Albert here not visit him, see if he can convince this Tyler to recant from the slave trade. Imagine the coup that would be?'

'So my idea to have Albert here may not be so bad after all. In fact, you even seem to agree with it now?'

'Not now, Thomas, this is hardly the time to gloat about your intellect,' Albert said.

'And we all know that is dangerous territory to pursue,' Mawson said.

'Aren't you getting tea?' Clarkson said.

'This is serious. We could get Tyler to turn from the trade, I really think so.'

'Alright. How?' Clarkson said. 'Albert you know him best, you have come closest to being in his shoes as it were. Could we do this?'

'He needs to do that because he wants to, not because we offer him the chance.'

'Oh for goodness sake, you're not still going on with that are you?'

'Yes, I am. I think Yorke may be right, I think George has genuine doubts about what he did. But I will not pursue such a course unless it's what George wants.'

Carrington looked at Albert and knew he was right. There was little point in forcing the issue, and then more out of pity and the hope of salvaging something for himself. 'I agree with Albert, Tyler has to want this.'

'But think of the opportunity that may be lost?' Clarkson said.

'Think of the man's soul,' Mawson said. 'If he reaches the point you both think he is near or at, then he will find us. Isn't that right, Albert?'

'Yes, Henry, it is. I will give him some time, perhaps write to him in a while and see how he is doing. If it comes up then I will pursue it, but only then.'

Clarkson sighed loudly. 'I think I will go and make some tea.'

'God help us all,' Mawson said.

*

Charles Pennington woke with a frightful hangover. He tried to find a bathroom but heard a man retching inside and walked up the stairs of the Bristol Club to his room. He washed slowly, careful not to turn or tilt his head too quickly. He picked up the razor but decided against shaving, all that moving of his head to see where he was using the razor felt beyond him.

Then he washed as best he could and dressed slowly, picked up his hat and cane and quietly walked back down the stairs. Slowly life was returning to the club, men bravely trying to convince their fellows and themselves that they were fine and that last night had not affected them at all.

Pennington slipped out the front door and walked to Simon Rubin's office. The lawyer was already at work on another case but did not look surprised when Pennington entered.

'Simon, I came by to thank you. You have won us all a mighty victory.'

'It was my pleasure, Mr Pennington.'

'I must say I had my doubts about your argument, but you pitched it perfectly. Tyler sends his regards too. The chap is so relieved he seems to have fallen into a bout of melancholy. Anyway send the account to me in Bristol and I will settle up.'

'Are you taking Tyler back with you? Will he captain more ships for you?'

'Absolutely. Now that he is the face of the trade one cannot cut him loose. How would that look?'

'Well, then it seems all is good in the world of the slave trade then?'

'The other owners a cock-a-hoop. This victory has done so much to boost the trade.'

'So it was worth it then?'

'Indeed it was. Again thank you, Simon.'

Pennington shook Rubin's hand and left the offices, walking down a flight of stairs to the street. He stood in the august sun and allowed it to seep deep into him. Tyler's acquittal was the greatest coup of his career and the sun's warmth amplified that feeling.

I have brought legitimacy to the trade, Pennington thought. He did not think about how many slaves had died to make that happen, nor how many he had sold into slavery to build his wealth, nor of any of the sailors involved. That is why a man had intermediaries, to keep the more inconvenient parts of wealth creation at arm's length.

The sun continued to warm him, its glow spreading deep inside. It lasted long after he left London and returned to Bristol and the trade he loved.

*

Tyler's return to Bristol left him cold. When Pennington had assured him the captaincy of the Charlotte was his again Tyler had jumped at the chance. The idea of familiar surroundings, captaining a ship on the sea stilled the doubts inside.

Now sitting in the carriage, bored and unsure of how much longer he had to sit, Tyler could not keep the doubts away. He knew none of the landmarks, what to expect. Memories of Micah surfaced, of descriptions of roadside altars and men walking strange roads forsaking their gods and lives. He tried to think of the sea but that only led to slaves in the water and the words of the judge, *'…the true sentence you will carry is the moral indictment brought upon yourself by your actions'*.

There was a noise inside, of African ports and moaning and whimpering slaves and funerary dirges sung at sea by slaves dead to their past lives and hopes. Unlike other slave cargoes, there was no hold to store the noise away, no barriers separating slaves from the crew.

'Time to get out, you walk the rest of the way,' the carriage driver said.

Tyler stood in the cramped carriage, leaning forwards, stooping over like in a slave hold.

He climbed down the ladder of the carriage and was on the outskirts of Bristol. He tried to clear his mind of slaves and set out towards the river and ports. From here it would be a short walk, past familiar landmarks, into a place he knew well and then aboard the Charlotte.

He walked faster like the Charlotte gaining pace on the Guinea current, smooth sailing ahead. Yet after what happened on the last voyage, who was to say the next would be different. Onwards he walked, almost in a daze, until at last the river came into view. He walked to it and then along the shore past the warehouses and bustling industry until at last he reached the wharves. Up ahead, he saw Pennington Trading Co on the side of a warehouse and moored beside the river the Charlotte, renamed now, as though the ship herself could no longer bear to remember the past.

He spoke to the guard on duty and was ushered aboard the Charlotte, now named the Emily. Tyler stopped on deck and looked around. The masts stood solid, surrounded by rigging and furled sails. He heard the water lapping against the sides, the familiar creaks and pops of a ship. A welcoming chorus. He walked to the stern and stopped and looked down, trying to see the name Emily but could not.

Then he climbed down the stairs and walked the short corridor that led to his cabin. It was largely as he left it, only with the bedding made up. He wondered if Pennington had organised that. It seemed out of sorts for the man.

Tyler sat at the small bureau desk and leaned back on the chair. It groaned and creaked under his weight. He sat a long time, unsure what to do. Perhaps there were instructions in one of the drawers, a clue as to when he would be sailing again.

He opened a couple of the drawers and rummaged through but there were only a few blank papers. Finally, he opened the main drawer under the table.

Ledger of the Charlotte, 1804 voyage to Africa and the Caribbean

Tyler opened the ledger, saw Pennington's letter of commission, took it and folded it up and put it in his pocket, then felt his fingers flicking through the pages despite himself. Opening on an entry—eleven slaves dumped overboard. The next, 50 slaves dumped overboard, and another and another.

He stared at the handwriting, so familiar to him. The only evidence left that those people had ever lived, stolen from their homes, sold, abused and finally drowned, and for what he asked himself. For money for Pennington, for the officers. For himself.

He felt sickened inside.

'You murdered them and for what, George?'

Had he said that aloud he wondered, murdered them?

No surely not, he thought. But that thought arose, like the bloated carcass of a slave from the deep. Murdered them.

'*...the true sentence you will carry is the moral indictment brought upon yourself by your actions'.*

I murdered those slaves. The thought was loose now, like the Charlotte gaining pace in the Guinea current, hunting a new cargo.

And Tyler knew then that he was a murderer. An idea that he had tried to suppress now free and running. No longer an abstract thing, but solid and real. Tipping the balance, as a ship tossed at sea by a storm until she could no longer right herself.

His world suddenly capsized, turning over into a barren place. Tyler stood and walked out of the cabin, the ledger still open with the final entry, *50 more dumped overboard, that should be enough!*

He climbed the stairs and walked out onto the deck heading towards the railing on the riverside of the Emily; no, the Charlotte. His partner in crime then and now.

He prowled the deck of the ship searching for a way to undo the thought now loose.

Wanting to undo the past, hoping to find on board the ship a way to do that. Yet the ship was now a stranger to him, seemingly having cast off the past as it did her old name. Easily, without fuss.

Night fell and still, he walked the deck, thoughts of murder filling his head. The blackness that had infiltrated his soul, gradually taking form now became real, solid. *Murderer! Murderer!*

He walked to the rail, looked into the dark and littered river water. He placed a foot on the rail and grabbed a rope that disappeared upwards into the rigging. Then he hauled himself up, the effort intense and physical as though the Charlotte was holding him down.

The darkness below in the waters slipping by, matched only by the darkness he felt inside. He sought communion with those dark waters. A way to free himself, of the judgement that he now knew he gave himself. *Murderer!*

Step forward and atone for the past, deny the future. The hand holding the rope now loosening, caressing the ropes. *Step forwards,* he thought, *find redemption, allow it to wash you away. Take you to that place in the deep where slaves now slept forever. Join them.*

A ship's bell rang out.

Shaken, Tyler looked down, stepped back and onto the deck of the Emily. Leaving one abyss behind and falling into another. A void inside him.

Come the morning and Tyler woke, having slept in a corner of the ship. He dreamt of slaves in the water, of the woman and child. The Emily was no longer his home, the sea no longer offering the hope of comfort and renewal. It had spurned him, ashamed of his crime.

Was this freedom? Feeling nothing inside, knowing he was a murderer and feeling nothing.

And all the while the water, lapping against the side of the ship, calling him, tempting him.

Thirteen

Tyler had no idea how many days had passed since he first boarded the Emily. He had taken a room above a pub, barely sleeping, walking at night near the river. Fighting the temptation it offered, to take him and wash his sins away and unite him with the deep, with the blackness.

When he slept the dreams broke him, shattered him anew. Dreams of slaves in the water and the woman and child, of unearthly cackling laughter and tears. Of hopelessness.

He woke startled, the late afternoon sun still shining. Had he dreamed the knock on the door or was it real?

Tyler looked around, seeing the envelope still sticking partly under the door. He contemplated what it might mean, afraid and uncertain. *Was it from Pennington? Was it a threat from someone who knew who he was and if it were would he allow that threat to be carried out? Welcome it even.* Finally, he sat up, then stood and walked to the door and stooped down and picked up the letter, unfolding it as he walked back and sat on the bed.

My dearest George,

I trust in God that this letter finds you.

My ministry with you, though you may disagree, feels incomplete. There is more to discuss between us, should you wish it, more than the judgements of the court to consider.

In our time together while you were imprisoned, I came to understand that your involvement in the slave trade was not, as I first believed, a wilful sin, undertaken knowingly. Rather I see now that you felt you were answering a calling, much as I answer a calling by serving the church.

I fear now, George, that you may be lost, uncertain of your calling, unsure of what to do now and in need, more than anything else, of a friend to talk to.

God has ordained for me to come to Bristol to undertake ministry amongst those who have suffered at sea, including, I firmly believe, you. Perhaps if you wish it, you could come and see me or let me know of where we can meet.

I will be working in and around St Stephen's Church, near the river ports. I would be most happy and grateful to see you.

May God bless you,

Albert.

Tyler turned the letter over and over in his hand, thinking about Albert. About Micah and the trial and the slaves and his dreams. He was drifting in oblivion and hadn't cared at all until now. Such things as life were mundane, unable to float to the surface against the blackness he felt inside.

He balled the letter up and threw it into a corner. Then he reached for the bottle of liquor and took a long pull and fell asleep. When he woke it was dark and he put a coat on and walked out into the night. He traced his usual steps to the river and contemplated jumping but knew that he was too much of a coward for that. There was more that was needed than simply jumping, disappearing into the dark waters. Joining the people he had murdered.

He thought again of Micah as he did more and more, remembering a man that he had last known during a quarrel. And that over the future of slavery. A trade that he had defended and that he now recoiled from. How many had he delivered into slavery, into death? Far more than he himself had killed.

He remembered Micah talking about those people sold into slavery wiping dirt on themselves and dying before their gods. Better to be forgotten than live a half-life. *A life like I am now living,* Tyler thought.

Already people had moved on from the trial. Had forgotten much of it and the sugar boycotts. All but the outrage. And yet Tyler remembered it all. He knew the faces in his dreams intimately, even if they were not the real faces of those that died at his hand. By his order. People that he did not honour. Nothing would honour them Tyler knew.

He sat by the river and watched it go by and then stood and walked on, following it past ships loading goods and ships sitting silently. *How many of those ships had carried slaves and would do so again?* he wondered. Even one was too many.

Tyler saw the church up ahead. St Stephens. It was small and slightly run-down, dwarfed by the warehouses and wharves nearby. There was a small flicker of light coming from the church, a flicker that he longed to experience himself.

Tyler walked up to the church, seeing the door slightly ajar. He peered inside but the church was empty.

'Help you?' a voice said from behind Tyler.

Tyler turned and saw a black man and for a moment thought it was Micah. 'Is Father Albert here?' Tyler said before he even thought about it.

'He'll be back tomorrow morning. Come then,' the man said.

'What is your name?' Tyler said.

'Luke, it's Luke.'

'Your name your parents gave you, do you remember it?'

'I told you, it's Luke.'

'That is probably what they told you after you were freed from slavery. I mean before that?'

'I wasn't ever a slave. I was born a couple of miles from here,' Luke said.

'I...I am sorry.'

'We aren't all slaves, even if that's how you see us,' Luke said. Then he turned and walked away.

*

'Father, there is a man here to see you,' Luke said.

'Thank you, tell him I will see him shortly.'

'He said his name is George,' Luke said to Albert as he walked away.

Albert stopped and turned. 'Where is he?'

'In the knave out the back,' Luke said. 'He came last night and came back this morning. He's a bit odd, thought I was a slave he did.'

'Did he?' Albert said smiling. Then he turned and walked up the aisle of the church and into the knave.

George Tyler stood looking at an icon on the wall. 'George,' Albert said.

Tyler turned, looking at Albert, uncertain of what to expect.

Albert walked over and embraced Tyler. 'I am so glad you are here, you have been on my mind for days now.'

'Any good thoughts or all bad?'

'I've been concerned. After the trial, Mr Carrington came to visit me. He is worried for you.'

'That's a strange way he has of showing it, trying to get me hung.'

'Yes, I suppose so. How are you, George?' Tyler looked at Albert and then looked away.

'That bad. Well, how does it feel to be an innocent man? It must be an immense relief?' Albert said.

'It's good.'

'Good. And when the judge said you were innocent, I imagine that must have been an incredible feeling?'

'It felt good, I suppose.'

'What was in your mind. I am fascinated by this, by those moments that define us.'

'It was…I would say knowing that I was right.'

'That is an odd way to put it. Was it elation too, pure joy or what?'

'I don't know!'

'I apologise, George, I did not mean to push you.'

'I should go,' Tyler said standing.

'Before you go I have something for you. Micah asked me that should something happen to him, I think he knew deep down that well, he knew, so he asked me to give this to you.'

Albert handed over a small carving, no more than two inches in size, made from animal bone. It depicted an elephant, crudely and broadly cut but unmistakably an elephant.

'He managed through all those years to hold on to it,' Albert said. 'I asked him about it once, soon after we met. His mother carved it for him and had given it to him as her own token of recognition that he was becoming a man. She told him that elephants can shake the ground and that a good man does that too, makes the earth shake before him. It was, Micah said a symbol of manhood and of being Tebou, his tribe.'

'Why would he give that to me?'

'Deep down he never really renounced his heritage or forgot his home. I have wondered since his death what he really believed and I think this elephant answers that. Somewhere inside, where no man could reach he held on to hope, of family and home. Perhaps even of the gods he said he renounced.'

'I did not think you believed in any god but the Lord?'

'I don't. God is God. But I have come to see that every man carries within him something that sustains him, no matter what we call it. I think that all Micah truly believed is in that carving.'

'But you still haven't said why me? Why not you?'

'Micah quite liked you,' Albert said with a smile. 'Here, take it.'

'There is nothing in me that's worthy of this. Men like me took Micah from his home. I don't want it.'

'I think that Micah saw something in you, something that you don't yet see. A goodness maybe. A hope that you could be more.'

Tyler started to cry. He tried to stop himself but could not. 'Do you know what I have missed most, George?'

'What?'

'Your struggle.'

'My struggle?'

'It helps me, to understand that there are others who struggle with what they do, who want to be better.'

'How can you say I want to be better, after what I've done?'

'Because you are here. You had the chance, I believe, to return to the sea and to slaving yet you are here. That says something, George.'

Tyler was quiet for a long time. 'At first, I was angry, after the trial. And I didn't understand that. How could I be found not guilty but be angry? Then it hit me. The judge said that I would have to deal with my own verdict, my own morality. And he was right. Pennington and the other slavers saw me as the face of the trade, but what was worse, I began to see all that was wrong in me was all that was wrong with the trade. A willingness to throw lives away, to steal people from their lives and for what? Money, my own satisfaction at captaining a slaver. And then came Bristol and the Charlotte. I found…'

Tyler looked at the floor, sobbed and sobbed again before regaining some composure.

'I found the ledger, the journal of that voyage. And my notes about throwing slaves, people overboard. They were so, casual, so uncaring. Since then it has been despair and blackness inside if that makes sense.'

'Do you believe you are innocent?'

'God no. I murdered those people.

'A court found you had no case to answer.'

'There are higher courts than those that make the laws of men, Albert.'

'And now that you know that, what are you going to do about it?'

'I...don't know what to do.'

'George, let the past go for a moment. Forget the future. What does your heart tell you?' Tyler was quiet for several moments.

'That what I did was—'

'This is not about what you did, it's about what you do now. You have turned your back on slavery have you not?'

'Yes.'

'So what now, what are you thinking, for surely you have had enough time to think?'

'I lack the courage to end it all, so I'm just getting through each day. There's nothing more.'

'As I said, you are here now. So beyond that pain, that blackness, what is there?'

Tyler sat and thought for a time.

'I want to make sure those people I killed are not forgotten.'

'Good, that's good.'

'I don't know how to do that. I don't know what to do?'

Tyler looked at Albert, pleading for guidance.

'I can't be the one to tell you what to do, George. It doesn't work that way. You need to find that path for yourself.'

The two sat in silence for a long time.

'That thing you told me, about that Zurara who said Africa was full of heathens, and that black men are less than us, is it true?'

'I don't know, George, why?'

'It's just that, meeting Micah, seeing a black man, an African who is...who was educated, it's harder to think of his fellows as slaves. And when I think of Micah, who never stopped remembering, hoping. He should not be forgotten. They all should be remembered, but as people, not as slaves. Like the book that Gustavus the former slave wrote, the one you gave me. He is so—'

'Human,' Albert said.

'Yes.'

'Because when you see Micah, when you read Olaudah's book, you see something of yourself in them, don't you?'

'Yes.'

'And you wonder why you never saw it before, during all those voyages?'

'Yes.'

'My friend, Thomas Clarkson speaks about this. He shows people art and tools made by Africans, he shows Africans as men and women and not beasts of burden. When people hear that and want to see that, they find it harder to justify slavery. They no longer see blacks, as many call slaves, but people. Is that what you see now, George?'

'Yes.'

'It's interesting to see how words and our thinking of Africa as a place of slaves and not people helps to make slaving easier. It depends on how you choose to see it, as Zurara did, to justify slavery, or as you see it now.'

Tyler said nothing, lost in thoughts of the people he had enslaved.

'Do not dwell on such things,' Albert said, surprising Tyler. 'Perhaps instead think about the future. To look backwards all the time would be to…well, I think you know that.'

'Yet, we build our future on the past, on where we have been and what we have done and that is not…an easy thing for me. My past is one of…as a slave boat captain, you make allowance, that what you do doesn't matter inside. You place a barrier between yourself and the slaves, both on the boat but also inside. That's why we called slaves cargo because then they aren't really people, they aren't us. It dehumanises them, turns them into something else. It's how the whole trade works, it's why it works. I can't do that anymore, they are people like us.'

'Like you?'

'Yes like me. That barrier, that difference is not just blurred, it's gone. I don't know how to do that anymore, I can't.'

'We make accommodations with ourselves all the time, many without understanding.'

'Where they lead?' Tyler said.

'Or how hard they are to give up. That is what makes you extraordinary, George, you have changed. That is amazing.'

Tyler smiled for the first time in days. 'So that still doesn't help me with what I do now.'

Albert chuckled. 'Sorry, George, I do not mean to mock you, but I have no idea either.'

Then in a moment of inspiration Albert remembered Clarkson's words, *'Albert, you know him best, you have come closest to being in his shoes as it were.'*

'George, there is a saying, not to judge another until you have walked a mile in their shoes. Few men would better understand what it is to be a slave than you, imprisoned, used by men for their gain and objectives. And few know this trade better than you. Perhaps there is something in there, a meaning perhaps?'

Tyler looked at Albert then looked away. For the first time he could remember he felt something inside that was not dark and painful. Dying would be easy, living would be hard, but in that lay a way forward. Rising from the darkness that he feared he would never escape, always trying to live despite his soul being enslaved.

Like Micah, never forgetting but finding a new path.

Late that evening, the two left the Church. Albert pulled the door to struggling to get it to close.

'It's always the same, this thing never wants to close,' Albert said with a rising tone of frustration.

Tyler helped and eventually the two men pulled the door closed.

'It's been that way since I got here and well before that,' Albert said. 'Anyway, you have a place to stay tonight, George?'

'Yes.'

'Will I see you tomorrow?'

'Yes, Albert, you will.'

*

Albert woke and for the first time in days said a quiet prayer that Tyler would come back to the church. Then he hurriedly washed and dressed and walked to the church. As he neared the church he thought the door was open but then as he got closer he saw that the door was gone.

Worried, Albert walked up the stairs and saw Luke.

'He's been here since early this morning,' Luke said. 'He said you wouldn't mind.'

Albert saw Tyler poke his head around the door frame and run a hand down the side of the door jam. Then Tyler crouched and used a chisel and hammer to gently remove the base of the door frame.

'Good morning, George,' Albert said.

'Albert,' Tyler said, not looking up.

Albert and Luke walked in through the space where the door should be and sat down at a nearby pew.

'I didn't know you knew carpentry, George?' Albert said.

'On ships there are always carpenters, to fix things, make repairs, reconfigure the ships. When I was younger, I spent a bit of time watching them. You pick things up along the way.' Tyler reached into a bag and pulled out a planer and then turned the door upside down, stood on a small bench and set to planning the top of the door. After a few minutes, he took the base off the door frame and placed it against the base of the door, carefully examining both.

Albert and Luke sat and watched Tyler on and off over the next hours as he gradually planed more from the door, and a touch off the frame's base. Then carefully, he nailed the frame back into its place at the base of the door and then rehinged the door and tested it. He opened it and closed it several times, taking care to note where it stuck, then pulled it from the hinges again and planed the door some more. Finally, on the fourth attempt at rehanging the door it opened and closed smoothly. Tyler had said little and that he did mainly to himself. Watching, Albert smiled, then he stood and walked away, over to the altar and stopped briefly. *Thank you,* he said in his head, nodding to the image of Christ. He turned back and Tyler was still busy with the door and for the first time, Albert felt happy for his friend.

*

The following afternoon, Luke came up to Albert. 'I think you should see this.'

'What is it?'

'It's the door.' Albert followed Luke to the door.

'See along the side of the door frame,' Luke said, opening the door and pointing at the crudely carved figures of people up and down the door frame. They were only visible when the door was open.

'I have counted them,' Luke said.

'There are one hundred and twenty-nine, right?' Albert said.

Luke looked at Albert in astonishment. 'How did you know that?'

Albert just smiled. He stood looking at the crude figures, little more than stick men.

Eventually, Luke walked away and Albert pulled the door open as far as was possible and looked at the inside of the door, where it joined the door frame when closed. He saw letters carved into the door, one above another.

Children of Africa, murdered aboard the slaver Charlotte. RIP.

Over the next few days, Tyler found things to do, to occupy his mind and still the doubts, a space to think. He and Albert began to talk about mundane things and about important things.

About food and life and the politics of slavery. About foreign ports and cities and religions and the weather. About Bonaparte and revolution and John Locke and philosophy. Mostly they talked about what needed doing around the church.

Tyler would then get on and do what he could with the things he knew. It was small but it was better than Tyler had dared hope for, a meaning where before none existed.

*

The sun was setting outside and the chill of winter was already in the air. Albert was kneeling at the altar praying. He stood and looked around the church and saw Tyler watching him.

'What?' Albert said.

'Nothing, it's just you seem to be spending longer praying, talking to God.'

Albert thought for a moment. 'Yes, I have been.'

'Is He talking back to you?'

'It doesn't usually work that way, George. Does He speak to you at all?'

Tyler laughed. 'I think I'm the last person He'd speak to.'

'George, where do you stand with God?' Albert said.

'I think you would know more about that than me.'

'Have you thought of atoning for your sins? Perhaps about embracing God in your life.'

'I have and always I come back to the same point, I cannot believe in a god that would bring me into the fold after what I did. How can killing 129 people be about my redemption. What about them?'

Albert looked at Tyler and said nothing. There was nothing to say. 'An atonement needs meaning, Albert.'

'That it does, George. But without God what else is there?'

'I suppose what we choose to make important.' Then Tyler smiled. 'Thank you, Albert, I know what I need to do now. What it is that's important for me to do. Can we see Carrington please?'

'I will arrange it.'

Fourteen

Yorke Carrington sat quietly after Tyler finished speaking. For the first time since the trial, he felt a genuine satisfaction.

'Use my story how you wish, but make it count. Make it mean something in the fight against slavery, promise me that,' Tyler said.

'I will. And thank you. What you have done here today will change how people see slavery. It will, well it's going to shake people. They will have to confront the realities of this trade.'

'You might say that it will shake the ground on which this trade stands,' Albert said.

'Yes, I think it will,' Carrington said.

Tyler smiled, his fingers touching Micah's elephant carving that hung around his neck. 'What will you do now?' Sophie said.

'I don't know. It really doesn't feel like it matters to me anymore,' Tyler said.

'We will find something for George, I think,' Albert said.

'Good, that's good,' Sophie said. Then she looked at her husband who smiled and nodded to her.

Carrington stood and walked over to Tyler and offered out his hand, an acknowledgement that said more than words. Tyler stood and shook Carrington's hand. 'Thank you, Mr Carrington, for all that you have done.'

'You can call me Yorke if you wish.'

*

That night, Tyler lay down to sleep. He closed his eyes and a slave chamber he had seen once, many years ago in Zanzibar, and yet yesterday, opened before him. A hut covered a hole in the ground. Below this, several feet down was a small room with two adjoining chambers opening in opposite directions. A channel was carved into the centre of each chamber finishing at a narrow opening at each end of the chambers, far smaller than any man could fit through, but allowing a nearby creek a spillway into the rooms. Water would fill this channel as the tides flowed into the creek, slipping without struggle into the chambers, washing away the worst of the excrement. Each chamber was low and dense, thick walls crowding in with only a narrow cut high in each wall for ventilation. The ceiling pressed down from five feet above towards the floor.

Surrounding the channel was a ledge, three feet up from the floor, two down from the ceiling and barely two feet wide. Slaves were piled sitting stooped over and laying on the ledge. Some could not reach the ledge, sitting in the channel, and others lay on the floor or upon the dead. More than fifty, perhaps seventy slaves were pressed and crowded into each chamber, where ten men would struggle to fit comfortably. On the main pillar between the chambers, a serpent of chains coiled out, tying the mass of humanity to their servitude.

The hope of sleep gathered Tyler, as in his mind he pushed into the chamber, led by no one. He slumped down in the filthy water that was pouring into the chamber, felt the chains slithering towards him, coiling around him, pulling him down and he knew that this was where he would spend his nights from here on.

Historical Note

The trans-Atlantic slave trade operated from the 16th to the 19th century. Trading in slaves from West Africa was underway as early as the 1480s, with Portuguese traders transporting slaves to the Madeira Islands and other locations on the eastern side of the Atlantic. The trade accelerated in the 16th century when Atlantic crossings became the norm before it finally was outlawed in the mid-1800s. During that time, many nations set up factories in Africa to house slaves before the sale, these growing into the systems and forts of Elmina, Cape Coast and elsewhere.

Historians have debated how many people were transported by this system, with the total number suggested being as high as 60 million and as low as 3 million people. These are the numbers found on the extremities of the debate, with most historians agreeing the figure is most likely somewhere between 10 and 13 million people transported into slavery. Another 6 million Africans were estimated to have died in conflicts to obtain slaves, with between 5 to 40 per cent of slaves taken in those conflicts estimated to have died before being forcibly embarked on ships. To put this into perspective the estimated population of Africa in 1820 was around 75 million people.

One of the many tragedies of the slave trade across the Atlantic is that the exact number of people transported into slavery will never be known, nor the number that died during the middle passage. Again estimates vary but the agreed figure is around 10 per cent of those transported did not live to see the end of their voyage. To put it simply from our perspective today, the Atlantic is both the graveyard of many Africans and the location of multiple crimes.

Yet one of the most difficult challenges in writing about the slave trade and the men who conducted that trade is putting aside our modern viewpoint on slavery, which is distinctly (if you will pardon the use of the term here) black and white. That is to say that from today's vantage slavery was wrong and has always been so. Yet there was a time when slavery was accepted as a normal practice.

Indeed the Bible says that slaves should obey their masters, reflecting the use of slavery in the Roman Empire, the dominant power during the birth of the early church. People in Europe from the Dark ages onwards could sell themselves into slavery, and during the apogee of Viking raids, many feared being taken and sold into slavery.

European nations including Portugal, Holland, Spain and France all transported slaves, while the Royal House of Stuart in England established the Royal Africa Company in 1660 led by the future king of England, James II and with Charles II as founder and patron. Until the 1700s and early 1800s, the trade was both accepted and highly profitable with Britain as the leading player in the trade. One of the wealthiest places on earth during the 18th century was Haiti, a country that today is one of the poorest. It was in Haiti that a slave rebellion began at the end of the 18th century that did much to raise awareness of the evils of slavery.

In England, where this story is set, the acceptance of the trade changed following a speech by William Wilberforce, before the House of Commons, on 12 May 1789. That day Wilberforce shook the foundations of the trade, although it would take another eighteen years until the trade was finally abolished in Britain, in January 1807. To understand just how entrenched the trade was, it is worth considering that in the early 18th century one estimate suggested that one-quarter of London's population was involved in the trade. In monetary terms, the trade was worth the equivalent of today's housing market, for all of England! The city of Liverpool saw £17 million of slave-related money flow into its economy in one year in the early 1700s, an amount worth around £1 billion today adjusted for inflation.

What Wilberforce did was focus attention on the morality of the trade, both in terms of the concept of slavery itself and what it did to British sailors involved in the trade. In doing so, Wilberforce tapped into an anti-slavery sentiment in Britain that began with Elizabeth I, who said that the trade would 'call down the vengeance of heaven'. Despite that nothing was done to outlaw the trade during her long reign.

The story presented here is fictional, as are most of the characters. Only Thomas Clarkson was a real person, and elements of the speech he gives in the Church, along with the box of African artefacts and implements of the trade in slaves, are factual. Clarkson toured England giving his speeches with the show box being a central component of his argument. You can find some of the speeches Clarkson gave online even today. Clarkson was an immensely important figure in the abolitionist movement and is considered as second only to Wilberforce in terms of shaping the debate around slavery at the end of the 18th century and the start of the 19th century.

The other characters are my invention, as is the story. The inspiration for the story is the slave ship *Zong*, which dumped many of its *cargo* of Africans, taken as slaves, into the Atlantic. There were attempts to prosecute the captain of the *Zong*, Luke Collingwood, for murder, but Collingwood died before such a prosecution took place. Today that leaves an interesting and awful what-if scenario that never played out, which is where this story begins.

Little is known about the thoughts of those engaged as sailors in the trade, nor what led them to be involved, or if they questioned the trade. This story seeks to elaborate on those questions, albeit from today's vantage point.

The characters involved, Tyler, Albert, Carrington, Micah and Mawson, Kemp, Pennington and Rubin, along with others are my invention. The story is also my invention. No trial took place in 1805 of a slave boat captain, nor was any trial influential in shaping the debate on slavery.

The use of newspapers and pamphlets, many printed on the newly developed iron printing presses of the day, did occur. In many ways, these represent the social media of the time, along with soap boxes and speaker's corners. What is fascinating is that many such papers and pamphlets were circulated, few owned by media moguls and many represented the views of those paying for the presses and ink and paper, including pro and anti-slavery groups.

The novel does not touch heavily on the role of the Quakers in the abolitionist movement, other than to have Clarkson speak in a Quaker church. It would be remiss not to mention here the vital role of the Quakers. Without the Quaker movement, the abolitionist cause may not have delivered the results it did. One of the key factors in the success of the movement involving the Quakers was humanising slaves. This was helped by the story of Olaudah Equiano, which was widely read in Britain at the time, and sugar boycotts, which did occur.

The issue of the humanisation or dehumanisation of Africans is important in discussing the slave trade. The mention of the work by Gomes Eanes de Zurara references a real historical work. Zurara was a Portuguese chronicler who lived in the fifteenth century working in the Portuguese Royal Library, who wrote about Prince Henry the Navigator and Africa.

Portugal established the fort of Elmina on what is now the coast of Ghana in 1482, as a means to establish a staging post to tap into the riches of Africa. At first, the focus was gold, but soon an agricultural plantation system was set up in Sao Tome, on the west coast of Africa. For that system to work effectively, slave labour was needed, and so the centuries-long exploitation of African humanity for slavery was rapidly accelerated. The reason demand for slaves remained so high is the plantation system, exported from Sao Tome to the Caribbean and then North America was intensely hungry for slaves. Plantation owners soon realised the economics of the model worked best if slaves were worked to death, a process usually taking around seven years. And with a plentiful supply from West Africa to replace those killed and no labour costs, that system revolutionised agricultural production, of cotton and sugar particularly. The only thing lacking at the establishment of that system was a justification for the use of slave labour.

The idea of Zurara's work being the basis for slavery, by suggesting Africans as inferior and in need of saving references the work of an American scholar, Ibram Kendi, amongst others. Kendi has won the American National Book Award for his work, *Stamped from the Beginning, The Definitive History of Racist Ideas in America* and has launched the Antiracist Research and Policy Centre at American University. Without diving too deeply into Kendi's work there are fascinating and sickening questions that are raised; what if racism is a deliberate invention and what if Zurara did portray Africans as *lesser,* to justify slavery? What if racism in America and elsewhere is built on these and other lies? I will leave these important questions for the reader to consider, along with a starting point in Kendi's work for those interested.

What is ultimately fascinating about Britain's decision to abolish slavery is why? For some historians, that decision represents one of the few truly altruistic acts by a government in history. For others, there are economic or geo-political imperatives involved. What is likely is that the views of everyday people in England who were entitled to vote started to become impossible to ignore. Only around one in every twenty men held the right to vote around 1800 in England. Women were not able to vote. Despite this Wilberforce's speech was widely read and highly influential, as was the work of Clarkson, reflecting in some ways the disenfranchisement of many.

What Wilberforce began, including through newspapers that printed his speech, and Clarkson continued, was the beginnings of a mass movement for morality, for an idea of equality and to end injustice, a movement that continues in many forms today.